LUCKY LEGS

ERLE STANLEY GARDNER

Printed in the United States of America
19 18 17 16 15   5 4 3 2 1

CONTENTS

A NOTE FROM PUBLISHER

The world in which Perry Mason was first introduced back in 1933 with the publication of *The Case of the Velvet Claws* was very different than the world in which we live today. Views on race and gender relations have dramatically evolved in the more than 80 years that have elapsed between the debut of Perry Mason and his resurrection today. While these classic novels are very much a product of the environment in which they were written, we believe that the stories themselves and the values that underlie them continue to have universal appeal today, and are indeed the bedrock for so many of the wonderful legal thrillers we have come to enjoy in the decades since.

With the reissue of this iconic series—many titles of which have not been in print for years—it is our hope at Ankerwycke to introduce a whole new generation of readers to the investigative brilliance of Perry Mason, and the masterful storytelling of Erle Stanley Gardner; drawing together a new and connected family of fans throughout the world.

Enjoy!

A NOTE FROM ERLE STANLEY GARDNER

Perry Mason shares the prerogative of all good fictional characters. They never grow old. Yet the lawyer's cases began years ago in what now seems almost a different world. *The Case of the Lucky Legs* deals with Perry Mason at a time in his career when there were three powerful "slick paper" magazines, *The Saturday Evening Post, Collier's* and *Liberty.* Only *The Saturday Evening Post* has survived. It occurred in a period when much of the best food was in speakeasies, when sliding-panel doors were standard equipment. Moreover, in these earlier cases Perry Mason had the great advantage of complete freedom of action.

Those of you who read Perry Mason's adventure of *The Case of the Lucky Legs* will, I think, agree that fame has disadvantages; that a young, relatively unknown fighting criminal lawyer can get into a series of most attractive escapades with skeleton keys and an impulsive disregard for the finer points of legal ethics. Nowadays when the celebrated Perry Mason dashes past a cornerstone of legal ethics without bothering to touch base, bar associations shiver with apprehension. In these earlier days when only a few people knew of the daring, resourceful Perry Mason, a bunch of skeleton keys in his pocket was standard equipment. After all, who dared to keep a locked door between a Perry Mason reader and the mystery on the other side? Certainly not the author!

So to those who wish to encounter Perry Mason in one of his earlier adventures, who have a nostalgic longing for the days of the speakeasy and individual initiative, I trust this reprinting of *The Case of the Lucky Legs* will give you your money's worth of excitement and entertainment.

E. S. G.

CAST OF CHARACTERS

PERRY MASON—Who wants to be the first to guess what happened and usually is

DELLA STREET—His devoted secretary, whose soft heart for the underdog is equalled only by her concern for Perry Mason's safety

MR. J. R. BRADBURY—A very substantial citizen, former President of the Cloverdale National Bank, and a fighter who refused to be underestimated

EVA LAMONT—Who signed the telegram that precipitated the hunt

MARJORIE CLUNE—Tricked, robbed, and betrayed by her not-so-lucky legs

FRANK PATTON—Motion picture promoter with a beguiling proposition

DR. ROBERT DORAY—Rising young dentist who ran afoul of the law in the big city

MAMIE—The blonde at the cigar counter

PAUL DRAKE—Owner of the Drake Detective Agency who knows how to turn question marks into exclamation points

THELMA BELL—Another girl whose legs were lovely but not lucky

DETECTIVES RIKER AND JOHNSON—Who thought they had finally caught up with Perry Mason

1

Della Street held open the door of Perry Mason's private office.

"Mr. J. R. Bradbury," she said.

The man who pushed past her, into the room, was around forty-two years of age, with quick gray eyes that surveyed Perry Mason with ready friendship.

"How do you do, Mr. Mason?" he said, extending his hand.

Perry Mason arose from his swivel chair to take the hand. Della Street stood for a moment in the door, watching the two men.

Perry Mason was taller than Bradbury. He was, perhaps, heavier, but his heaviness was the result of big bones and heavy muscles, rather than the heaviness of fat. There was in his motions, as he arose from the chair and shook hands, a suggestion of finality. The man seemed as substantial as a granite rock, and there was something of the appearance of rugged granite in his face, which was entirely without expression as he said:

"I'm pleased to meet you, Mr. Bradbury. Have a chair."

Della Street caught Perry Mason's eye.

"Is there anything you want?" she asked.

The lawyer shook his head. Then, as Della Street closed the door, turned to his visitor.

"You told my secretary that you had sent me a telegram," he said, "but our files fail to disclose any telegram by a man named Bradbury."

Bradbury laughed and crossed one well-tailored leg over the other. He seemed very much at ease.

"That," he said, "is easily explained. I filed the telegram from an office where my name was known. I didn't want to use my name, so I signed the telegram Eva Lamont."

Perry Mason's face showed quick interest.

"Then," he said, "you are the one who sent the photograph by air mail. The photograph of the young woman."

Bradbury nodded and fished a cigar from his waistcoat pocket.

"All right if I smoke?" he asked.

Perry Mason nodded an answer. He picked up the telephone on his desk, and when he heard Della Street's voice, said, "Bring me that photograph that came yesterday, also the telegram that was signed 'Eva Lamont.'"

He hung up the telephone, and, as Bradbury clipped the end from his cigar, Perry Mason took a cigarette from a humidor on his desk. Bradbury scraped a match along the sole of his shoe and jumped from his chair to hold a light to Mason's cigarette, then, still standing, he applied the flame to the end of his cigar and was just dropping the match into the ashtray on the desk when Della Street opened the door from the outer office and laid a legal jacket on Perry Mason's desk.

"Anything else?" she asked.

The lawyer shook his head.

Della Street's eyes turned appraisingly to the well-tailored figure of the man who stood puffing on his cigar. Then she turned and left the room.

As the door clicked shut, Perry Mason turned back the jacket and picked up a photograph which had been printed on glossy paper. It was the photograph of a young woman, showing her shoulders, hips, arms and legs. The photograph did not show the young woman's face, but there could be no doubt of her youth from the willowy shape of her body, the graceful contours of her hands, and the sweep of leg which was displayed in the picture.

The woman's hands held her skirts very high, showing a pair of slim legs. Underneath the picture was a typewritten caption which had been pasted to the photograph and which read "THE GIRL WITH THE LUCKY LEGS."

Clipped to the photograph was a telegram which read:

"SENDING YOU SPECIAL DELIVERY AIR MAIL PHOTOGRAPH OF UTMOST IMPORTANCE IN CASE I AM ABOUT TO PRESENT KEEP PHOTOGRAPH AND AWAIT ME IN YOUR OFFICE WITHOUT FAIL

(Signed) "EVA LAMONT"

Bradbury crossed to the desk, stared down at the photograph.

"The girl who posed for that photograph," he said, "was tricked, robbed and betrayed."

Perry Mason looked not at the photograph but at Bradbury's face, his eyes holding that steady, watchful scrutiny which seeks to uncover truth beneath a veneer of stage setting. It was the scrutiny of an attorney who has handled clients of all types, and who has learned to calmly and unhurriedly brush aside layers of falsehood in order to get at the real facts.

"Who is she?" Mason asked.

"Her name," said Bradbury, "is Marjorie Clune."

"You say she was tricked, robbed and betrayed?"

"Yes."

"And who is the person who is responsible for that?"

"Frank Patton," said Bradbury.

Perry Mason waved his hand toward the big leather chair which faced his desk.

"If," he said, "you'll sit down and tell me about it from the beginning, we can probably make faster progress."

"There's one thing I want understood," Bradbury said, sitting down, "and that is that whatever I tell you is going to be in confidence."

"Certainly," said Mason.

"My name is J. R. Bradbury. I live in Cloverdale. I was a heavy stockholder in the Cloverdale National Bank and was its president for many years. I am forty-two years of age. Recently I retired, to devote my time exclusively to private investments. I am a substantial citizen of Cloverdale and can furnish you with any number of first-class references."

Bradbury's voice held the close-clipped articulation of a man who is dictating. The lawyer watched him with eyes that seemed to penetrate the man's mind as X-rays penetrate human tissue.

"Marjorie Clune," went on Bradbury, "is a young woman of character and beauty. She is an orphan. She was employed as a stenographer in my bank. She would probably have agreed to marry me within another month. Frank Patton came to town. He was a promoter. He claimed to be representing a motion picture company that was searching for a young woman of personality and beauty, who could stand being advertised as 'THE GIRL WITH THE LUCKY LEGS.' They were going to insure her legs for two million dollars; release publicity about the most beautiful legs in the world."

"Did Patton say he had authority to act for such a motion picture company?" Mason asked.

Bradbury smiled wearily, as though he were telling something that he had repeated on many occasions.

"He had a contract with a motion picture producing company with offices here in the city. The contract was signed in blank by the picture company. Patton was empowered to select the other party to the agreement. Ostensibly, it was an agreement by which the actress was to be employed for forty weeks out of the year, at a salary of three thousand dollars a week. It contained, however, a joker by which the company could terminate the contract if it decided not to go ahead with the picture in which it contemplated starring the actress."

"How did Patton make his money out of it?" Mason asked.

"Through the Chamber of Commerce. He sold them on the idea of the advertising that would result to Cloverdale if the young woman was selected there. He sold scrip to the merchants; the merchants passed it out to customers. The scrip entitled the holder to share in the profits of the picture."

"Wait a minute," Perry Mason said, "let's get that straight. The scrip holders became partners in the production?"

"Not in the production," Bradbury said, "but in the earnings from the production. There's a vast distinction. We didn't realize it at the time. The actress was to sign a contract with Patton to act as her manager on a percentage of her earnings. The earnings were to include a share in the picture. Patton assigned that share of the earnings to the scrip holders."

"And the scrip holders," asked the lawyer, "were to assist in the selection of the actress?"

"Now," Bradbury said, "you've got the idea in a nutshell. The scrip was sold to the merchants; the merchants gave it out with purchases. The holders of the scrip cast ballots to determine who should be the actress selected. There were half a dozen candidates. They appeared in bathing suits, posed in the stores, modeled stockings in the windows, appeared in the local picture shows, allowed their legs to be photographed and the photographs placed in store windows. It stimulated business. Naturally, it exploited the young women. Patton made a bunch of money out of it."

"Then what happened?" asked Perry Mason.

"Marjorie Clune was selected as the most beautiful of the contestants, or candidates, if you want to call them that. Patton gave her a big send-off. There was a banquet. The secretary of the Chamber of Commerce presented her with the contract. It was signed with a fountain pen which was placed in a glass case and returned to the Chamber of Commerce to be kept in the city hall. Cloverdale was to be put on the map. It was to be the home of the biggest motion picture actress in the industry; the most beautiful girl in America. Patton had engaged a drawing-room on the night train. Margy was escorted to the drawing-room by more than fifteen hundred cheering citizens. The drawing-room was banked with flowers. There was a brass band. The train pulled out."

Bradbury paused for a moment, then said dramatically, "That was the last anyone ever heard of Marjorie."

"You think she was abducted or something?" Mason asked.

"No; she was swindled and her pride wouldn't let her return. She had left Cloverdale to take her place among the big motion picture stars. She didn't have courage enough to return and admit she had been the victim of a legal fraud."

"Why do you say a legal fraud?" Perry Mason asked.

"Because it's air-tight. There were no false representations made that the district attorney of Cloverdale is willing to act on. He wrote the motion picture company; they stated that they were in search of such an actress; that they had empowered Patton, in whose judgment they had the greatest confidence, to discover such an actress; that Marjorie Clune had appeared at their studios; they had employed her for two days while they started to film the picture, and then had decided to scrap it, due, in part, to the fact that Miss Clune did not screen well."

"The contract was limited to one picture?" asked Perry Mason.

"To three pictures, but they were all of them predicated on the satisfactory completion of the first."

"And the title of the first was specifically set forth so that there was nothing to prevent the motion picture company from abandoning production on that play, changing the name and employing another star for the same picture?" Perry Mason asked.

"Now," Bradbury said, "you've got the sketch."

"What do you want me to do?" Mason inquired.

"I want to put Frank Patton behind the bars," said Bradbury. "I think he's had some very shrewd legal advice; I want to get some that's just as shrewd. I want to find him. I want to find Marjorie Clune. I want to force him to make restitution to Marjorie Clune, and, incidentally, I want to make him confess to a fraudulent intent."

"Why?" Perry Mason asked.

"Because then," Bradbury said, "the district attorney here will proceed against the picture company, and the district attorney in Cloverdale will proceed against Patton; but they claim they have to prove his intent beyond a reasonable doubt. It's a mixed-up case. If he claims good faith, they can't convict him. They want some sort of an admission from him."

"Why don't they get it then?" Mason asked.

"The district attorney in Cloverdale," Bradbury said, "for some reason simply won't have anything to do with the matter. The district attorney here says that he isn't going to wash Cloverdale's dirty linen; that if I want to work up a case against Patton, he'll take some action, but he won't waste county time and money trying to pull chestnuts out of the fire for Cloverdale; that it was Cloverdale money that was taken, and the representations were all made in Cloverdale."

"What else do you want me to do?" asked Perry Mason.

"I want you," Bradbury said, "to see that I don't get put in jail for blackmail."

"You mean when we find Patton?"

Bradbury nodded and pulled a wallet from his pocket.

"I am prepared to pay," he said, "a retainer of one thousand dollars."

Perry Mason turned to Bradbury.

"You'll need a good detective," he said. "Paul Drake, head of the Drake Detective Bureau, is a very good friend of mine. I'll give you a card to him."

He picked up his desk telephone.

"Della," he said to his secretary, "make a receipt to J. R. Bradbury for one thousand dollars. Get Paul Drake on the line, and then get me Maude Elton, the district attorney's secretary, on the line."

2

Maude Elton, the general secretary at the district attorney's office, was reputed to know more about the inside history of criminal matters than any one in the court house. Her complexion was slightly sallow; her features were hardly the kind to get motion picture producers raving over screen tests, but her face showed a quick vitality, an alert watchfulness which made her seem as restless as a canary hopping about in bright-eyed scrutiny of a stranger who has approached too close to its cage.

"Hello, Mr. Mason," she said.

Perry Mason grinned at her.

"After seeing some of these dumb-bells," he said, "who can't think of anything except getting their powder on smoothly, it's refreshing to look into a pair of eyes like yours."

"I presume," she told him, "that means you're going to try to pump some information out of me that you can't get from any one in the office."

"This is once," he told her, "that your environment has betrayed you."

"Why my environment?"

"Because you always see the seamy side of life. You deal with crooks and with persons who have ulterior motives. My errand today is merely that of a peaceful citizen, a taxpayer if you wish, who comes to the office of a public servant, seeking legitimate information."

She twisted her head slightly to one side as she stared at him.

"I believe you're right, at that," she said.

"I am," he told her.

"You're not kidding?"

"No. On the square."

"Well, I've seen lots of things in my time, but I never expected to see this. What is it you want?"

"I want to find out what deputy was consulted by a man named Bradbury who came here from Cloverdale to see about a racket that was pulled on the Chamber of Commerce in Cloverdale."

She frowned.

"Bradbury?" she said. "Why, it was Dr. Doray who was in here about that—Dr. Robert Doray."

"No," he said, "I'm after a Bradbury—that's the name—J. R. Bradbury."

"Wait a minute," she said, "I'll take a look through the appointment book."

She ran her finger down the pages of a daybook, then nodded.

"Yes, he saw Carl Manchester. They both saw Carl Manchester."

"And Dr. Doray," said Perry Mason, "being young, handsome and impressionable, is remembered without consulting the records, whereas Bradbury, being fattish and forty, is relegated to the limbo of forgotten names. Once more psychologists are vindicated in claiming that we remember that which we are interested in, and—"

"Carl Manchester," she said, interrupting him, "is the third door down the corridor on the left. Shall I tell him you're coming? If you start probing the secrets of my heart, I'm going to bang this law book at you, and there's a sadfaced man who was defrauded out of the savings of a lifetime sitting there in the waiting-room, who'll think it's conduct unbecoming a lady and as out of place as an accordion at a funeral."

"Tell him I'm on my way in," Perry Mason said, smiling, and walked through the gate which separated the waiting-room from the long corridor of offices.

Carl Manchester looked up from a law book, a half-smoked cigarette hanging from his lips, as Perry Mason opened the door.

Manchester gave the impression of being one whose body was always on an angle of forty-five degrees. He seemed to put in his entire waking time leaning over a law book in rapt concentration, or else looking up at a visitor with the manner of one who trusts that the interruption will not cause him to lose his place in the book he is reading.

"Hello, Perry," he said. "What brings you here?"

"Doing my duty to a client," said Perry Mason.

"Don't tell me you're retained in that hammer murder!" Manchester said. "We've got a good case against that woman, but if you start in—"

"No," Mason said, "I'm working on the same side of the street you are this time."

"How do you mean?"

"Bradbury was in to see you about Frank Patton, who put on a racket in Cloverdale," Mason said.

"So was Dr. Doray," Manchester told him. "Doray's coming back in half an hour."

"Why coming back?"

"I told him I'd look up a little law."

"Have you looked it up?"

"No, but it's going to make him feel better handling it that way."

"In other words, you're washing your hands of the whole affair?"

"Of course. We aren't washing Cloverdale's dirty linen, and there was nothing pulled here. This is where the girl is, that's all."

"The motion picture company's here," Mason said.

"What of it?"

"Nothing, perhaps; again, perhaps quite a bit of it."

"It's Cloverdale's money, and the Cloverdale merchants are the ones to make a squawk," Manchester went on. "We've got enough troubles of our own. What are you going to do, Perry?"

"That depends," Mason said, "on what I *can* do."

"What are you driving at?"

"If," Perry Mason said, "I could get a confession from Patton, stating that this was the general scheme he had built up to defraud merchants in Cloverdale and elsewhere, it might change the complexion of the situation."

"Listen," Manchester said, "that bird, Patton, is a smooth individual. He knows what he's doing. He isn't going to make any such confession."

"That depends," Perry Mason said.

"Depends on what?"

"Depends on the way he's approached."

Carl Manchester looked shrewdly at Perry Mason, then took the cigarette from his lips and ground out the end in an ashtray.

"Now," he said, "I'm commencing to get your drift."

"I hoped you would," Mason said.

Manchester looked frowningly thoughtful.

"Look here, Mason," he said at length, running his fingers over the corners of the law book, and letting the pages riffle through his fingers, "we're not washing Cloverdale's dirty linen; that doesn't mean that we're sticking up for Patton. The man's a crook; there's no question of that. I've gone into the evidence enough to know it. I don't know whether we can prove anything; I doubt it. The district attorney at Cloverdale passed the buck; that's a bad sign. We don't want to monkey with it. We've got enough stuff to bother us, as it is, without borrowing trouble. But if you want to take this man to pieces, you go ahead."

"How strong can I go?" asked Perry Mason.

"Just as strong as you damn please."

"Suppose he makes a squawk?"

"Get me right on this," Manchester said. "I know the set-up. It's one of those legalized rackets. A lawyer has advised Patton just how far he can go and keep out of jail. Perhaps the lawyer was right; perhaps he's wrong. It's all a question of intent, and you know as well as I do that it's damn near impossible to prove intent by a preponderance of the evidence as it's required in a civil case, let alone to prove it beyond all reasonable doubt, as is required in a criminal case.

"But if you want to get in touch with Patton and try to take him apart and see what makes him tick, you go right ahead."

"And the limit?" asked Perry Mason.

"So far as this office is concerned," Manchester said, "the sky's the limit. That is, we couldn't countenance mayhem. We couldn't overlook beating up with a club, but a rubber hose might be different. In other words, if Patton shows up at this office and tells any story of sharp practice or abuse at your hands, we'll scrutinize that story with a great deal of skepticism and we'll ask him a lot of questions about his occupation. Our attitude toward him won't be exactly friendly."

"That," said Perry Mason, with his hand on the knob of the door, "is all I wanted to know. And don't tell Doray about me."

"Get a confession out of him," Manchester called as Mason was stepping through the doorway to the corridor, "and I think Cloverdale will do something with him."

"When I get a confession out of him," Perry Mason said grimly, "I'll show all of you fellows something."

He closed the door behind him, paused for a joking comment with Maude Elton, left the court house and took a taxicab to his office.

The blonde girl who operated the cigar counter in the lobby of the building, twisted crimson lips into a flashing smile.

"Hello, Mr. Mason," she said.

Perry Mason paused to lean against the counter.

"Marlboros?" she asked.

"A package," he told her.

"Going to shake for them?" she asked.

"No," he said, "I'll pay cash."

He counted out the money, took the package of cigarettes, tore off a corner and leaned with one elbow on the glass of the showcase.

"You work *all* the time?" he asked.

She smiled and shook her head.

"You're on evenings," he said.

"Yes," she told him, "I come down evenings to catch the theater trade."

"And you're on mornings and afternoons?"

She smiled, and shook her head slightly from side to side.

"What are you trying to do," she asked, "make me feel sorry for myself? When a woman has a child to bring up and a mother to take care of, she has to work. And she's mighty lucky to find work."

"How old's the girl now?" asked Perry Mason.

She laughed. "Just the same as she was the last time I told you—five and a half. You ask me regularly about once a month."

Perry Mason's grin was sheepish.

"I keep forgetting," he said, "in between times."

He pulled out a wallet from his inside pocket, took out a twenty-dollar bill.

"Put that in the kid's savings account, will you, Mamie?"

There were swift tears in her eyes.

"Listen," she said, "why do you always do that? I don't like it. I can't refuse for the kid, but I'm getting by here all right, making a living, and—"

"It's just like I told you the last time, Mamie," he said.

"Superstition?" she asked, staring at him with eyes that were hard and bright as those of a wild duck.

He nodded his head.

"I guess all gamblers get that way, Mamie, and I'm one of the biggest gamblers in the world. I gamble with human emotions instead of with cards. Every time I've made a little deposit for the kid's account, it's brought me luck."

Slowly her hand came out and the fingers closed over the bill. Tears once more softened her eyes.

"You're commencing to get me half sold that it *is* superstition," she said, "and that shows how good you are."

Perry Mason started to say something, but turned as he heard some one call his name.

Paul Drake, the detective, and J. R. Bradbury were just emerging from the lobby of the office building.

Paul Drake was a tall man with drooping shoulders. He carried his head thrust slightly forward. His eyes were glassy and prominent. His face was twisted into an expression of droll humor. The eyes held no expression whatever.

"Hello, Perry," he said, "were you just going out?"

Mason looked at his wristwatch.

"I was just coming in," he said. "I've been down for a chat with the D.A.'s office. I see you and Bradbury have had your heads together. What did you accomplish—anything?"

Bradbury's quick gray eyes glinted to Perry Mason's face with swift affirmation.

"I'll say," he said. "This man knows more about the case now than I ever did." His eyes shifted over to the smiling blonde back of the cigar counter.

"Hello, sister," he said, "I'm buying some cigars. Pull out that box over there in the right-hand corner."

He tapped on the glass of the showcase with his finger.

Mamie brought out the box of cigars.

"Ever try these?" asked Bradbury. "They're a fine twenty-five-cent cigar."

Mason nodded, picked out a cigar.

"Take a couple," said Bradbury.

Mason took two cigars.

Bradbury slid the box toward Paul Drake.

"Take a couple," he said.

Drake took two of the cigars and Bradbury took two, and clinked a couple of silver dollars on the glass showcase.

"I'd like to talk with you about this case, Perry," said the detective, as Mamie rang up the sale in the cash register, and pulled change from the compartment of the cash drawer.

"When?" asked Mason.

"Right now, if you can spare the time."

Mamie handed Bradbury the change. Bradbury's gray eyes stared directly at her. His face was twisted into a friendly grin.

"Nice day," he said.

She nodded brightly.

Perry Mason looked at his watch.

"Okay," he said, "I can run up to the office, I guess."

Bradbury turned away from the blonde.

"You folks will want me there?" he asked.

"No," Paul Drake said, "it won't be necessary. I just want to talk over some of the legal points with Mr. Mason and find out just where we stand."

"In other words," Bradbury said, "you'd prefer not to have me there?"

"You don't need to be there," Paul Drake told him. "And you can't do any good by being present. I've got all the information that you have, I think."

"You should have," Bradbury told him, and laughed lightly. "You've asked enough questions."

He reached up with his left hand and took the lapel of Perry Mason's coat, pulling him gently away from the cigar counter and lowering his voice confidentially.

"There's one thing," he said, "that I want to make certain about."

"What is it?" Mason asked.

"I've learned," said Bradbury, "that Bob Doray is in the city. I want you to understand that the employment you have taken from me precludes you from accepting any employment from him, except with my consent."

"Who's Bob Doray?" asked Perry Mason.

"He's from Cloverdale. He's a young dentist—rather impecunious. I don't like him."

"And what's he doing in the city?"

"He's here because Margy is here."

"A friend of hers?" asked Mason.

"He would like to be."

"And you think he'll offer me employment?"

"Hardly," said Bradbury. "I happen to know that he borrowed two hundred and fifty dollars at his bank just before he came to the city. He had some trouble getting the money."

"But you said," Mason pointed out, "that you didn't want me to accept any employment from him."

"I mean," Bradbury said, "that I want you to understand the situation. That if he should approach you, I want you to remember that you are employed by me. He might offer you a note, or something."

"I see," Perry Mason said. "In other words, I'm to remember that *you're* the one who arranged that Miss Clune should have the benefit of my services, and that the credit goes to you exclusively. Is that it?"

A frown of annoyance came to Bradbury's face, which was speedily dissipated by a smile.

"Well," he said, "that's putting it rather directly, but I guess you have the idea."

Mason nodded.

"Anything else?" he asked.

"That's all. I've given Mr. Drake all of the details, a complete mass of details."

Paul Drake nodded to Perry Mason.

"Let's go," he said.

"You can reach me at any time," Bradbury said, "at the Mapleton Hotel. I'm in room 693. Your secretary has a note of the address and the telephone number, Mr. Mason; and Drake also has the information."

Drake nodded.

"Come on, Perry," he said.

The two men turned toward the elevator. Bradbury watched them for a moment, half turned toward the cigar counter, ran his eye over the file of magazines on display; then strode briskly out to the sidewalk.

"I owe you one on that," said Paul Drake to Perry Mason in the elevator.

"Got a good fee?" asked Mason as the cage stopped at his floor.

"Pretty fair. He's rather tight on money matters, but I've worked out a good arrangement with him. The case is a cinch."

"You think so?" Mason asked.

"I know it," said Drake as Mason pushed open the door of his office.

"This man Patton has put on the same kind of a racket other places. It's too well thought out and too smooth to have been tried out just once. I won't bother about the Cloverdale angle. I'll pick out some of the other places.... Hello, Miss Street. How are you today?"

Della Street smiled at him.

"I presume," she said, "you came in to look at the photograph."

"What photograph?" asked Paul Drake, trying to look innocent.

She laughed.

"Oh, well," Drake said, "I may as well look at it while I'm here."

"It's in on Mr. Mason's desk," she told him.

Perry Mason led the way to his private office, dropped into the swivel chair and picked up the legal jacket which was on the desk. He passed it over to the detective. The detective looked at the photograph and whistled.

"Plenty of class," he said.

"Yes," Mason said, "that's one thing about Patton, he's a good picker. What was it you wanted to see me about, Paul?"

"I want to know what's going to happen in this case," the detective said.

"Nothing in particular," Mason remarked. "You're going to find Patton; you're going to find Marjorie Clune. We're going to interview them. We're going to get a confession out of him, and the district attorney here is going to prosecute, and the district attorney in Cloverdale is going to prosecute."

"When you say it fast," Paul Drake said, blinking his expressionless eyes, "it sounds easy."

"I believe in working fast," Mason told him.

"I think I can find Frank Patton," Drake said. "I've got a good description of him. He's tall, heavy-set, dignified, fifty-two years of age, has gray hair and a close-clipped gray mustache. There's a mole on his right cheek. Bradbury has a file of the *Cloverdale Independent* in his rooms at the hotel. There are ads in there that will be evidence, and a photograph we can use.

"My theory is that this racket is too well thought out to have been used in one town. I can find where it's been used in other towns and through some of those other towns I can get a line on Patton."

"All right," Perry Mason said, lighting a cigarette, "go ahead."

"But," the detective inquired, "then what's going to happen?"

"How do you mean?"

"Just how far can we go?"

Mason grinned and said, "That's what I've been down to the district attorney's office for. The sky's the limit."

"Should we tell Bradbury that?" asked Paul Drake.

"We should not," Mason told him, speaking with swift emphasis. "We'll tell him nothing of the sort. When we locate Patton, we keep that location to ourselves. We interview him. After we've interviewed him, we tell Bradbury what we have done; we don't tell him what we are going to do, at any stage of the game."

"I'm supposed to make reports to my client," Drake said uneasily.

"That's easy," Mason said. "I'm your client's attorney. You make the reports to me, and I'll take the responsibility."

The detective watched Perry Mason with meditative speculation.

"Can we get away with that?" he asked.

"I can," Mason said.

"And the district attorney doesn't care how we get a confession?"

"Not a bit," Mason said. "You understand, the district attorney's office can't use improper methods; we can use almost any method."

"You mean violence?"

"Not necessarily; there are better ways. We can put him in a spot where he'll have to start talking. Then we'll crowd him into a position where he'll think we're working on a charge of using the mails to defraud in connection with the picture show contract, and get him to make some admissions about the picture business."

"Why didn't the district attorney of Cloverdale go ahead with this?" Drake asked.

"In the first place," Mason said, "he didn't have a case. In the second place, all the big business men in Cloverdale were the suckers. The more moves the district attorney made to clear up the situation, the more he showed the credulity of the small town business man. Naturally, he passed the buck."

"And you're not going to let Bradbury know what we're doing?"

"Not until after it's done."

"In other words," Drake said, "you intend to get rough with him?"

Mason's tone was quietly emphatic.

"You're damn right I intend to get rough with him," he said.

3

Afternoon sun was slanting in through the windows of Perry Mason's office and casting reflections on the glass doors of the sectional bookcases as Perry Mason pushed through the office door and tossed a brief case to a table.

"I got a plea in that knife case," he said. "They reduced it from assault with a deadly weapon with intent to commit murder, to simple assault, and I grabbed at the chance."

"Get any fee?" she asked.

He shook his head.

"That was a charity case," he said. "After all, you couldn't blame the woman; she'd been goaded beyond human endurance. She didn't have any money and she didn't have any friends."

Della Street stared at him in smiling appraisal, her eyes warm.

"You would," she said.

"Anything new?" he asked.

"Paul Drake has been trying to get you on the telephone. He wants you to call just as soon as you come in."

"All right," Perry Mason said, "get him on the line. Anything else?"

"Just a lot of routine," she said, "I've made a memo on your desk. The Drake call is the only one that's important. Bradbury has called a couple of times, but I think he's just trying to find out how the case is going."

"Be sure," Perry Mason said, "that he doesn't get me on the line until after I've talked with Paul Drake."

He walked through to the inner office and had no sooner seated himself at the desk than the telephone rang. He scooped the receiver to his ear and heard Paul Drake's voice:

"I've got the dope on Frank Patton, Perry," said the detective. "That is, I'm going to have it by eight o'clock tonight; perhaps a little before. Can I run in and tell you about it?"

"Okay," Mason said. "Just stay on the line a moment."

He clicked the receiver rest with his finger until he heard Della Street's voice.

"You on the line, Della?" he asked.

"Yes."

"Paul Drake's on the line," he said. "He's going to run in to tell me about this Bradbury matter. He thinks he's got the information that we want. It's important that no one disturbs me until I've finished with Drake. That means, particularly, that I don't want to talk with Bradbury."

"Okay, chief," she said.

"Come right on up," Mason told Drake, and slid the receiver back into place.

Two minutes later, Paul Drake pushed his way through the door to Perry Mason's private office.

"What have you got?" asked the lawyer.

"I think I've got the thing sewed up," Paul Drake said, dropping into the big leather chair and lighting a cigarette. "I've found out that fellow Patton put on the same sort of a racket in Parker City. The peculiar thing is that he didn't use an alias. That is, he pulled the same racket in Parker City and gave his name as Frank Patton. The motion picture company that signed the contract was the same as the one that figured in the Cloverdale contract."

"Who did he hook in Parker City?" asked Perry Mason curiously.

"The same outfit—the Chamber of Commerce and the merchants."

"No, that isn't what I mean. Who was the girl that got gypped?"

"That's where we're going to get our lead on Patton," the detective said. "She's a girl named Thelma Bell, and she's living here in town. We've got her address and telephone number. She's living at the St. James Apartments, a cheap apartment at 962 East Faulkner Street, and the telephone number is Harcourt 63891. She's got apartment 301, but she's out right now. We've been telephoning and trying to get in touch with her. We've got evidence that leads us to believe she's keeping in touch with Frank Patton."

"When can you get in touch with her?" Mason asked.

"Around eight o'clock some time. She's working somewhere, I don't know just where. She's been in chorus work, and I gather that she may be a bit hardboiled. She won the leg contest in Parker City and came on here with a picture contract, the same as Marjorie Clune had. When she found out she was stung, she went into chorus work and has done some posing as an artist's model."

"And she's kept in touch with Frank Patton?" asked Perry Mason, frowning.

"Yes, apparently she's the kind of a kid that takes things as they come. She figured that Patton was running a racket and couldn't be blamed for that. She put it up to him to do the best he could for her here in the city. That's the way we figure it out, according to the story we get from the girl's friends."

"And she's going to be in around eight o'clock tonight?" Mason asked.

"Yes, perhaps a little before that."

"And you think she'll give us Frank Patton's address?"

"I'm certain she will. I've got a good man waiting to catch her as soon as she comes in. He can hand her a line about wanting to keep other girls from being lured to the city by false promises, and all that sort of stuff."

"Well," Perry Mason said, pulling a Marlboro from the desk humidor, "that's swell."

"Oh, no, it isn't," the detective said. "Not yet."

"How do you mean?"

"I want to know," Paul Drake said, "exactly what you're going to do when we've located Frank Patton."

Perry Mason faced Paul Drake with an expression that was grim as granite.

"When I find that man," he said slowly, "I'm going to break him."

"Just how are you going to break him?"

"I don't know," Perry Mason said. "The element of surprise is going to enter into it in some way. You understand, Paul, that this racket he's pulling may be on the up and up, and again it may not be. It's a question of intent.

"Now, that's where all criminal prosecutions break down. District attorneys get frightened to death to take a case where they've got to prove the element of fraud or an intent to defraud. It's an element of the crime. Therefore it has to be established beyond a reasonable doubt. It's hard enough to establish what's in a man's mind by evidence of others, let alone to establish an intent beyond a reasonable doubt.

"Therefore what I want out of this man is a confession. I want to force him to betray himself; to admit that the whole thing is a racket; that his intent from start to finish is to defraud the merchants with whom he is doing business and the girl who is given the phony picture contract. In order to do that, we've got to crash in and surprise him. We've got to get him off his guard and rush him off his feet before he gets a chance to figure just how much of our talk is bluff and how much of it we can prove."

"And I take it we don't want Bradbury there?"

Perry Mason stared steadily at Paul Drake.

"Get this, Paul," he said. "We don't even want J. R. Bradbury to know anything about what we're doing."

The telephone on his desk rang.

Perry Mason picked up the receiver.

Della Street's voice said cautiously, "J. R. Bradbury is calling. He says that he's found out you've left the court house for your office and that he's coming over unless he can talk to you on the telephone."

"Tell him," said Perry Mason, "that I am just coming in the door; that I will be occupied for five minutes; that if he will call at the end of five minutes, I will talk with him over the telephone; that he is not to come to the office until I send for him. Have you got that?"

"Yes, chief," she said.

Mason slammed the receiver back into place, looked up at Paul Drake.

"That guy," he said, "could become a first-class nuisance."

"Bradbury?" asked the detective.

"Bradbury," said Perry Mason.

"He seems affable enough," the detective said.

Mason nodded wordlessly.

"Suppose Bradbury should call *me*?" Paul Drake asked.

"Tell him that you have reported in detail to me and that I have told you not to discuss what you have discovered."

"You mean refuse to tell him anything?"

"Certainly that's what I mean. What did you suppose I meant?"

"He may get sore."

"Leave that to me," Mason said. "Now, here's what I want: I want you to be in readiness to make a dash out to Patton's place with me just as soon as we get him located.

I want you to be prepared to back my play, but I want to take the lead."

"I'm not worrying so much about that," Drake said, "as I am about the position it puts me in with my client. I've really collected information that I'm refusing to give him."

"You've given it to me," the lawyer told him, "and I'm taking the responsibility."

The telephone rang.

Perry Mason frowned at it, picked up the receiver and said, "What is it this time?"

"I want to come in. May I?" asked Della Street.

"Sure," he told her, and dropped the receiver back into place. He sat motionless, his eyes on the door to the outer office.

The door opened and Della Street slipped into the room.

"Dr. Doray is out there," she said quietly. "He insists that he must see you. I wanted you to know before Bradbury called back."

Perry Mason slitted his eyes in thought, then turned quickly to Paul Drake.

"Anything else, Paul?" he asked.

"That just about covers it," the detective said. "I'll know around eight o'clock tonight. Will you be here in your office?"

Mason nodded.

"You can go out," he said, "by that door which opens into the corridor."

Paul Drake slid his legs from the arm of the leather chair, got to his feet and moved toward the door.

"Bradbury," he said, "is almost certain to call me."

"Tell him what I told you," Mason said, and, turning to Della Street, he jerked his head toward the outer office.

"Tell Dr. Doray to come in," he said.

Paul Drake slipped out through the door into the corridor. Della Street held open the door to the outer office.

"You may come in, Doctor," she said.

Dr. Doray was tall, with dark hair, black eyes, high cheekbones, a mouth which was shapeless and a jaw which was thrust aggressively forward. He seemed oddly uncertain of himself as he stood in the doorway.

"Come in," said Perry Mason.

Dr. Doray entered the room, and Perry Mason indicated the big leather chair.

As Della Street closed the door of the outer office behind her, Perry Mason let his eyes sweep over Dr. Doray in frank appraisal.

"What was it?" he asked.

"You're the attorney who's been engaged to locate Marjorie Clune," said Dr. Doray without preliminaries.

"Who told you?" asked Perry Mason.

"That is something that I can't tell you," Dr. Doray said, fidgeting uneasily.

Perry Mason stared at him.

"Well?" he asked.

"I wanted," said Dr. Doray, "to have you give me some information. I thought that perhaps I could arrange to have you represent Margy—Miss Clune—in the matter. I don't know just what Bradbury has hired you to do."

"Unfortunately," said Perry Mason, "I can't accept any employment from you. I am, however, interested to learn how you knew that I had been employed, and what made you think it was Mr. Bradbury who had employed me."

Dr. Doray smiled with his mouth. His eyes remained black, glittering and unsmiling.

"You're not going to answer the question?" asked Perry Mason.

Dr. Doray shook his head.

"Under those circumstances," said Perry Mason slowly, "I would say that you had purchased a box of candy for Miss Maude Elton, the secretary in the district attorney's office."

Dr. Doray flushed and hastily averted his eyes.

Perry Mason nodded. "I think, Doctor," he said, "we understand each other perfectly."

"I'm not certain that we do," said Dr. Doray. "What I am particularly anxious to find out is—"

"Nothing that I can tell you," Perry Mason said.

The telephone rang twice. Perry Mason picked up the receiver.

"Excuse me a moment," he said to Dr. Doray, and then said into the transmitter, "Hello."

Bradbury's voice came over the wire.

"Have you learned anything?" he asked.

"Yes," said Perry Mason in a guarded voice, "I think that I am going to have some important information for you around eight o'clock tonight. I want you to be at my office by eight fifteen at the latest. I want you to bring with you the file of newspapers that you have."

"Have you located Patton?" asked Bradbury eagerly.

"I have not," Mason said.

"You've talked with Mr. Drake?"

"Yes."

"Has Drake located him?"

"No," said the lawyer. "He reports, however, that he is making progress."

"Can't you tell me anything more than that?"

"That's all. I want you to be in my office by eight fifteen, and I want you to have those newspapers with you."

"Can I see you before that?" asked Bradbury.

"No," said Perry Mason, "I'm busy. I'll see you tonight."

"Will you be there when I arrive?"

"I don't know. If not, you are to wait until I telephone for you to join me, or until I return to the office."

"I want to talk with *you*," Bradbury said.

"You can talk with me tonight," Mason told him. "Good-by." He pushed the receiver back into position.

Doray's black eyes were glittering as though with a fever.

"Was that Bradbury?" he asked hoarsely.

Perry Mason smiled at him.

"As I was saying, Doctor," he said, "I think we understand each other perfectly. There is nothing that I can tell you. You might, however, leave your address with my secretary."

"I have already done that," Dr. Doray said. "I had to do it before she would announce me. I'm staying at the Midwick Hotel. The telephone number is Grove 36921."

"Thank you," said Perry Mason, arising and indicating the exit door to the outer corridor. "You can go out through that door."

Dr. Doray got to his feet, hesitated a moment, took a quick breath as though about to say something, then changed his mind, turned and walked to the door.

"Good afternoon, Counselor," he said.

"Good afternoon, Doctor."

The door slammed shut. Perry Mason picked up the receiver of his telephone.

"Della," he said, "I want you to be at the office by eight fifteen tonight; perhaps a little bit before that. Have plenty of freshly sharpened pencils and a clean notebook. I may want you to take a statement."

"A confession?" she asked.

"It may amount to that," he told her, and smiled grimly as he dropped the receiver back into position.

4

Perry Mason latch-keyed the outer door of his office and switched on the lights. He looked at his wrist-watch. The time was precisely seven fifty. He pushed off the latch of his office door, crossed the outer office, opened the door of his private office and pushed on the light. He sat on the edge of the desk and picked up the telephone receiver. A buzzing sound announced that Della Street had left the instrument plugged in on the outer line through the switchboard in the other office. Perry Mason dialed the telephone number which he had seen on Della Street's memorandum in the file of the case of the girl with the lucky legs. His memory for telephone numbers was almost photographic, and his fingers moved swiftly and unhesitatingly.

"Mapleton Hotel," said a woman's voice.

"I want to talk with Mr. J. R. Bradbury, of Cloverdale," Perry said.

"Just a moment."

There was a moment during which the receiver made singing noises, then the click of a connection, and a woman's voice said, "Yes?"

"I wanted Mr. Bradbury," said Perry Mason.

"Ring room 693," the woman's voice said irritably, and there was the sound of a receiver slamming on the hook at the other end of the line.

At that moment, the door of the outer office opened and closed. Perry Mason looked up. The receiver was still making singing noises. A shadow formed where the ribbon of light came through the bottom of the door of Perry Mason's private office, then the door opened.

Perry Mason dropped the receiver back into place.

"Hello, Bradbury," he said, "I was just calling you."

Bradbury entered the office, smilingly suave.

"Are you going to tell me," he asked, "what you've got?"

"I haven't got anything," Mason said.

"Not yet?" asked Bradbury.

"Not yet."

"I called Paul Drake this evening," said Bradbury. "He told me that you had instructed him to give all of the information he uncovered to you and that you would be responsible to me."

Perry Mason made little drumming motions with the fingers of his right hand on the top of the desk.

"Let's get this straight once and for all, Bradbury," he said. "You hired me to represent your interests. I'm hired as an attorney, not as an employee. I occupy the same position that a surgeon would occupy. If you employed a surgeon to operate on you, you wouldn't try to tell him how to perform the operation."

"I'm not kicking," Bradbury said smilingly. "You know your business. I looked you up thoroughly before I came here. Anything that you say is okay with me."

Perry Mason heaved a sigh.

"That," he said, "simplifies matters."

He took a cigarette from the humidor, turned it toward Bradbury. Bradbury shook his head and reached for his waistcoat pocket.

"No," he said, "I'll smoke one of my cigars."

"You're early," Perry Mason said.

Bradbury indicated a copy of *Liberty* which he held under his left arm.

"I picked up one of the new *Libertys*," he said. "They're just on the stand. I don't need to bother you at all; I'll sit in the outer office and read. You go right ahead with whatever work you have in mind."

Perry Mason moved away from the desk and toward the door to the outer office.

"I was just going to suggest that," he said. "I've got some matters that I want to work on without being disturbed. I'll let you know just as soon as I'm ready for you."

Bradbury nodded, his keen gray eyes surveying Perry Mason.

"Do you think," he said, "that you're going to be able to get sufficient facts on which to base a criminal prosecution?"

"I don't think," Perry Mason told him, "until I've got something to work on. You can't build up a case without facts. I haven't got all of the facts yet."

Bradbury walked back into the outer office. The door clicked shut behind him. Perry Mason read a copy of the *Advance Decisions* of the Supreme Court for ten minutes, then softly tiptoed to the door which led to the outer office, opened it and looked out.

J. R. Bradbury was seated in one of the chairs to the right of Della Street's desk, immersed in the periodical he was reading. He did not even look up. Perry Mason turned the knob with his fingers as he closed the door, so that the latch slipped silently into place.

He walked back to his desk, tossed the *Advance Decisions* to one side and smoked in silent contemplation.

The telephone rang.

Mason scooped the receiver to his ear with a hasty motion.

"Mason talking," he said.

Paul Drake's voice came to his ears:

"Okay, Perry," he said. "I've heard from my man who was out at this woman's apartment, waiting for her to come back. He's got all the information."

"Have you located Patton?" Mason asked.

"Yes, we've located him, and we're pretty certain that he's in his apartment. We've got quite a bit of dope on the racket he runs, perhaps enough to make it look as though we could start a criminal prosecution.

"He's living at the Holliday Apartments out on Maple Avenue, 3508 is the number. He's got apartment 302.

"I've looked the place up. It's an apartment house that pretends to have a hotel service, but doesn't have very much. There's an automatic elevator and a desk in the lobby. Sometimes there's some one on duty at the desk, but not very often. I have an idea we won't have any trouble getting up there unannounced. We can give him a third degree, and we can probably get a confession out of him."

"Okay," Mason said. "Where are you now?"

"I'm telephoning from a drug store at Ninth and Olive. I'm ready to start whenever you are. I think you'd better take Della Street along. He'll probably make a statement."

"No," Perry Mason said, "I don't want to take her right now. I don't want her to hear the way we work on him. I'll have her where she can grab a taxi and come out the minute we telephone."

"You'll join me here, then?" asked Paul Drake.

"Yes, you stay there. I'll be with you in ten or fifteen minutes, perhaps less."

Perry Mason dropped the receiver into place, paused for a moment, frowning thoughtfully, then he strode across the office and opened the door which led to the outer office.

Bradbury looked up from his magazine expectantly.

"Will it be much longer before you are ready for me?"

"Not very much longer," Mason said. "Della Street hasn't come in yet, I see."

Bradbury looked over at her vacant desk.

"Was there something I could do?" he asked. "I'm willing to do anything. You know, I—"

He suddenly stared at Perry Mason with his eyes wide, a look of consternation on his face.

"What's the matter?" asked the lawyer.

"Those newspapers!" said Bradbury. "By Gosh! I came away and forgot them!"

Perry Mason nodded his head slowly.

"That's okay," he said. "I wish I had them, but a delay of an hour or so won't make any difference. How long will it take you to get them?"

Bradbury looked at his watch.

"I could get them," he said, "in perhaps thirty minutes. A taxicab would get me to the hotel in about fifteen minutes, and it would take about the same to come back. I can put my hand on them even in the dark. I remember I rolled them up and left them on the bed."

"Any wrapper around them?" asked Mason.

"No, they're just rolled and tied with a string."

Perry Mason shook his head in silent rebuke.

"Don't ever do that," he said. "Whenever you're commencing to put the screws on a crook you want to take care of every bit of evidence you've got. Those newspapers represent evidence, and if Patton should learn that you had them, he'd steal them."

"We could, of course, get the back files of the newspaper," Bradbury said, "but these are complete files that we can introduce as evidence if we have to."

"I don't want to introduce them as evidence," Perry Mason told him, "I want to spread them out on a table in front of that crook and make him realize just what he's up against. You go and get them."

Bradbury dropped his magazine and started for the door. At that moment, the door opened and Della Street smiled at them.

"Am I late?" she asked.

"No," Mason told her. "Every one else is early. I'm just going out, Della."

She glanced meaningly at Bradbury.

"Mr. Bradbury," said the lawyer, "is going to his hotel to get some papers that he forgot. He'll be back with them within half an hour. You'll probably hear from me within half an hour—within an hour, anyway. Wait here until you hear, and have a shorthand book and some pencils ready. Mr. Bradbury will return to the office, and he'll wait for instructions here."

Bradbury's face was eager.

"You think you're going to get somewhere, Mr. Mason?" he asked.

"Perhaps," said Perry Mason.

"Look here," Bradbury said, "I'll telephone just as soon as I get to the hotel, so that if you've learned anything you can leave word for me."

Perry Mason turned his head slightly so that the wink of his right eye was visible only to Della Street.

"Okay," he said. "It may be that I'll want you to meet me somewhere."

He turned to Della Street.

"I'm on my way," he said.

"By the way," Bradbury said, "there's one question I wanted to ask you."

Perry Mason turned impatiently at the door.

"Has Dr. Doray called on you?" asked Bradbury.

"Yes," Mason said, "he has. Why?"

"You didn't accept any employment from him?"

"No, certainly not. That was part of the understanding I had with you. I wasn't to represent him under any circumstances."

"That is," Bradbury said, "without my consent."

Mason nodded.

"Why?" he asked.

"I want to warn you," said Bradbury, "that Doray is rather a peculiar character. If you get in touch with Marjorie Clune, bear that in mind, and under no circumstances let Doray know where Patton is, if you locate Patton."

"Why?" Mason asked. "You're afraid that Doray might do something violent?"

"I am quite certain he might," Bradbury said. "I happen to know of some statements he's made."

"Okay," Mason said. "There's no particular hurry, Bradbury. I think you've got half an hour anyway, but I'll keep in touch with the office, and you can do the same."

He pushed his way out into the corridor and slammed the door behind him, leaving Bradbury bending over Della Street's desk, a look of keen interest in his eyes as he offered her a cigarette.

5

Perry Mason left his taxicab at Ninth and Olive.

"I'm going to want you for a while. You stick around," he told the driver.

He crossed the street to a drug store and found Paul Drake leaning against the marble slab of the soda fountain, smoking a cigarette.

"You were long enough getting here," the detective said.

"Bradbury was in the office," Mason told him, "and he wanted to tell me a lot of stuff about Doray."

"Yeah?" asked Paul Drake.

"And then," said Perry Mason, "he was offering Della Street a cigarette. He was doing it with something of a manner."

The men looked at each other and laughed.

"Well," Paul Drake said, "I don't know how you feel about it, but as far as I'm concerned, I don't care how impressionable he is. That's what's giving me the butter on my bread. Personally, I'd say he was laboring under the impression he was quite a ladies' man. Did you notice the way he smirked at Mamie down at the cigar counter?"

Perry Mason nodded curtly.

"However," Paul Drake went on, "you can't blame him. He's evidently a bachelor with plenty of money. You notice the way he dolls himself up. His tie must have cost more than five dollars. His tailored suit is a wonderful piece of work. And the particular shade of brown has been chosen with some care. You can tell, because it matches his complexion. And then he wears socks, shoes, tie and shirt all in a general color scheme of—"

Perry Mason made a gesture of disgust.

"Forget it," he said. "Let's get down to brass tacks. What about Patton?"

"I don't know much more than I told you over the telephone, but I want to work out a plan of campaign."

"All right," Perry Mason said, "here's the plan of campaign. You've got your car here?"

"Yes."

"You get in it and go on out to the Holliday Apartments. I've got a taxicab waiting out here. I'll go out in it. You may make a little better time in your car than the cab, so you'd better give me a start of about five minutes. I'll go out there and break the ice. You come busting into the apartment without knocking. I'll try and arrange things so the door is open."

"What do I do after I come in?" Paul Drake inquired.

"You follow my lead," Perry Mason said. "I'm going to start browbeating him. He'll either get frightened or righteously indignant, one of the two. You can tell which it is when you open the door.

"You can pretend you haven't got any connection with me, if you want to. Or you can put up any kind of a stall you want. Bradbury is going to be at my office within half an hour with original newspapers that we can use any way we want to. We can tell him that part of the newspaper subscription list went through the mail, and that therefore he'd used the mails to defraud."

"That'll be a good line," Drake said. "We should have the newspapers with us."

"I know it," Mason said, "but Bradbury forgot them and I didn't want to wait. Della Street is in the office, all ready to grab a taxi and come out as soon as we get him softened up a bit. He'll probably be hard at first, and I don't want Della to hear what goes on.

"Now, remember that I'm to take the general lead, but we can pull almost anything we want to. The district attorney can't use improper methods to get a confession; but *we* can use almost anything *we* want to get a confession. And then he can confirm it later on to the district attorney."

"And you're going to try to make him admit that his intention was to defraud?" asked the detective.

"That's the gist of the whole business," Perry Mason said. "We keep plugging away at him until we get that admission. After we get it, we don't care what happens."

"All right," Paul Drake said, "let's go. I'll give you five minutes. It'll take you almost twenty minutes to get out there."

"Not much over fifteen," Mason said. "You just give me five minutes' start, and don't worry about the time at the other end."

Paul Drake nodded, motioned to the attendant at the counter.

"A bromo seltzer," he said.

Perry Mason turned and flagged his taxicab from the opposite curb. As the cab swung around to him, he said, "The Holliday Apartments on Maple Avenue; 3508 is the number. Step on it."

He settled back in the cushions of the cab as the vehicle lurched into motion, and lit a fresh cigarette from the butt of his old one. He sat perfectly calm and steady, with no outward indication of tension or nervousness. He gave the impression of a fighter who would jockey his adversary about with the utmost patience until there was an opportunity to end the fight with one terrific punch.

He was just finishing his cigarette when the cab slowed down and pulled toward the curb.

Perry Mason leaned forward and tapped on the glass. As the driver turned and slid the glass partition back, Perry Mason said, "Don't stop right in front of the Holliday Apartments. Better stop half a block this side."

The driver nodded, crossed an intersection and pulled in toward the curb.

"How's this?" he asked.

"This is fine," the lawyer said. "Now, I may be gone an hour—perhaps longer. I may not want you at all, but if

I do want you, I'll want you in a hurry. Here's ten dollars. Park right along in here some place and start your motor every five or ten minutes so it'll be warm. I may want you to go places in a hurry."

The cab driver grinned and pocketed the bill. Perry Mason got to the curb and located the illuminated sign which marked the location of the Holliday Apartments. He pounded down the pavement with quick, aggressive, purposeful strides, and was within twenty feet of the entrance when he saw a young woman emerge hastily from the door.

She was in the early twenties. She wore a white coat with a fox fur collar, white shoes and a small white hat with a red button on the top. Her figure was trim and graceful, and there was a certain subtle ease about her stride which made her walk with an effortless glide.

Perry Mason caught a brief glimpse of a very white face with wide blue eyes; then the face was hastily averted, and remained averted as she walked past Perry Mason, her heels clicking on the pavement.

Perry Mason paused to stare at her. There had been something almost of panic in the blue eyes, and the face was held so rigidly averted that she might have been some one who was acquainted with the attorney and trying to keep him from recognizing her.

The coat fitted snugly around the back and hips, and Perry Mason could see the smooth play of her muscles beneath the cloth as she walked.

He watched her until she had crossed the intersection, and then pushed his way into the Holliday Apartments.

There was a desk in the lobby but no one was at the desk. Back of the desk was a rack of pigeonholes over each of which was the number of a room. In some of the pigeonholes were keys, and in some were bits of paper or envelopes.

Perry Mason looked at number 302 and saw that there was no key in the box. He walked to the elevator, opened the door, entered the smelly cage, pushed the button for the third floor, and rattled slowly upward.

When the elevator came to a jarring stop, Perry Mason opened both doors, walked out into the corridor. He found a right angle turn in the corridor, turned to the left, walked the length of the corridor, and came to apartment 302. He started to rap with his knuckles when he noticed a bell button to the right of the door. He pushed his thumb against the bell button and heard the whir of a buzzer on the inside of the apartment.

There was no sound of motion.

Mason waited and pushed his finger on the buzzer once more. When there was no response, he pounded with his knuckles on the panels of the door. He saw light in the apartment and bent to the keyhole.

He waited for a few silent seconds; then, frowning, tried the knob. The knob turned readily, the latch clicked and the door swung open.

Perry Mason stepped into a room which was fitted as a combination sitting and dining-room. There was a small kitchenette on the right. On the left was a closed door. The room was empty. On the table lay a man's felt hat, a cane, a pair of gray gloves, and two slips of paper.

Perry Mason walked over to the table and picked up the slips of paper. Both of them were telephone calls which had been received and evidently placed in the pigeonhole at the desk, to be given to the occupant of apartment 302 when he should call for his key.

One of the messages simply said, *"Mr. Patton: Call Harcourt 63891 and ask for Margy—6:05 P.M."*

The other message read, *"Mr. Patton: Tell Thelma Margy will be about twenty minutes late—8:00 P.M."*

Perry Mason stared frowningly at the two slips of paper, dropped them back on the table, picked up the gray hat and looked at the initials on the band. They were F.A.P.

Perry Mason stared toward the closed door on his left. He let his right hand drop to the edge of the stained table and made little drumming motions with his fingers. Then, reaching a decision, he strode toward the door and opened it.

There were lights burning in the bedroom just as they had been burning in the room he had entered. To the left of the door was the door of the bathroom, which was open. In the opposite corner was a bed and across from the bed was a dresser. The mirror on the dresser showed a reflection of the corner beyond the bathroom which Perry Mason could not see from the door in which he stood.

The reflection in the mirror showed the slippered feet of a man, the toes pointed upward at an angle. Above the slippers was a glimpse of bare leg, and then the fringe of a bathrobe.

Perry Mason stood absolutely motionless for a second or two, his eyes staring at the reflection in the mirror.

He looked over toward the bed and saw a man's coat, shirt, tie and trousers flung on the bed, apparently without any attempt whatever at order. The coat was wrinkled and one sleeve was pulled up inside of itself, the trousers were flung in a heap. The shirt was at the opposite corner of the bed.

Underneath the bed were shoes and socks. The shoes were tan oxfords, the socks were gray. Mason looked at the necktie. It too was gray. The trousers and coat were gray.

Perry Mason stepped into the room and walked around the corner of the bathroom.

He stood staring at the body which lay on the floor.

The body was that of a man approximately fifty years of age, with gray hair, close-cropped, grizzled mustache, and a mole on his right cheek.

The body was attired in underwear, with a silk bathrobe thrown over the shoulders, the right arm through the sleeve, the robe lying loose over the left shoulder, and the left arm bare. One hand was sprawled out with the fingers clutched; the other hand was lying across the chest. The man's body lay on its back, and the eyes were partially open and glazing in death.

There was a stab wound in the man's left breast from which blood had spurted and was still welling in a thick viscid pool which stained the bathrobe and discolored the carpet. A few feet away from the body there lay on the carpet a long-bladed knife of the sort that is frequently used for cutting bread. It was a knife that had a blade some three inches wide at the base, and which tapered uniformly to a point. The blade was some nine inches long. The knife was covered with blood, and had evidently been dropped after it had been pulled from the man's body.

Perry Mason carefully avoided the blood, bent down and felt of the man's wrist. There was no pulse. The wrist was still warm.

The lawyer looked about the room at the various windows. One of them—the one by the bed—opened on a fire escape, and the bed was slightly indented, as though a person had either lain on it, or had crawled across it. Mason tried the door which led from the bedroom to the hallway. It was locked and bolted from the inside. He took his handkerchief and carefully wiped off the door-knob where his fingers had touched it. He walked back to the door which led from the sitting-room to the bedroom and polished the knob of that door with his handkerchief. Then he did the same thing to the knob of the door which led from the living-room to the corridor.

As he was polishing the doorknob, his eye noticed some object lying on the floor near the comer of the room. He walked to it. It was, he saw, a leather-covered billy, or blackjack, with a leather thong on the end to be looped over the wrist.

He bent to examine it, without touching it, and noticed that there was blood on it.

Lying on the floor, near the table on which the hat, gloves and stick reposed, was some brown wrapping paper which had not been crumpled, but had evidently been dropped to the floor and was stiff enough to have retained something of its original shape.

Perry Mason noticed that the wrapping paper was creased as though it might have been wrapped about the knife that he had seen in the other room.

He opened the door to the corridor, taking care to hold his handkerchief over his finger-tips as he did so. He started to polish the outer knob of the door, then thought better of it. He stepped into the corridor and pushed the door shut with his right hand, making no effort to keep his fingers from touching the outside knob.

He was just closing the door when he heard the clang of the elevator door and a woman's voice saying, "...you can hear her just as soon as you get opposite the door. She's crying and laughing and saying something about lucky legs."

There were pounding steps in the corridor, and a man's gruff voice said, "Probably just a woman having hysterics over a love affair."

"But I heard something fall, Officer. It sounded like a body. It was a jarring thud..."

Perry Mason looked toward the far end of the corridor. It was a blind corridor with no window. He looked back toward the bend in the corridor, whipped some passkeys from his pocket, selected one and inserted it in the lock of the door. The key worked smoothly. The bolt clicked into place, and Perry Mason was slipping the key back into his pocket as an officer in uniform barged around the bend in the corridor and came to an abrupt stop as he saw Perry Mason in front of the door of apartment 302.

Perry Mason raised his knuckles and pounded upon the panel, keeping his face toward the door.

From the corner of his eye, he saw the officer hold out his left hand and restrain a rather fleshy woman of middle age who had rounded the corner in the corridor just back of the officer.

Perry Mason banged on the panels of the door; then pressed his thumb against the button on the buzzer.

After a moment, he turned away with an air of dejection, raised his eyes and then, apparently for the first time, saw the officer and the woman.

He stared at them.

"Just a minute, buddy," said the officer, moving forward. "I want to talk with you."

Perry Mason stood still.

The officer turned to the woman.

"That apartment?" he asked.

The woman nodded.

Perry Mason turned to face the woman. She wore a rather wrinkled dress, shoes, and no stockings. Her hair was badly disarranged. There was no make-up on her face.

"Who were you looking for, buddy?" asked the officer.

Perry Mason jerked his head toward the door of apartment 302.

"I wanted to see the man who lives in there," he said.

"Who's the man who lives there?" asked the officer.

"His name is Frank Patton," Perry Mason said, "—that is, I have reason to believe that's his name."

"What did you want to see him about?"

"About a matter of business."

The officer turned to the woman.

"Do you know this man?" he asked.

"No," she said, "I've never seen him before."

Perry Mason frowned irritably.

"You don't need to wonder about who I am," he said.

He pulled a leather card case from his pocket, took out one of his business cards, and handed it to the officer.

The officer read it, and there was a note of respect in his voice as he looked up and said, "Oh, you're Perry Mason, the big lawyer, eh? I've seen you in court. I remember you now."

Mason nodded, smiled affably.

"How long you been trying to get in the apartment?" asked the officer.

"Oh, perhaps a minute, perhaps a little longer," Mason said.

"There's no one home?" the officer inquired.

"I couldn't hear a sound," Mason said, "and it's strange, because I had every reason to believe that Patton was in. I pushed the button on the buzzer, and I could hear the buzzer sounding in the apartment. Then I pounded on the door, but I didn't get any answer. I thought perhaps he was in another room, or changing his clothes or something, so I waited a little while and then started all over again. I was just giving up in disgust when you came around the bend in the corridor."

"This woman," said the officer, "heard a girl having hysterics in there and then she heard something bang, as though some one had fallen to the floor. You didn't hear anything, did you?"

"Not me," Mason said. "How long ago was it?" he asked the woman.

"Not very long ago," she said. "I was in bed. I hadn't been feeling well and I went to bed early. I jumped up and pulled on a dress and put on some shoes and went out to find the officer. I brought him up here just as soon as I found him."

"Did you try the door?" the officer inquired.

"I rattled the knob," Perry Mason said. "I think the door's locked. But I didn't really turn the knob and press against it to find out. I just rattled it. I don't mind telling you, Officer, that I'm very much interested. I'm anxious to see Frank Patton. If he's in there, I'd like very much to see him."

The officer regarded the woman with frowning contemplation; then moved over to the door of apartment 302 and banged with his knuckles on the panel. When there was no answer, he took out his night stick and rapped sharply with the end of that. Then, he tried the knob of the door.

"Locked," he said.

He turned away from the door and said to the woman, "You've got the apartment across the hall?"

She nodded.

"Let's go in there," he said. "I want to locate the manager and see if he's got a passkey, and will let us in."

Perry Mason looked impatiently at his wristwatch, then faced the woman.

"Would you say that it was as much as ten minutes ago that you heard the noise in there?" he asked.

"Just about, I guess," she said.

"Just what did you hear?"

"I heard a girl sobbing. She kept saying something about lucky legs, or about her legs being lucky."

"Was she talking in a loud tone?" Mason asked.

"Yes, you know the way a woman does when she's having hysterics. She was sobbing and crying out words."

"You couldn't hear all the words?"

"No."

"Then what did you hear next?"

"Then I heard something bang to the floor."

"You didn't hear any one go in the apartment?"

"No."

"Didn't hear any one go out?"

"No. I don't know as I would have heard that. You see, the way the apartment is arranged, I can hear sounds that come through the bathroom window, but I can't hear things that go on in the apartment."

"But you heard the sound of the jarring fall?"

"Yes, that even jarred the pictures on the wall."

"And you heard this girl sobbing about her lucky legs?"

"Yes."

"She must have been in the bathroom."

"I think she was."

Perry Mason looked over toward the officer.

"Well," he said, "I guess there's nothing more I can do. If there was a woman in there, it doesn't look as though she's there now, and, anyway, I wanted to see a man. I've got to go back to my office."

"I can reach you there any time?" asked the officer. "You may be wanted as a witness. I don't know what's in there. Maybe nothing, but I don't like this business about the jar that shook the pictures on the wall."

Perry Mason nodded, extended his hand with a five dollar bill folded between the fingers, holding it in such a position that the officer could see the bill but the woman could not.

"Yes, Officer," he said, "I can be reached at my office any time. There's nothing that I know. There was no commotion when I got up here. The apartment was silent just the way it is now."

The officer slipped the five dollar bill from between Perry Mason's fingers.

"Very good, Counselor, we'll reach you if we should want you for anything. I'm going to get a passkey and see what's in the apartment anyway."

The woman took a key from her purse and opened the door of the apartment opposite 302. The officer stood aside for her to enter, then followed her in and closed the door. Perry Mason moved swiftly down the corridor and didn't bother to wait for the elevator, but found the stairs and took them two at a time. He slowed to a leisurely walk as he went through the lobby of the apartment house. There was, however, no one at the desk.

Perry Mason walked rapidly down the street and picked up his taxicab.

"Run straight down the street. Keep your eye open for a place where I can telephone, after you've gone about a dozen blocks, but I don't want to telephone from any place in the neighborhood."

The driver nodded.

"She's all warmed up ready to go," he said, and slammed the door as the lawyer settled into the cushions, and jerked the cab into almost immediate motion. He ran for eight or ten blocks; then slowed.

"The drug store over there on the corner," he said.

"That'll be fine," Mason said.

The cab pulled in by a fire plug.

"I'll keep the motor running," the driver said.

"It may be a little while to wait," Mason told him, and entered the drug store. He found a telephone booth, dropped a coin and dialed the number of his office.

Della Street's voice answered.

"Is Bradbury there, Della?" asked Perry Mason.

"Not right now," she said, "he's due any minute. He called up from the Mapleton Hotel about fifteen minutes ago; said that he had the newspapers and that he had some other stuff, some communications that had been written to the Chamber of Commerce, some contracts that were used by the merchants, and some samples of the scrip, and a lot of that stuff. He asked if I thought you'd want that as well as the newspapers. He said he had it all in a brief case."

"What'd you tell him?" asked Mason.

She laughed.

"I didn't know whether you wanted it or not," she said, "but I figured it would keep him out of mischief, so I told him sure to bring it along. He should be in—here he comes now."

"Put him on the phone," Perry Mason said, "I want him."

Mason could hear the sound of her voice, coming faintly over the line.

"Mr. Mason is on the line, Mr. Bradbury," she said, "and he wants to talk with you. You can take the call from that phone over there on the table."

There was a click in the connection; then Bradbury's eager voice.

"Yes?" he asked. "Yes, what is it?"

Perry Mason's voice was low and impressive.

"Now listen, Bradbury," he said, "I'm going to tell you something, and I don't want a fuss made over it."

"A fuss," Bradbury asked, "what sort of a fuss?"

"Shut up," Mason told him, "and keep quiet until I can tell you just what the situation is. Just answer yes or no. I don't want my secretary to know what's going on. Do you understand?"

"Yes," said Bradbury.

"You've been to your hotel?"

"Yes."

"Did you get the papers?"

"Yes."

"You have them there with you?"

"Yes."

"And there was a brief case with some other stuff in it that you brought?"

"Yes."

"The one you telephoned my secretary about?"

"Yes."

"All right," Mason said. "Now we located Frank Patton a little while ago."

"You did," exclaimed Bradbury. "That's great. Have you talked with him yet?"

"He's dead," Mason said.

"What?" yelled Bradbury, his voice shrill with excitement. "What's that? You mean to say you found him—"

"Shut up," barked Perry Mason into the telephone. "Use your head. I told you to sit tight and listen. Don't make a lot of exclamations."

There was a moment of silence. Then, Bradbury's voice, lower in tone, said, "Yes, Mr. Mason. Go ahead. I couldn't hear you very well."

"Now get this," Perry Mason said, "and get it straight, and don't make a commotion about it. We located Frank Patton. He's living at the Holliday Apartments and he has apartment 302. Those apartments are out on Maple Avenue. I went out to see him. I wanted to try and get a confession out of him before you entered the picture. I figured your presence might simply lead to argument, and not do any one any good.

"Frank Patton had been killed about ten minutes before I got there. Some one had stuck a bread knife into his chest. He was lying in his apartment, stone dead."

"Good God," said Bradbury, and then added, almost immediately, "Yes, Mr. Mason. I was just thinking of something. Go ahead and tell me some more."

"Just as I was about to go into the apartment house," Mason went on, "I saw a girl coming out. She was around twenty-one or twenty-two. She had snaky hips and wore a white coat, with a fox collar. She had on white shoes, and a little white hat with a red button on it. Her eyes were very blue, and she looked as though she might be running away from something.

"Now, I want to know if that was Marjorie Clune."

Perry Mason could hear the gasping intake of Bradbury's breath over the line.

"Yes, yes," he said, "that description fits. I know the coat and hat."

"All right," Perry Mason said, "figure it out."

"What do you mean?"

"She may be in a jam."

"I don't understand."

"She was leaving the apartment house just as I went up. There was a woman in an adjoining apartment who had heard quite a racket in Patton's apartment and had gone out to get a cop. She showed up with the cop about five minutes after I got there. There's a pretty good chance the cop may have seen Marjorie Clune. There's also a chance that they may find out she was in the apartment. There was some girl in the bathroom having hysterics and screaming about her lucky legs. That would seem to tie in with Marjorie Clune. Now, what do you want me to do about it?"

Bradbury's excitement burst the bounds of self-control.

"Do about it?" he screamed. "You know what I want you to do about it. Go ahead and represent her. Go ahead and see that nothing happens to her. To hell with Frank Patton. I don't care anything about him, but Margy means everything in the world to me. If she's in a jam, you go ahead and get her out of it. I don't care what it costs. You send the bill to me and I'll foot it."

"Wait a minute," Perry Mason told him. "Keep your shirt on. Don't throw a fit. And, after you hang up the telephone, if Della Street starts asking you questions, don't tell her anything. Tell her that I told you I thought I was going to have some news for you in about an hour, or something of that sort. Stall her along and tell her to wait there. Do you understand?"

"Yes," Bradbury said, but his voice was still high-pitched with excitement.

"You wait right there," Perry Mason said.

"Not here," Bradbury told him, "I'll go to my hotel. You can call me there at my room. You know the number, room 693. Be sure and ask for my room number. I'll be there."

"You'd better wait there in the office."

"No, no, I want to be where I can talk. I've got a lot to tell you, and I want to find out all about what's happening. Will you call me at my room in fifteen minutes, and tell me exactly what's happened?"

"Snap out of it," Perry Mason told him. "I told you not to spill all this information. I'm busy, and I haven't got time to argue with you."

He slammed the receiver savagely on the hook, and strode out of the drug store.

"Go to the St. James Apartments," he told the cab driver. "That's at 962 East Faulkner Street, and drive like the devil."

6

Perry Mason tapped on the door of apartment 301 at the St. James Apartments.

Almost instantly he heard the quick rustle of motion from the interior of the apartment, then footsteps on the floor, then silence as the person on the other side of the door stood motionless, listening with an ear against the door.

Perry Mason knocked again.

He thought he could hear the sound of quick feminine whispers. Then, after a moment of silence, a voice said, "Who is it?"

Perry Mason said gruffly, "Telegram."

"Who for?" asked the feminine voice, louder and more confident this time.

"Thelma Bell," said Perry Mason.

There was the sound of a bolt clicking back. The door opened a crack and a bare arm thrust out through a loose sleeve that appeared in the crack in the door.

"I'll take it," said the voice.

Perry Mason pushed the door open and entered the apartment.

He heard the swirl of motion, the patter of footsteps. A door slammed shut before he could turn his head in the direction of the noise. There was water running in the bathroom, and Perry Mason could hear the steady churning of the water in the tub.

A woman wearing a kimono which had apparently been thrown hastily about her stood staring at Perry Mason with warm brown eyes which now held a trace of angry defiance as well as a trace of panic.

She was, perhaps, twenty-five years of age, well formed, and poised.

Perry Mason stared at her.

"Are you Thelma Bell?" he asked.

"Who are you?"

Perry Mason let his eyes drift over her, noticing the dampness of the fine hairs of her temples, the bare feet, hurriedly thrust into slippers, the pink coloring of the skin at the ankles.

"Are you Thelma Bell?" he again inquired.

"Yes," she said.

"I want to see Marjorie Clune."

"Who are you?"

"Is Marjorie here?" he asked.

She shook her head.

"I haven't seen Margy in ages," she said.

"Who's in there taking a bath?" Mason asked.

"There's no one in there," she said.

Perry Mason stood quietly, staring at the woman. The water in the bathroom had been turned off, and there could plainly be heard the sounds of hurried splashings as some one performed a quick, vigorous scrubbing. Then there was the sound of bare feet thudding to the floor.

Perry Mason let his smiling eyes contradict the girl's statement by calling her attention to the physical proof of her falsehood.

"Who are you?" she demanded again.

"Are you Thelma Bell?" he asked.

She nodded.

"I am Perry Mason, an attorney," he told her. "It's imperative that I get in touch with Marjorie Clune right away."

"Why?" she asked.

"I'll explain that to Miss Clune."

"How did you know she was here?"

"That is something I don't want to tell you right now," Perry Mason said.

"I don't think Miss Clune would wish to see you. I don't think she wants to see any one."

"Listen," Perry Mason said, "I'm an attorney. I'm here to represent Miss Clune. She's in trouble; I'm going to help her out."

"She isn't in any trouble," Thelma Bell said.

"She's going to be," Perry Mason retorted grimly.

Thelma Bell wrapped the kimono more tightly about her, moved to the bathroom door, tapped on the panels.

"Margy," she said.

There was a moment of silence, then a voice said, "What is it, Thelma?"

"There's a lawyer out here," she said, "who wants to see you."

"Not me," said the voice from the other side of the bathroom door. "I don't want any lawyer."

"You come on out," Thelma Bell said.

She turned back to Perry Mason.

"She'll be out in a minute.

"I wish you'd tell me how you knew Margy was here," Thelma Bell said. "There was no one who knew she was here. She came in this afternoon."

Mason frowned, crossed to a chair, dropped into it and lit a cigarette.

"Let's come down to earth," he said. "I know you; you're the young woman who won the leg contest Frank Patton held in Parker City. Patton gave you a fake motion picture contract and brought you here. You were too proud to go back. You've been getting by the best way you could. You met Marjorie Clune through Frank Patton. She was in the same kind of a jam that you were. You wanted to help her out.

"Marjorie Clune was at Frank Patton's apartment tonight. I've got to talk with her about what happened there, and I've got to talk with her before the police do."

"The police?" said Thelma Bell, her eyes widening.

"The police," Perry Mason repeated.

The door of the bathroom opened. A young woman with very blue eyes clasped a flannel bathrobe about her, stared at Perry Mason and then gave a quick little gasp.

"Oh, you recognize me, then," Perry Mason said.

Marjorie Clune said nothing.

"I saw you coming out of the Holliday Apartments," Perry Mason told her.

Thelma Bell's voice was quick and positive.

"You didn't see her coming out of the Holliday Apartments," she said. "She's been with me all the evening, haven't you, Margy?"

Marjorie Clune continued to stare at Perry Mason, her big blue eyes showing a hint of panic. She said nothing.

"The idea,"Thelma Bell went on in a louder voice, "of you making such a statement as that! What would she be doing in Frank Patton's apartment? Anyway, she was with me all evening."

Perry Mason stared steadily at Marjorie Clune.

"Listen, Marjorie," he said in a kindly tone, "I'm here to represent you. You're in a jam. If you don't know it now, you will know it pretty soon. I'm a lawyer. I'm retained to represent your interests. I want to do what's best for you. I want to talk with you. Do I talk now, or do you want to wait until you can talk with me alone?"

"No," she said, "I want to talk now."

"Go ahead," Perry Mason told her, "and get some clothes on."

He turned to Thelma Bell.

"You, too," he said.

There was a small dressing-room which opened on one side of a swinging mirror, on the back of which was a wall bed. The girls exchanged glances, then moved swiftly toward the dressing-room.

"Don't take too much time comparing notes," Perry Mason said. "It won't do you any good. We've got to get down to brass tacks. The police may be here any minute. Make it snappy."

The door of the little dressing-room slammed.

Perry Mason got up from the chair in which he had been seated. He looked around the apartment. He went to the bathroom and opened the door. Water was draining from the tub. There was a bath mat on the floor with wet stains on it. A wet towel lay in a heap near the bath mat. Perry Mason looked around. There were no clothes in the bathroom. He walked back to the apartment, saw a closet door, walked to the closet and opened the door. There was a long white coat with a fox fur collar hanging close to the door. Perry Mason picked up the bottom of the coat and ran it carefully through his fingers.

There was a puzzled frown on his face as he finished with his examination and let the coat drop back into position on the hanger. He noticed a shelf of shoes, and took down the shoes one at a time. There were no white shoes on the shelf.

He stood for a moment with his legs spread apart, standing with his weight slightly forward, his eyes squinted in thought, staring meditatively at the white coat with the fox fur collar. He was still standing in that position when the door of the dressing-room opened and Marjorie Clune entered the room, tugging her dress into position. A moment later, and Thelma Bell followed.

"Do you want to talk in front of her?" asked Perry Mason, jerking his head toward Thelma Bell.

"Yes," she said. "I haven't any secrets from Thelma Bell."

"Do you want to talk frankly and tell me everything?"

"Yes."

"I'll tell you first about me," Perry Mason told her. "I'm a lawyer. I've handled some pretty big cases here and I've been fairly successful. J. R. Bradbury is in this city. He's looking for you. He wanted to build up a case against Patton. He wanted to put Patton in jail if he could. He went up to see the district attorney; they told him nothing doing, that they didn't have enough evidence. Then he came to me. I think he wanted me to try and get a confession of some sort out of Patton. I think the district attorney had told him that he'd have to have something like that before he could do anything.

"Anyhow, I got a detective and we started locating Patton. We finally located Thelma Bell. She gave us a lead on Patton."

Perry Mason turned to Thelma Bell.

"You talked with some one from the detective agency tonight," he said.

She nodded.

"I didn't know he was a detective," she said. "I didn't know what he wanted. He wanted some information. I gave it to him. I didn't know what he wanted to use it for."

"Well," Perry Mason said, "that's the story. I was retained to represent you. I was retained to try and bring Patton to justice. I went out to Patton's apartment, when I found out his address from the detective who had been talking with Thelma Bell. I saw you, Marjorie, leaving the apartment."

The two young women exchanged swift glances.

Marjorie Clune took a deep breath, turned to stare steadily at Perry Mason.

"What," she asked, "did you find in Frank Patton's apartment, Mr. Mason?"

"What," asked Perry Mason, "did you leave there, Marjorie?"

"I couldn't get in," she said.

Perry Mason shook his head wordlessly in chiding negation.

"I couldn't!" she flared. "I went up to his apartment and pressed the buzzer. There wasn't any answer. I came back down."

"Did you try the door?" asked Perry Mason.

"No," she said.

"When you left the apartment," he said, "there was—"

"I tell you I wasn't *in* the apartment!"

"We'll let it go at that," he told her. "When you left the apartment house there was a woman bringing an officer to the apartment. She'd heard quite a bit of commotion in the apartment. She'd heard a girl screaming something about her legs being lucky, and having hysterics. Then she'd heard the sound of something falling, a heavy fall that had jarred the pictures on the wall."

Perry Mason stopped and stared steadily at Marjorie Clune.

"Well?" she asked, and her voice contained just the right amount of polite disinterest.

"Well," said Perry Mason, "what I want to know is whether you met the cop as you walked along."

"Why?"

"Because," he said, "you looked guilty. When you looked at me and saw I was looking at you, you turned your head the other way and acted as though you were afraid I was going to nab you and charge you with the theft of a thousand dollars."

Perry Mason watched her with his eyes slitted in shrewd contemplation.

The girl bit her lip.

"Yes," she said slowly, "I saw the officer."

"How far from the Holliday Apartments?"

"Quite a way; perhaps two or three blocks."

"You were walking?"

"Yes, I was walking. I wanted to . . ."

She broke off.

"Wanted to what?" asked Perry Mason.

"Wanted to walk," she said.

"Go ahead," he told her.

"That's all there was to it."

"You saw the officer. What happened?"

"Nothing."

"Did he look at you?"

"Yes."

"What did you do? Did you walk rapidly?"

"No," she said.

"Think again," Perry Mason told her. "You were almost running when I saw you. You were walking as though you were trying to win a walking race. Now, are you sure you didn't do that when the officer saw you?"

"Yes."

"What makes you so sure?"

"I wasn't walking at all."

"Oh, you stopped then?"

"Yes."

Perry Mason stared steadily at her and then said slowly and not unkindly, "You mean that when you suddenly saw the officer you turned faint. You stopped, perhaps put your hand to your throat, or something of that sort. Then you turned to look into a store window. Is that it?"

She nodded her head.

Thelma Bell slipped an arm around Marjorie Clune's shoulder.

"Lay off the kid," she said.

"What I'm doing," Perry Mason told Thelma Bell, "is for her own good. You understand that, Marjorie. You *must* understand that. I'm your friend. I'm here to represent you. There's a possibility that the officers may come here even before I've finished talking with you. Therefore, it's important to know just exactly what happened, and to have you tell me the truth."

"I am telling you the truth."

"You're telling the truth about not getting into that apartment?"

"Of course. I went to the apartment and couldn't get in."

"Did you hear any one moving around in there? Did you hear any one screaming? Any one having hysterics? Any one making reference to lucky legs?"

"No," she said.

"Then you came back down the elevator and out to the sidewalk?"

"Yes."

"And you're positive you didn't get in that apartment?"

"Positive."

Perry Mason sighed and turned to Thelma Bell.

"How about you, Thelma?" he said.

She raised her eyebrows.

"Me?" she asked in a tone of polite surprise.

"Sure, you," Perry Mason said, with a savage drive to his voice.

"Well," Thelma Bell said, "I'll bite. What about me?"

"You know what I mean," Perry Mason said. "Were you at the apartment tonight?"

"You mean Frank Patton's apartment?"

"Yes."

"Certainly not."

Perry Mason regarded her with calm appraisal, as though considering just what sort of an impression she would make on the witness stand.

"Tell me some more, Thelma," he said.

"I was out with a boy friend," she told him.

Perry Mason raised his eyebrows.

"Good girl," he said.

"What do you mean?"

"For coming home so early."

"That's my business," she told him.

Perry Mason regarded the toes of his shoes with casual interest.

"Yes," he said, "it's your business."

There was a period of silence. Perry Mason suddenly faced Marjorie Clune.

"Did you girls have an appointment with Frank Patton tonight?" he asked.

They looked at each other and raised their eyebrows.

"An appointment with Frank Patton?" said Marjorie Clune, as though it was a physical impossibility for her to believe her ears.

Perry Mason nodded.

The young women exchanged glances, then laughed in high-pitched, patronizing amusement.

"Don't be *silly*," said Marjorie Clune.

Perry Mason settled back in the chair. His features were utterly without expression. His eyes were calm and tranquil.

"All right," he said, "I was trying to give you a break. If you don't want to take it, there's nothing I can do except sit here with you and wait for the police."

He lapsed into a calm, meditative silence.

"Why should the police come *here*?" asked Thelma Bell.

"Because they will know Margy is here."

"How will they know?"

"They'll find out the same way I did."

"How did you find out?"

He yawned, stifled the yawn with four fingers gently patting his lips, and, as he yawned, shook his head, but made no audible comment.

Marjorie Clune's glance toward Thelma Bell was distinctly uneasy.

"What will the police do?" said Marjorie Clune.

"Plenty," said Perry Mason grimly.

"Look here," said Thelma Bell suddenly, "you can't put this kid in a spot like that."

"What kind of a spot?" Perry Mason asked.

"Get her involved in a murder and stand by and not do anything to protect her."

The mask of patient tranquillity dropped from Perry Mason. He flexed his muscles. His eyes became hard, like the eyes of a cat slumbering in the sun who suddenly sees a bird hop unwarily to an overhanging branch.

"How did you know it was a murder, Thelma?" he asked, straightening in the chair and swinging about so that his hard eyes bored steadily into hers.

She gasped, recoiled slightly, and said with quivering lips, "Why . . . why . . . you acted that way. From something you said, I guess."

He laughed grimly.

"Now listen," he said, "you can either take this from me or you can take it from the police. You girls had an appointment with Frank Patton tonight. Marjorie called up and left her telephone number. It was this number. The police will trace the number and come out here. Also, Margy telephoned a message Patton got just before he arrived at the Holliday Apartments, telling him to tell Thelma that she would be about twenty minutes late.

"Both of you girls have won contests that Frank Patton put on; both of you have been chosen as having the most beautiful legs in a small town. One of you, at any rate, has been referred to in the newspapers as having lucky legs—probably both of you. It's a line of publicity that Patton hands out to the local press.

"Now, there was a girl in the bathroom at Frank Patton's apartment who was having hysterics about her legs. She kept using the words 'lucky legs.'

"I saw Marjorie Clune leaving Frank Patton's apartment house. She says she didn't see him. That's what *she* says. Perhaps she did and perhaps she didn't. The police are going to be very interested in finding out. Their methods of finding out are going to be quite direct and not very pleasant.

"I'm the only friend you kids have got in the whole world so far as this business is concerned. I'm trying to help you. I've had the experience and I have the knowledge. You won't accept my help. You sit there and arch your eyebrows at each other and exclaim, 'What? Us go to see Frank Patton? Ha, ha, ha! Don't be *silly*.'

"Then I come up to the apartment and find both of you girls in a lather of cleanliness. You've got bathtub hysteria. You can't get into the bathtub quick enough. You've drawn two baths, and one of you has hardly jumped out of the bathtub before the other jumps in."

"What's wrong with that?" demanded Marjorie Clune aggressively. "I guess we can take baths if we want them."

"Oh, certainly," Mason remarked. "Except that the police will see the evidences of those baths this early in the evening and wonder if you didn't have some reason for taking them."

"What reason could we possibly have for taking a bath that the police would be interested in?" Marjorie Clune demanded in that same haughty tone she had used previously.

Perry Mason turned on her savagely.

"All right," he said, "if I've got to hand it to you, I'll hand it to you. The police would say that you were washing off blood stains; washing blood off your stockings; washing off blood that had spattered on your legs when you stood over Frank Patton."

The girl recoiled as though he had struck her a physical blow.

Perry Mason pulled his big boned frame from the chair, stood towering over the two young women.

"My God!" he said, "have I got to pick on two women in order to get the truth from them? Why weren't there any clothes in the bathroom? What did you do with the clothes you took off? And you, Marjorie Clune, what did you do with the pair of white shoes that you were wearing when you came from the apartment house?"

Marjorie Clune stared at him with eyes that were wide and frightened. Her lips quivered.

"Do . . . do the police know that?"

"They'll know plenty," he told her. "Now, let's come down to earth. I don't know how much time we've got, but we might just as well face the issue frankly."

Thelma Bell spoke in even, expressionless tones.

"Suppose we *were* there? What difference does it make? We certainly wouldn't have killed him."

"No?" asked Perry Mason. "You wouldn't have any motive, I suppose?"

He turned back to Marjorie Clune.

"How long had you been here before I arrived?" he asked.

"Just a m-m-m-m-minute," she quavered. "I didn't take a c-c-c-cab. I came on the street car."

"You were in Frank Patton's apartment, in the bathroom, having hysterics, talking about your lucky legs?"

She shook her head mutely.

"Look here," said Thelma Bell quickly, "will the police know anything about Marjorie being there if the officer who saw her on the street doesn't connect her in some way with the crime?"

"Perhaps not," Perry Mason said. "Why?"

"Because," said Thelma Bell, "I can wear that white coat with the fox fur collar. I can wear the little cap with the red button on it. I'll swear they belong to me."

"That will just put you on the spot," Perry Mason said. "The officer probably didn't remember the face as much as he did the clothes. He'll see the clothes and figure that you were the one he saw. He'll identify you as being the one."

"That's what I want him to do," said Thelma Bell slowly.

"Why?" asked Perry Mason.

"Because," she said, "I wasn't anywhere near the place."

"Can you prove it?" Mason inquired.

"Of course I can prove it," she said savagely. "You don't think I'd put myself in a spot like that unless I could prove it, do you? I want to give Marjorie a break, but I'm not foolish enough to get myself mixed up in a murder rap in order to do it. I'll wear those clothes. The officers can identify me all they want to. The officer on the beat can swear I'm the one he saw coming from the apartment. Then I'll prove to them that I wasn't there."

"Where were you?" Perry Mason asked.

"With a boy friend."

"Why did you go home so early?"

"Because we had a fight."

"What about?"

"Is it any of your business?"

"Yes."

"About Frank Patton."

"What about Frank Patton."

"He didn't like Frank Patton."

"Why? Was he jealous?"

"No, he knew the way I felt toward Patton. He thought Patton was dragging me down hill."

"In what way?"

"The contacts he was making for me."

"What, for instance?"

"Modeling," she said. "Artists, illustrators, and such stuff."

"Your boy friend didn't like it?"

"No."

"What's his name?" Perry Mason wanted to know.

"George Sanborne is his name."

"Where does he live?"

"In the Gilroy Hotel—room 925."

"Listen," said Perry Mason, "you wouldn't try to kid me?"

"Try to kid my lawyer? Don't be silly."

"I'm not your lawyer," he said. "I'm Marjorie Clune's lawyer. But I want to give you a fair break."

She waved a hand toward the telephone.

"There's the telephone," she said. "Go ring up George Sanborne. The number is Prospect 83945."

Perry Mason strode to the telephone, jerked the receiver from the hook.

"Get me Prospect 83945," he said when the exchange operator in the lobby asked for his number. And, as he spoke, he was aware of swift feminine whispers behind him.

Perry Mason did not turn. He held the receiver against his ear, stood with his feet planted far apart and his chin thrust forward. There was the buzzing of the line, the click of a connection, and a feminine voice said, "Gilroy Hotel."

"Give me Mr. Sanborne in 925," said Perry Mason.

A moment later a masculine voice said, "Hello."

"Thelma Bell," said Perry Mason, "was hurt in an automobile accident about an hour ago. She's at the Emergency Hospital, and we find your name on a card in her purse. Do you know her?"

"What's that again?" asked the masculine voice.

Perry Mason repeated his statement.

"Say, what sort of a fake is this?" the masculine voice answered. "What do you think I am?"

"We thought here at the hospital that perhaps you were a friend who'd be interested," Mason said.

"Hospital hell!" said the man's voice. "I was out with Thelma Bell all the evening. I left her not more than half an hour ago. She wasn't hurt in no automobile accident then."

"Thank you," said Perry Mason, and hung up.

He turned to face Marjorie Clune.

"Look here, Marjorie," he said, "we're not going to do any talking now. You may think Thelma Bell is the closest friend you've got in the world, but there's only one person who's going to hear your real story—that's your lawyer. Do you understand that?"

She nodded her head.

"If you say so," she said.

"I say so."

He turned to Thelma.

"You're a loyal friend," he said, "but you won't misunderstand me. Anything Marjorie Clune tells *you* can be dragged out of you in front of a grand jury or in a court room. Anything she tells *me* is a privileged communication, and no power on earth can unseal my lips."

"I understand," said Thelma Bell, standing very erect and very white-faced.

"Now, you're willing to help Marjorie out on this thing?"

"Yes."

"Get those things on," he said. "Let's see how you look."

She went to the closet and took down the coat. She put it on, fitted the hat into place.

"Good enough," he said. "Got any white shoes?"

"No," she said.

"He probably won't remember the shoes anyway," Perry Mason said. "What I want you to do is to get out of the apartment and walk around on the other side of the street. Some time tonight you'll see a police car drive up here. You can probably tell it by the license. If you can't, you can tell it by the kind of a car it is. It'll either be a car from the homicide squad, and, in that event, three or four broad-shouldered men who look like cops in plain clothes will get out of it; or else it'll be a radio car. In that event, it'll be a light roadster or coupé, and there'll be two men in it. One of them will get out and the other one will stay in the car to keep track of the radio calls."

"I think I can spot it all right," she said. "What am I supposed to do then?"

"As soon as you see the men head for this apartment building," Perry Mason said, "you'll come walking across the street as though you had just returned from an errand somewhere. You can say you've been to the drug store for some aspirin, or any other kind of a stall that you want to make. Walk right into the arms of the police. They'll start asking you questions. Don't tell them that you've got an alibi too soon. Pretend that you're all confused. Answer the questions in a way that'll arouse their suspicions. Get angry with them and tell them that you don't have to tell anybody where you were and what you were doing.

"If the officer on the beat saw anything particularly suspicious about the way Margy acted, he'll have turned in her description. The probabilities are it'll be a description not so much of the girl as of the clothes. She saw his uniform and that threw her into a panic. She stopped and turned her back to him, looking in the display windows. It probably registered with him at the time, but he was going on another job with this woman who had pulled him in to see what was happening in the apartment, and he didn't pay too much attention to her. But after he got in Patton's apartment and found those telephone messages in there, with Margy's name and Thelma Bell's name, he's going to start thinking back, trying to see if he remembers seeing any woman who acted as though she'd been mixed up in a murder. He's pretty likely to remember the coat and the hat.

"Now, that's going to put you right square on the spot. It isn't going to be pleasant. It's going to mean notoriety, and it's going to mean a lot of things. The question is, Can you do it?"

"I can," she said, "and I will."

Perry Mason turned to Marjorie.

"Go through this apartment," he said. "Pick out anything in here that belongs to you. Put it in a suitcase. Beat it out of here just as quick as you can. Go to a hotel somewhere. Register under your own name, but do it in a way that won't make you too easy to find—what's your middle name?"

"Frances," she said.

"All right," he said, "register as M. Frances Clune, also remember not to give your address as Cloverdale. You're here in the city now. Figure that you're a resident of the city, and put that as your address. Here's one of my business cards. The telephone number is on there, Broadway 39251. Call up my office, ask for Miss Street—she's my secretary—she'll know who you are. Don't mention any names over the telephone, simply say that you talked with me earlier in the day, and that I asked you to leave your address. Tell her the hotel that you're registered at. Then lock yourself in your room. Don't go out at all; don't get away from the telephone. Be where I can reach you at any hour of the day or night. Have your meals sent into your room. Don't try to communicate with me unless something happens. If the police should find you, put on your best expression of baby-faced innocence and don't answer a single question, except as to whether you've got an attorney. Tell them that I'm your attorney. Demand that you be allowed to communicate with me."

She nodded slowly, her eyes fastened steadily upon him.

"You understand all that?"

"I think so."

"Get started then," said Perry Mason. "And remember that no matter what happens, you aren't to make any statement to any one until you have talked with me. You aren't even to answer questions. You won't even tell them who you are or where you came from. The minute any one puts you under arrest, you demand to be placed in communication with your attorney. Show them the card. Demand that you be allowed to telephone me. If they let you telephone me, I'll talk with you over the telephone and tell you not to say anything. If they don't let you telephone me, get sulky. Tell them that if they won't do what you want them to do, you won't do what they want you to do; that if they won't let you telephone me, you won't answer the questions they ask. And every time they ask you a question and you refuse to answer, use that same formula, that you won't answer questions unless they let you call me. You understand?"

"I understand," she said.

Perry Mason strode to the door. As he passed Thelma Bell, he patted her on the shoulder.

"Good kid," he said.

He stepped out into the corridor and heard the door close behind him and the bolt click into position.

7

J. R. Bradbury was seated in the lobby of the Hotel Mapleton when Perry Mason pushed his way through the door.

Bradbury looked cool, capable, and efficient, in a suit of gray tweeds which matched the gray of his eyes. He wore a gray shirt, a gray tie flecked with red, gray woolen socks and black and white sport shoes. He was puffing meditatively at a cigar, when his quick eyes lit on Perry Mason's figure.

Bradbury got to his feet and pushed his way toward Mason.

"Tell me about it," he said quickly and eagerly. "How did it happen? Have you found Marjorie? What can you do for her? What—?"

"Take it easy," said Perry Mason. "Let's go where we can talk. How about your room?"

Bradbury nodded, turned toward the elevator, then paused suddenly.

"There's a swell little speakeasy around the corner," he said. "We can get something to eat there, and we can get a drink. I need it, I haven't got anything in my room."

"You lead the way," Perry Mason said.

Bradbury pushed his way through the swinging doors of the lobby, waited a moment for Mason on the sidewalk, caught the lawyer's arm with his hand and said, "Are there any clews that don't point toward Marjorie?"

"Shut up," Perry Mason said. "Let's wait until we can get where we can talk, and if we can't get privacy in this speakeasy, we aren't going to talk there."

"Don't worry," Bradbury said, "we can get a quiet booth. It's very exclusive. I got a card from the bell captain of the hotel."

He rounded the corner, paused before a door, and pushed a button. A panel slid back, a pair of beady black eyes surveyed Bradbury, then the face vanished. There was a sound of a bolt clicking back, and the door opened.

"Right on upstairs," said Bradbury.

Perry Mason led the way up the carpeted stairs. A head waiter bowed a welcome.

"We want a booth," Mason said.

"Just the two of you?" the waiter inquired.

Mason nodded.

The waiter hesitated for a moment. Then at the steady insistence of Perry Mason's eyes, turned and led the way across a small dining-room in which tables had been crowded, across a small square of waxed dance floor, and down a carpeted corridor. He pulled back a curtain and Perry Mason went in and sat down at a table. Bradbury sat opposite him.

"I want some good red wine and some hot French bread with lots of butter," Perry Mason said, "and that's all."

"I'll have a rye highball," Bradbury told the waiter. "In fact, you'd better bring a pint of rye, some ice, and a couple of bottles of ginger ale. Mr. Mason will probably have a highball when he finishes his wine."

"Not me," said Perry Mason, "wine and French bread, that's all."

"Make it one bottle of ginger ale then," Bradbury told the waiter.

As the curtain clicked back into place, Bradbury looked at Mason and raised his eyebrows.

Perry Mason leaned forward with his elbows on the table, and spoke in a low, confidential, yet rapid voice.

"I located Marjorie Clune. I went out there. She's mixed up in it; I don't know just how badly. There was a friend of hers there, a girl named Thelma Bell. Thelma Bell is in the clear; she's got an alibi, she's going to help Marjorie Clune out.

"I didn't get Marjorie's complete story. I got the story she told me, but it wasn't the complete story. I didn't dare to get the complete story in front of Thelma Bell, and I didn't dare to take Marjorie Clune into another room to talk with her, because I was afraid Thelma would think we were planning some sort of a double-cross. Thelma is going to shoot square with Marjorie. I can't tell you all the details. It's one of those cases where the less you know the better off you'll be."

"But Margy is all right?" asked Bradbury. "You can promise that you're going to keep her in the clear?"

"I can't promise anything," Perry Mason said. "I've done the best I could, and I got to her before the police did."

"Tell me about Frank Patton," said Bradbury. "How did it happen?"

"I don't know how it happened," said Mason. "I found out where he lived and went out there."

"How did you find that out?" Bradbury asked.

"Through the detective you employed."

"When did you find it out?"

"This evening."

"Then you knew where he was living when you started out of your office tonight?"

"Yes."

"Why didn't you take me along?"

"Because I didn't want you along. I wanted to try and get some sort of a confession or an admission out of Patton. I knew that you'd lose your temper and start making a lot of accusations that wouldn't get anywhere. I wanted to talk to him and lay a trap or two for him and see if he wouldn't walk into one of the traps. Then I was going to get rough with him; after I had softened him up some, I was going to get you and my secretary to come out. My secretary would have taken down the conversation in shorthand."

Bradbury nodded.

"That sounds all right," he said. "I was a little bit hurt at first."

"There's nothing to get hurt over," Mason said. "I'm handling this case for the best interests of all concerned. You've got to have confidence in me, that's all."

"Go ahead," Bradbury said, "tell me what happened."

"Well, I got out there," Mason went on, "and pounded on the door of the apartment. There was no answer. I dropped down and took a peek through the keyhole. There was a light on in the apartment. I looked through the keyhole and saw a table with a hat, a cane and some gloves on it. I feel certain they belonged to Patton. They looked the part, they fitted in with the description of Patton that we had.

"I pounded on the panel again, and went to work on the buzzer. I stopped in between times to listen, but couldn't hear a thing. I was just ready to go away when I noticed a cop standing at the corner of the corridor, he'd evidently been watching me for a little while, I don't know just how long.

"Right away, I figured that perhaps something was wrong and I'd walked into it, but there was nothing I could do then except put a bold front on it, so I walked right on toward the cop, he stopped me and wanted to know what I'd been doing, trying to get in the apartment, I told him that I was looking for Frank Patton. That I understood he lived in the apartment there and that I thought he'd be home. I told the cop who I was and gave him my business card.

"There was a woman with the cop; she said she lived in the apartment across the way. I think she's on the up and up. She looked as though she'd tumbled out of bed and dressed in a hurry. She said she'd gone to bed and hadn't been feeling well. That some woman was raising hell in the next apartment and having hysterics about lots of things, among which she was mentioning the words 'lucky legs.' I told you that part on the phone."

"Then what happened?" asked Bradbury.

"Then," said Perry Mason, "the cop went into the woman's apartment and they held a pow-wow. The cop finally managed to get the room opened. He found that Patton had been stabbed with a big bread knife, one of those triangular-bladed affairs that are big and long. I got in touch right away with you because I wanted to find out what you wanted me to do about Margy."

"How did you know Margy was mixed up in it?" Bradbury inquired.

"I saw her—that's what I called you about," Mason told him. "She was coming out of the apartment house just as I went in, and she looked so guilty that she caught my attention. It wasn't guilt as much as it was panic. There was fear in her eyes. She had on that white coat with the white hat, and the red button on the hat, but you're not supposed to know anything about that. It's in confidence. Keep it to yourself."

"Of course I'll keep it to myself," Bradbury said, "but why didn't you speak to her?"

"I didn't know her," said Perry Mason. "I didn't have any idea who she was until afterwards. She looked panic-stricken when she went by me and when I checked up what this woman told the cop about the girl having hysterics over her legs, I figured that it must have been Margy who was in the bathroom."

"What would she be doing in the bathroom?" Bradbury asked.

"You can search me," Mason said. "It looks as though the party had got a little rough. Patton had a bathrobe half on, but his outer clothes were off. There's a chance he tried to pull something and Marjorie had barricaded herself in the bathroom. That's the way I figure it."

"Then Patton followed her into the bathroom and she stabbed him?" asked Bradbury.

"No," Mason said, "the body wasn't in the bathroom. The body was in a bedroom on the other side of the bathroom. There's a chance that the girl was in the bathroom and Patton managed to get the door open. They might have had a struggle of some sort, and then she stabbed him in self-defense. There's another chance that while she was in the bathroom with the door locked, some one else entered the apartment and stabbed Patton."

"Was the door locked?" asked Bradbury.

"Sure," Mason said, "the door was locked. Didn't I tell you that the cop had to go hunt up a janitor or something to get the door open."

"Then," said Bradbury, "if the door was locked, how could any one have walked into the apartment while Margy was in the bathroom?"

"That's easy," Mason said. "Whoever did it, could have locked the door behind him when he went out."

Bradbury nodded again.

"How about the detective, Paul Drake," he said. "Was he around there?"

"Paul Drake was to have followed me out," Perry Mason said. "I told him to give me a five-minute start. I went down to meet Drake at Ninth and Olive and that took a little while. We figured out our plan of campaign and Drake was to leave Ninth and Olive five minutes after I did. Drake was driving his car. I went in a taxicab. Drake would probably make better time than I did; I haven't had a chance to talk with him. The way I figure it is, that just about the time he started toward the building, he saw the woman and the uniformed policeman going into the building. He figured right away that something was wrong, so he played foxy and jumped in the background until he found out what it was. At any rate that's the way I figure it; I haven't had a chance to talk with him."

The curtains clicked back and the waiter brought in their orders. Bradbury poured himself a stiff jolt of whiskey from the flask, dropped ice into the glass, poured in ginger ale, stirred it with a spoon, and drank half of the glass in three big gulps.

Perry Mason critically inspected the wine bottle, moved the neck of the bottle under his nostrils, poured out a glass of the red wine, broke off a piece of the French bread, took a mouthful of the hot bread and sipped the wine.

"Was there anything else?" asked the waiter.

"That's all for the present," Bradbury said. "We'll ring when we want the check. In the meantime, will you see that we're not disturbed?"

The waiter nodded.

"I've said about all I have to say," Perry Mason said.

Bradbury nodded.

"I want to do some talking," he said.

Perry Mason shot him a quick glance.

"You do?" he asked.

Bradbury nodded.

"Go ahead," said Mason.

The waiter stepped out and the curtains fell back into position.

"In the first place," said Bradbury slowly, "I want you to understand one thing, Mason. That is, that I'm going to stand back of Marjorie Clune in this thing, no matter what happens."

"Why, sure," said Mason, tearing off another piece of the French bread with his fingers. "That's the impression I've had all along."

"Furthermore," said Bradbury, "I am going to see that Marjorie Clune gets out of this, no matter who gets hurt."

"Yeah," said Perry Mason, "you haven't told me anything new yet."

Bradbury leaned forward and stared intently at Perry Mason.

"Understand me, Counselor," he said, "I don't want any misunderstandings about this. I am going to see that Marjorie Clune gets out of this, no matter who gets hurt."

There was a beating, steady insistence about his tone, and Perry Mason held the wine-glass halfway to his lips. His eyes suddenly snapped to focus upon Bradbury with a new light in them.

"Huh?" he said.

"Marjorie Clune," said Bradbury, "comes first. I love her more than I love life itself. I would do anything for her. I don't know the particulars as yet, you don't know them yourself, but I want it definitely understood that Marjorie Clune is not going to be placed in any danger. I am going to fight for her against the whole world. I don't care who I have to fight against."

"Go on," Perry Mason said, still holding the glass of wine halfway to his lips.

"I was wondering," said Bradbury, "just how long you had been knocking at the door before the officer got there."

"A minute or two," said Perry Mason. "Why?"

"Do you remember exactly what time it was when the officer arrived?"

"No," Mason said, "I didn't look at my watch."

"That," said Bradbury, "is something that can be ascertained, of course."

"Of course," Mason said, and set down his wine-glass. "Go ahead, Bradbury, I'm listening."

"I was wondering just what time the murder was committed, with reference to the time that you got to the apartment?" Bradbury went on. "The time element may be important there."

"It may be," agreed Perry Mason.

"It seems funny to me," Bradbury said, "that if Margy had been in the bathroom and some one had killed Frank Patton, that the door would have been locked."

"Why?" asked Perry Mason.

"In the first place," said Bradbury, "it is utterly impossible for me to believe that Marjorie Clune had a key to Frank Pattern's apartment. That is simply out of the question."

"Go ahead," Mason told him, "I'm listening."

"In the event," said Bradbury, "Marjorie Clune was barricaded in the bathroom, and Frank Patton broke in through the door, and there was a struggle and Marjorie killed him in self-defense, she would have been the last one to go through the door."

"Yes," said Mason, "what of it?"

"In that event, the door wouldn't have been locked. Since Marjorie Clune didn't have a key to it, and since the dead man could hardly have locked the door.

"On the other hand," went on Bradbury, his eyes boring into those of Perry Mason with steady insistence, "if Marjorie Clune had been in the bathroom, and Patton had been trying to get in the bathroom, but hadn't been able to do so, and some other person had walked through the door into the apartment and killed Patton, and then walked out as you suggest, locking the door behind him, how could Marjorie have got out of the apartment?"

Perry Mason kept watching Bradbury in silent speculation.

"The only other possible solution," said Bradbury, "would be that Marjorie Clune ran out of the bathroom while the two men were struggling. That is, while Frank Patton was struggling with the intruder who had entered through the door of the apartment. In that event, Marjorie Clune would have seen this murderer, and would undoubtedly either have recognized him if she had known him, or been able to give something in the line of a description of him if she hadn't known him."

"And then?" asked Perry Mason.

"Then," said Bradbury, "the murderer would have stabbed Patton and run from the apartment. In that event, he would probably have seen Marjorie Clune, either when she emerged from the bathroom, or while she was in the corridor, or in the elevator."

"You," said Perry Mason, "are a pretty good detective yourself, Bradbury. You've reasoned the thing out quite clearly."

"I simply wanted to impress upon you," said Bradbury slowly, "that just because I came from a smaller city is no reason that I can't stand up and fight when the occasion arises. I don't want you to underestimate me, Counselor."

Perry Mason's eyes were filled with interest and with the glint of a dawning respect.

"Hell, no, Bradbury," he said, "I'm not going to underestimate you."

"Thank you, Counselor," said Bradbury and picked up his highball glass. He finished draining the highball.

Perry Mason watched him attentively for a few moments, and then raised his wine-glass, sipped, and refilled the glass from the bottle.

"Are you finished talking?" he asked.

"No," said Bradbury, "there's one other point I wanted to make. That is, that I am satisfied Marjorie Clune must have seen the murderer, that in the event she didn't make an outcry or an alarm, it was because the murderer was known to her, and she desired to protect him."

"You're referring to Dr. Doray?" asked Perry Mason.

"Exactly," said Bradbury with a tone of cold finality in his voice.

"Look here," Mason said, "I may be able to set you right on one thing, Bradbury. I saw Marjorie Clune when she came out from the apartment house. I stood and watched her until she had walked a little over a half a block and then I turned and went into the apartment house. I took the elevator. After I left the elevator, I went down the corridor directly to Frank Patton's apartment. I didn't notice any one else coming from the apartment where Patton lived. I stayed at the door until after the officer arrived there. The officer wouldn't have let any one leave the apartment without his knowledge until he had made the search. Therefore, it is reasonable to assume that the apartment was empty when I arrived there. There is, of course, the possibility that a murderer might have gone down the stairs while I was coming up in the elevator. That is only a possibility. I had met Dr. Doray. If I had seen him there in the apartment house, I would have recognized him."

"How about the windows?" asked Bradbury. "Were there windows?"

"Yes, there's a window that opens on a fire escape," Mason said slowly.

"There you are," Bradbury triumphantly pointed out.

"But," said Perry Mason, "if Dr. Doray had been in the room, if Marjorie Clune had run from the bathroom and out of the door, why would Dr. Doray have locked the door of the apartment and then gone through the window and down the fire escape?"

"That," said Bradbury, "is one of the things we are going to determine."

"Yes," Mason agreed, "there are a lot of things we will have to determine when we've got more facts, Bradbury. You understand that it's a physical impossibility for a man to reconstruct the scene of a crime, unless he knows *all of the facts.*"

"I understand that all right," Bradbury said, "but the point I'm getting at is that the facts as we know them don't seem to check up with certain things that must have happened."

"That," Mason said, "is something for us to figure on when we come into court and start analyzing the case of the prosecution."

"I would prefer," Bradbury said, "to figure on them right now."

"Then," Perry Mason said, "you think that Bob Doray is the one who is guilty of the murder?"

"To be frank with you, I do. I have told you all along that the man was a dangerous man. I feel certain that he is the one who is implicated in the murder, and I feel equally certain that Marjorie Clune will try to shield him, if it is possible for her to do so."

"Do you think she loves him?"

"I am not certain as to that. I think she is fascinated by him. It may be that she *thinks* she is in love with him. You understand, Counselor, there's a distinction."

Perry Mason regarded the hard glittering eyes of J. R. Bradbury with a new-found respect.

"I understand," he said.

"Furthermore," Bradbury said, "in the event Marjorie Clune tries to sacrifice herself, in order to give Dr. Doray a break, I propose to see that she doesn't do it. Have I made myself plain on that point?"

"More than plain," Perry Mason said.

Bradbury tilted the flask over his glass and poured in another generous shot of rye, which he diluted with ginger ale from the bottle.

"No matter what happens," he said, "Marjorie must not be allowed to sacrifice herself for Dr. Doray."

"Then you want me to try and show that Dr. Doray did the crime?" asked Perry Mason.

"On the contrary," said Bradbury slowly. "I want to impress this upon you, Counselor, that in the event it turns out that I am right, and Dr. Doray is either implicated in this or it should appear that he is the one who actually committed the murder, I think I shall instruct you to represent Dr. Doray."

Perry Mason sat bolt upright in his chair.

"What?" he asked.

Bradbury nodded slowly.

"I shall ask you," he said, "to represent Dr. Doray."

"If I'm representing him," Perry Mason said, "I'm going to do my best to get him off."

"That would be understood," Bradbury told him.

Perry Mason ceased eating, and his fingers made drumming motions on the edge of the tablecloth as he stared across at Bradbury.

"No," he said slowly, "I don't think that I'll underestimate you, J. R. Bradbury—that is, never again."

Bradbury smiled. "And now, Counselor," he said, "that we understand one another perfectly, we can proceed to forget business and eat and drink."

"You can," Mason told him, grinning, "but I've got to get in touch with my office, and I have an idea there'll be some detectives prowling around the office."

"What will they want?" Bradbury inquired.

"Oh, they'll know that I was out at the apartment, and they'll want to find out what I went there for, and all about it."

"How much are you going to tell them?"

"I'm not going to tell them about you, Bradbury," Mason said. "I'm going to keep you very much in the background."

"That's all right," Bradbury remarked.

"And," Perry Mason said, "if there's any kind of a chance to build up newspaper publicity about a romance with Dr. Doray, I'm going to do that."

"Why?"

"Because," Mason told him, staring steadily at him, "you're an intelligent man, Bradbury, I can be frank with you. You're an older man, much older than Marjorie Clune; you've got money. In the event that Marjorie gets in a jam, and the first newspaper notoriety features her as a woman who won a leg contest, and further, features the rich sugar daddy who came to town to hunt her up, it's going to convey an entirely different impression, than handling it the other way."

"What other way?" Bradbury asked.

"On the theory that Marjorie Clune came to town. That she was bitterly disillusioned. That Dr. Robert Doray, a young dentist, only a few years older than herself, abandoned his practice, borrowed what money he could and came on to the city, determined to find her. That is going to make an entirely different picture, one of young romance."

"I see," Bradbury said.

"We're handicapped in this case," Perry Mason went on, "because of the leg contest. The minute the newspapers get wind of what it's all about, they'll start in publishing pictures of Marjorie Clune and the pictures naturally will be run to leg. That's going to attract the attention of readers, but it isn't going to build up exactly the sort of publicity for Marjorie that we want."

Bradbury nodded his head slowly.

"There is one thing, Counselor," he said, "that we can agree upon."

"What's that," asked Mason.

"That we are determined not to underestimate each other," Bradbury said, smiling. "And don't think for a minute that you have to apologize to me for anything you are doing, Counselor. You go ahead and handle the publicity on this any way you want to, only," and here Bradbury's eyes fixed upon Perry Mason with a hard glitter of businesslike scrutiny, "don't think for a minute that I'm going to let Marjorie Clune take the rap on this without fighting tooth and toe-nail. I'll drag any one into it in order to get her out. *Any one,* do you understand?"

Perry Mason sighed as he poured the last of the wine into his glass, and tore off another piece of bread, on which he placed a generous slab of butter.

"Hell," he said smoothly, "I heard you the first time, Bradbury."

8

Perry Mason waited until Bradbury had entered the elevator in the Mapleton Hotel, and been whisked upward, before he turned to the telephone booth and called his office.

Della Street's voice was low and cautious.

"What's wrong?" she asked.

"Why?" he wanted to know.

"There are two detectives up here."

"That's all right, tell them to wait. I'm coming."

"Are you all right, chief?"

"Of course I'm all right."

"Nothing's happened?"

"Nothing that need bother you."

Her voice came in a rapid rush.

"They're suspicious; they hear me talking on the telephone. They're going to plug in on the other line. . . ." Then, in a higher voice, she said, ". . . simply can't tell you when he *will* be in. I think he's going to be in sometime tonight. He told me to wait until I heard from him. I haven't heard from him yet. If you'll leave your name, I'll tell him that you called, or you can leave your number, and he'll call you back if he wants to talk with you."

Perry Mason disguised his voice, said, "No message," and slid the receiver back on the hook.

He paused as he emerged from the telephone booth, to light a cigarette and stare at the glowing end with eyes that were fixed meditatively upon the curling smoke. Then, he suddenly nodded his head as though he had reached some decision, strode across the lobby, hailed a taxicab and went at once to his office. He was serene and jaunty as he pushed the door open, and said, "Hello, Della."

"These two gentlemen . . ." she began, and turned her head toward the two men who sat in chairs and had them tilted back against the wall.

One of the men flipped back his coat and pulled his suspender through the armhole of his vest far enough to show a gold shield.

"We want to talk with you a minute," he said.

Perry Mason let his face light up with a smile of welcome.

"Oh," he said, "from headquarters, eh? That's fine. I thought perhaps you were a couple of clients, and I'm tired tonight. Come on in."

He held open the door to the inner office and let the detectives go in ahead of him. In closing the door, he caught Della Street's white face, her troubled eyes resting upon him, and closed his own right eye in a swift wink. Then he closed the door to the private office, indicated chairs with a wave of his hand, walked over to the big swivel chair, sat down and put his feet up on the desk.

"Well," he said, "what is it?"

"I'm Riker," said one of the men, "and this is Johnson. We do some work with the Homicide Squad."

"Smoke?" asked Mason, shoving a package of cigarettes across the desk.

The men both took cigarettes.

Perry Mason waited until they had lighted up, and then said, "Well, what is it this time, boys?"

"You went out to see a man named Frank Patton, in the Holliday Apartments on Maple Avenue."

Mason nodded cheerfully.

"Yes," he said, "I went out there and played around, but couldn't get any answer. A police officer showed up with a woman leading him along and jabbering a string of stuff about some girl having hysterics in there. I figured perhaps there was a petting party and the man didn't want to be disturbed."

"There was," said Riker, "a murder committed."

Mason's tone was casual.

"Yes," he said, "I heard that the officer broke open the door and found a murder had been committed. I didn't have a chance to find out the details. The man was lying in the room, wasn't he?"

"Yes," said Riker, "he was found dead. He was lying on the floor in his underwear. He had a bathrobe half on and half off. There was a carving knife stuck in his heart."

"Any clues?" asked Perry Mason.

"Why do you ask that?" Johnson wanted to know.

Mason laughed.

"Don't get me wrong, boys," he said. "This man is nothing in my young life, except that I wanted to interview him. As a matter of fact, his death leaves me sitting pretty."

"Just what do you mean by that?" Riker wanted to know.

"You can find out all about it, as far as I'm concerned, by talking with Carl Manchester in the district attorney's office," Perry Mason told him. "We were working together on the case. I was going to be a special prosecutor to put Patton over the hurdles."

"On what kind of a charge?" Riker asked.

"Any kind of a charge we could put against him," Mason said. "That was where I came in. I was supposed to get some sort of a charge framed up that would stick. Carl Manchester wasn't certain that he could put one against him."

"Never mind the legal end of it," Johnson said. "Give us the low-down."

"This fellow was in a racket that victimized girls with pretty legs," Mason said. "He would pick out a girl with pretty legs, and work a racket that would leave her holding the sack. It was something he worked in the small towns, picking on the Chamber of Commerce as the big sucker, and incidentally victimizing the girl."

"You mean to say he'd out-slick the Chamber of Commerce boys?" asked Johnson.

Perry Mason nodded.

"Sure," he said. "Why not?"

"Aren't they supposed to be pretty wise babies?"

"They think they are," Mason said. "As a matter of fact, there are a whole bunch of rackets that are worked on them. If you ask me, they're pretty easy."

Riker's eyes were shrewd in their appraisal.

"You're pretty high-powered," he said.

"What do you mean?" Mason asked.

"I mean that it costs money to get your services."

"Fortunately," said Perry Mason, grinning, "it does."

"All right. Somebody was interested enough to put up the money to have you prosecute this fellow."

Mason nodded.

"Sure," he said, "that goes without saying."

"All right," Riker said, "who was it?"

Mason shook his head, smiled, and said, "Naughty, naughty."

"What do you mean?" Riker demanded.

"I mean," Mason said, "that you boys are all right. You're working for your living, just the same as I am. You've asked me something that perhaps you'd like to know. If I thought it had anything to do with the murder, I might tell you. But it hasn't got anything to do with the murder, and, therefore, it becomes none of your damned business."

He smiled cheerfully at them.

"It goes to establish a motive," Riker said. "Anybody who would pay you money to put that man in jail would have a good motive for murder."

Mason grinned.

"Not after he'd given me a one thousand dollar retainer to prosecute him," he said. "If he had intended to murder the man, he'd have hung onto his one thousand dollars; he wouldn't have decorated the mahogany with me, and then gone out and killed the man so that I didn't have to do any work in order to earn my fee."

Johnson nodded slowly.

"That's so," he said.

"Just the same," Riker said, "I'd a whole lot rather know who it was that employed you."

"Perhaps you would," Mason said, "but I'd a whole lot rather not tell, and it happens that under the law, this is one of those little things that is known as a professional confidence. You can't make me testify, and therefore you can't make me answer any question. But there are no hard feelings about it."

Riker stared moodily at the toe of his boot.

"I'm not so sure that there ain't," he said.

"Ain't what?" Mason asked.

"Hard feelings about it."

"Don't get off on the wrong foot," Mason told him. "I'm giving you boys a break. I've told you as much as I can without betraying a confidence."

"So he was getting girls on the spot, was he?" Johnson demanded belligerently.

Perry Mason laughed.

"Go ask Manchester about it," he said.

Riker stared moodily at Mason.

"And you're not going to give us a break?"

Mason said slowly: "Riker, I'd like to help you boys out, but I can't tell you the name of the man who employed me. I don't think it would be fair. But I can tell you this much . . ."

He stopped and drummed with his fingers on the edge of his desk.

"Go on and tell us," Riker said.

Perry Mason heaved a deep sigh.

"There's a girl," he said, "from Cloverdale—his last victim—a girl named Marjorie Clune. She's here in the city somewhere."

"Where?" asked Riker.

"I'm sure I couldn't tell you," Mason said.

"All right, go on," Johnson told him. "What about her?"

"I don't know so much about her," Perry Mason said. "But she's got a sweetheart who came on from Cloverdale—a Dr. Robert Doray. He's staying at the Midwick Hotel; that's out on East Faulkner Street. He's a heck of a nice chap. I'm sure he wouldn't have any murder ideas in his system. But if he had run across Patton, he might have given him an awful beating."

"Now," said Riker, "you're giving us a break."

Mason's expression was wide-eyed in its baby-faced innocence.

"Sure I am," he said. "I told you I was willing to give you all the breaks I could. Shucks, you fellows are working for a living, just the same as I am. As a matter of fact, I've got nothing against the police on *any* of my cases. The police build up the best case they can, and I come into court and try to knock it down. That's business. If you fellows didn't build up your cases so you could make arrests, there wouldn't be any possibility for me to make fees by defending a man. A guy doesn't pay a lawyer fee before he's in trouble."

Riker nodded.

"That's so," he said.

"Can you tell us anything else about this Marjorie Clune?" asked Johnson.

Perry Mason rang for Della Street.

"Della," he said, "bring me that file in the Case of the Lucky Legs, will you?"

The girl nodded, stepped to the files and a moment later returned with a legal jacket.

Perry Mason nodded to her.

"That's all," he said.

She closed the door to the outer office with an indignant bang.

Perry Mason pulled the photograph out of the jacket.

"Well, boys," he said, holding up the photograph, "that photograph is of Marjorie Clune. Think you'd recognize her if you saw her again?"

Riker whistled.

Both men got up from their chairs and came closer to look at the photograph.

"A girl with legs like that," Johnson proclaimed, "was just born to cause trouble. I'll bet she's mixed in this murder case."

Mason shrugged his shoulders.

"Can't prove it by me, boys," he said cheerfully. "I got a fee to prosecute Patton. Now he's dead and I don't have to prosecute him. You can check up on all of my statements by getting in touch with Manchester. In the meantime, you'd better make a check on this Dr. Doray. By the time the news gets into the papers, Doray may decide there's nothing to keep him here, and go on back to Cloverdale."

"I thought he came for the girl," Riker said.

Mason raised his eyebrows.

"Did he?" he asked.

"Didn't you say so?"

"I don't think so."

"Somehow I got that impression."

Mason sighed and made an expressive gesture with his hands.

"Boys," he said, "you can't prove anything by me. I've told you all I know about the case that isn't a violation of a professional confidence, and you can talk from now until two o'clock in the morning without getting me to tell you any more."

Riker laughed and got to his feet.

Johnson hesitated a moment, then pushed back his own chair.

"You can go out this way," Mason told them, and opened the exit door into the corridor.

When he heard their steps diminish in volume as they turned the angle of the corridor toward the elevator, Mason slammed the door, made certain that the spring lock was in place, walked to the door which led to the outer office, opened it and smiled down at Della Street.

"What's happened, chief?" she asked, with a throaty catch in her voice.

"Patton was murdered," he told her.

"Before you went out there, or afterwards?"

"Before," he said; "if he had been murdered afterwards, I'd have been mixed up in it."

"Are you mixed up in it now?"

He shook his head, then sat down on the edge of her desk, sighed, and said, "That is, I don't know."

She reached out and dropped her cool, capable fingers over his hand.

"Can't you tell me?" she asked in a low voice.

"Paul Drake telephoned just before you got here," he said. "He gave me Patton's address. It was out in the Holliday Apartments. I busted on out there. Drake was to follow me in five minutes. Just before I went into the place, I saw a good-looking Jane coming out. She had on a white coat and a white hat with a red button; also white shoes. She had blue eyes. The eyes looked frightened. I noticed her particularly because she seemed to look guilty, and frightened to death. Then, I went on up to the apartment, and knocked at the door. Nothing happened. I tried the buzzer. There was no response. I tried the doorknob and it clicked back and the door opened."

He paused for a moment, with his head bent forward, and the fingers of her hand made gentle pressure on the back of his.

"Well?" she asked.

"I walked in," he said. "Something looked a little fishy to me. There was a living-room. There were hat, stick and gloves in the living-room. I'd seen them through the keyhole before I walked in. It made me think some one was home."

"Why did you have to go in?" she asked.

"I wanted to get something on Patton," he said. "He didn't answer the door. I thought it might be a break for me."

"Go on," she told him.

"There wasn't anything in the living-room," he said, "but when I went through the door into the bedroom, I found Patton lying on the floor, dead. He'd been stabbed with a big-bladed knife. It was a messy job."

"In what way?" she asked.

"He died instantly, all right," Mason told her, "but it was a big cut. It caught an artery right over the heart, and those things spurt, you know."

She fought back a spasm of horror from her face, and said calmly, "Yes, I can imagine. Then what?"

"That was about all," he told her. "There was a blackjack lying in the other room. I haven't figured that one out yet."

"But if he was killed with a knife," she said, "what was the blackjack there for?"

"That's what I can't figure," he told her. "There's something funny there."

"Did you notify the police?" she asked.

"That," he said, "is where the cards turned against me. I wiped my finger-prints off the doorknobs and started out. I knew that Paul Drake was going to come in about five minutes. I was going to let Drake be the one to discover the body. I had other things to do. I knew that Drake would notify the police.

"Just as I was leaving the apartment, I heard the slam of the elevator door, and voices. I heard a woman saying something about a girl having hysterics and gathered from what she said she was talking to a cop. I figured right away what must have happened. If I had been seen walking away from the apartment where the man was murdered, I'd have been in a hell of a fix. If I'd have stood my ground there and told the story of exactly what happened, I'd never have been believed. Not that they'd necessarily have accused me of the murder, but it would have looked as though one of my clients had committed the murder and had telephoned me, and that I had rushed up to suppress certain evidence, or something of that sort. You can see what a spot that would put me in. I figured that some of the people I had been paid to represent might be mixed up in it. After the cop had seen me *coming out* of the apartment, or standing at the door of the apartment as though I had just come out, I could never have represented any one charged with the murder, because the jury would have figured that my client must have been guilty and had given me a tip-off to what had happened."

"What did you do?" she asked, with quick interest. "You *were* in a spot."

"There was only one thing to do," he said, "the way I figured it. I had to think fast. I might have played it differently, I don't know. It was one of those times when a man has to make decisions and make them fast. I jerked a passkey out of my pocket and locked the door. It was a simple lock. Then, I pretended I didn't know there was a cop within a mile, and started banging on the door. The cop came around the corner in the corridor and saw me standing in front of the door and pounding on the panel. I jabbed my finger on the button a couple of times; then made a gesture of disgust and turned to walk away. Then I pretended to see the cop for the first time."

"Clever," she exclaimed.

"That part of it was all right," Perry Mason said judiciously, as though he had been commenting on the manner in which he had played a hand in a bridge game after the cards were all played. "But then, I made the mistake of my life."

"What?" she asked, her eyes slightly widened and staring steadily at his face.

"I underestimated the intelligence of J. R. Bradbury."

"Oh," she muttered, with a distinct feeling of relief, and then said, after a moment, "Has he any . . .?"

"You're damned right he has," Perry Mason said.

"I can say one thing about him," she said, "he has a roving eye and a youthful disposition. He was offering me a cigarette when you went out of the door, remember?"

"Yes."

"He leaned forward to give me a light."

"Did he try to kiss you?"

"No," she said slowly, "and that's the funny part of it. I thought he was going to. I still think he intended to try to, but something made him change his mind."

"What was it?"

"I don't know."

"Thinking perhaps you'd tell me?"

"No, I don't think it was that."

"What *did* he do?"

"He leaned close to me, held the match to the cigarette; then straightened, and walked to the other side of the office. He stood staring at me as though I had been a picture, or as though he had perhaps been trying to figure just where I'd fit into a picture. It was a peculiar stare. He was looking at me, and yet not looking at me."

"Then what?" Perry Mason asked.

"Then," she said, "he snapped out of it, laughed, and said he guessed he had better be going after the newspapers and the brief case."

"And he left?"

"Yes."

"By the way, what did he ever do with them?"

"He left them here."

"Did he say anything about the brief case when he went out?"

"No, that was what he telephoned about from the hotel."

"What did you do with them?"

She motioned toward the closet.

Perry Mason got up, walked to the closet, opened the door and took out a leather brief case and a pile of newspapers. He looked at the top newspaper. The heading showed that it was the *Cloverdale Independent* of an issue dated some two months earlier.

"Got a key to the closet?" asked Mason.

"Yes, it's on my key ring."

"Let's lock this closet door and keep it locked while we've got the stuff in here," Mason said.

"Should we have it in the safe?"

"I don't think it's that important, particularly. But just the same, I'd like to have it under lock and key."

She crossed to the closet door and fitted the key to the lock, and snapped the bolt into position.

"You still haven't told me," she reminded him, "about how you underestimated Bradbury's intelligence."

"I had seen a girl walking away from the place. I figured she was mixed up in the murder in some way. I didn't know just how. I didn't care particularly, unless the girl happened to be Marjorie Clune. But I wanted to make certain about it, so I telephoned Bradbury."

"And told him Patton was murdered?"

"Yes, and asked him about Marjorie Clune. I knew that if it had been Marjorie Clune that was leaving the apartment, I had to work fast and keep ahead of the police."

"But there wasn't anything else you could have done, was there?" she asked. "You had to find out about it, and find out what Bradbury wanted done."

"I guess so."

"I *thought*," she said, "there was something wrong. He acted so absolutely startled when you telephoned to him. I don't know what there was in what you said, but it seemed to knock him for a loop. I thought he was going to drop the telephone. He started breathing through his mouth, and his eyes got so big I could have knocked them off with a stick."

"Well," Mason said, "that's the situation in a nutshell."

"And how does that get you in bad?" she asked.

"It gets me in bad," he said, "because I don't dare let the cops know that I was in that room. If I should tell them the truth now, they'd probably suspect me of the murder. I've got to stand by my story of the locked door. On the other hand, that locked door may figure in the case quite prominently. A whole lot more prominently than I want."

"Well," she said, "isn't that up to the police to figure out?"

"I'm not so certain," he said, "but I am certain that Bradbury is going to be a dangerous antagonist."

"An antagonist," she said, "why, he's a client. Why should he become an antagonist?"

"That," he said, "is just the point. That's where I overlooked my hand."

"How do you mean?"

"The girl who left the apartment *was* Marjorie Clune. She's mixed up in the thing some way. I don't know just how much. Bradbury is crazy about her. He's desperately in love with her, and he's served notice on me that if she gets mixed in it, he doesn't care whom he has to sacrifice. He's going to clear her at any cost."

Della Street squinted her eyes thoughtfully; then suddenly turned to her notebook.

"Did you," she said, "expect a message from a young woman who was to ring up and leave an address?"

"Yes," he said, "that's Marjorie Clune. She's going some place where I can talk with her. I haven't had a chance to talk with her yet and find out what happened. She had an audience all the time."

"Just before you came in," Della Street said, "a young woman's voice came over the telephone and said, 'Simply tell Mr. Mason I'm at the Bostwick Hotel, room 408, and to check that alibi.'"

"That was all?" he asked.

"That was all."

"Check what alibi?"

"I don't know. I figured you would."

"There's only one person who has an alibi in this case," he said, "and I've checked it."

"Who's that?"

"That's Thelma Bell. She was out with a fellow named Sanborne, and I checked it before she got in communication with him."

"Perhaps that's the alibi she wanted you to check."

"I've already checked it."

He frowned thoughtfully at her; then shook his head slowly.

"That's the only thing it could mean," he said. "I'll check it again as soon as I've talked with Paul Drake. He'll be waiting around for me. He was to have met me out at Patton's apartment, but he got wise to what had happened, and kept back under cover."

"You want me to wait?" she asked.

"No," he said, "you go on home."

As she put on her hat and coat, and added touches of powder to her cheeks and lipstick to her lips, Perry Mason hooked his thumbs in the armholes of his vest, and started pacing up and down the floor.

"What is it, chief?" she asked, turning away from the mirror to watch him.

"I was thinking," he said, "about the blackjack."

"What about it?"

"When you can tell me," he said, "why a man should kill another man with a knife; then walk into another room and throw a blackjack in the corner, you'll have given me the solution to this whole case."

"Perhaps," she said, "it's one of those cases where a man planted evidence. He might have had a blackjack that had some one's fingerprints on it, some one that he wanted to implicate in the crime. The fingerprints might have been made months before he carried the blackjack, and then—"

"And then," he said, "he certainly would have killed the victim with the blackjack. There wasn't a mark on Patton's head. The thing that killed him was that knife thrust, and it killed him instantly. That blackjack had no more to do with the man's death than the revolver that's in the upper right-hand drawer of my office desk."

"Why was it left there then?" she asked.

"That's what I want to know," he told her, and then suddenly laughed.

"You've got enough to puzzle your brains over without trying to turn detective."

She stood with her hand on the knob of the door, regarding him curiously.

"Chief," she said, "why don't you do like the other lawyers do?"

"You mean plant evidence, and suborn perjury?"

"No, I don't mean that. I mean, why don't you sit in your office and wait until the cases come to you? Let the police go out and work up the case, and then you walk into court and try and punch holes in it. Why do you always have to go out on the firing line and get mixed up in the case itself?"

He grinned at her.

"I'm hanged if I know," he said, "except that it's the way I'm built. That's all. Lots of times you can keep a jury from convicting a person because they haven't been proven guilty beyond a reasonable doubt. I don't like that kind of a verdict. I like to establish conclusively that a person is innocent. I like to play with facts. I have a mania for jumping into the middle of a situation, trying to size it up ahead of the police, and being the first one to guess what actually happened."

"And then to protect some one who is helpless," she said.

"Oh, sure," he said, "that's part of the game."

She smiled at him from the door.

"Good night," she said.

9

Perry Mason dialed the number of Paul Drake's office, and heard the voice of the detective saying cautiously, "Hello."

"Don't mention any names in case you're not alone. The coast is clear up here."

"I'll be in to see you in about ten minutes," Paul Drake said. "Can you wait?"

"Yes," Mason told him.

The lawyer dropped the receiver back into place, tilted back in his swivel chair and lit a cigarette. Then he took the end from his mouth and held the cigarette so that he could watch the smoke as it curled slowly upward. He sat entirely without motion, watching the curling smoke with eyes that seemed half dreamy. Not until the cigarette was more than half consumed did he nod his head slowly as though he had reached some decision; and then he returned the cigarette to his mouth. He smoked steadily until he had finished the cigarette, then pinched it out, dropped it in the ashtray, and looked at his watch.

It was at that moment that he heard a rattle on the knob of the door which opened into the corridor.

Perry Mason walked to the door, stood with his hand on the knob.

"Who is it?" he asked.

"Open up, Perry," said Paul Drake's voice, and Perry Mason opened the door to let the detective walk in.

"You covered the situation?" asked Perry Mason.

"Sure," Paul Drake told him. "I figured that was what you'd want me to do."

"How did you get wise to what had happened?"

"In the first place," Paul Drake said, "I was delayed a little with starting trouble. The starter went haywire. The whole thing seemed locked. I couldn't figure out what was the matter. I kept trying it both with the crank and with the starter; then some pedestrian came along who knew his onions. He said one of the gears had dropped out of position. That if I'd put the car in high gear and rock it back and forth, it would work all right. I tried it and it did."

Perry Mason watched Paul Drake narrowly.

"Go on," he said.

"I'm just telling you," Paul Drake said, "why I was a little late."

"How much late?"

"I don't know.

"I got out there just as you were headed away in a taxi. I got a glimpse of you going down the street. You looked as though you were going places in a hurry. I figured something was wrong; that there'd either be a message for me at Patton's apartment, or that you were up against an emergency. I went up, plenty cautious. A uniformed cop was just getting the door open as I came down the corridor."

"You didn't tip your hand?" asked Perry Mason.

"No. I didn't know whether you'd want me for an alibi or not. There were a few curious roomers forming a circle of spectators, and I joined them."

"You didn't get in?"

"You mean to Patton's apartment?"

"Yes."

"No. I couldn't get in. They got the homicide squad right away. But I was friendly with a couple of the boys, and then there were the newspaper photographers. I got all the dope."

"Let's have it," Perry Mason said.

"In the first place," Paul Drake told him, "and before I go ahead with it, have *you* got anything to tell *me*?"

"Only that I was a little bit delayed myself," Mason told him, "and when I got there, I found the door locked. I looked through the keyhole; saw a hat and stick and gloves. I knocked on the door, and—"

"I know all about the story you told the officers," Paul Drake said.

"Well," Mason told him, "what else would there be?"

Drake shrugged his shoulders.

"How should I know?" he asked.

"Well," the lawyer said, "if you know my story, that's all there is to it."

"It's a good story," Paul Drake said, and then added after a moment, "except for one thing."

"What's the one thing?" Mason wanted to know.

"I'll tell you the facts," Drake told him, "and then you can put two and two together."

"Go ahead," said the lawyer curtly.

Paul Drake squirmed about in the big leather chair so that his long legs were swung over the arm of the chair. The opposite chair arm braced the small of his back.

"Hat, gloves, and cane on the table in the living-room. Those were Patton's. A woman—the one you met, by the way—whose name happens to be Sarah Fieldman, occupying the opposite apartment, heard a girl having hysterics; figured the sounds must have come from the bathroom; thinks the girl was locked in the bathroom and perhaps some man was trying to get in. The body was lying in the bedroom, clad in underclothes, a bathrobe thrown over one shoulder, one arm through the sleeve, the other arm not in the sleeve; death almost instantaneous; a single stabbing puncture with a large bread knife. The knife was new. The wound was directly over the heart. It was a messy murder, a lot of blood spurting around; the doors both locked, the door from the bedroom bolted on the inside. An open window leading to a fire escape; marks on the bed indicating a man might have gone across the bed and out on the fire escape, or might have climbed in through the fire escape.

"In the bathroom, the police find a girl's handkerchief, all wet as though it had been used as a wash rag, or had been dropped in blood and then an attempt made to wash it out. There was bloody water spattered around the sides of the wash bowl. It had been a hasty job. Looks as though some woman had tried to clean the blood on her clothes, or herself, without much success. In the outer room, the police found a blackjack."

"Wait a minute," Mason interrupted. "You say the knife was a new knife. How could the police tell that?"

"Evidences of a chalk price mark on the blade. Also, the knife was brought to the apartment wrapped in paper. Apparently the wrapping paper is the same paper that was wrapped around the knife when it was purchased. The police have some fingerprints on the paper. They're not so good—mostly smudged. Knobs of the doors on the inside contain no fingerprints. Looks as though some one had wiped them off. The outer knob has too many prints to be of any value—the police, Mrs. Fieldman, perhaps yours, and lots of others."

"Any suspects?" asked Perry Mason.

"How do you mean?"

"Any one seen leaving the apartment?" asked the lawyer.

Paul Drake looked at him with that expression of droll humor on his face, his eyes glassy and utterly without expression.

"What makes you ask that?" he inquired.

"Just a routine question," Perry Mason told him.

"The officer on the beat," said Paul Drake, "reported a woman who acted suspiciously. There were a couple of telephone messages from women on the table. The police would have attached more importance to those, if it hadn't been for one thing."

"What was the one thing?" the lawyer inquired.

"Your friend, Dr. Doray," the detective said. "His car was parked out in front of the place at the time of the murder. That is, it was parked within half a block of the place."

"How do the police know?"

"It was parked in front of a fire plug. The traffic officer tagged the car. He noticed that it came from Cloverdale. When the report of the murder went in to the homicide squad, they got in touch with the district attorney's office, and some bright boy in the district attorney's office remembered that Carl Manchester had been working on a case involving a man named Patton. They got hold of Manchester, found out it was the same chap, found out that you were interested in it, that Bradbury was interested in it, and that a Dr. Doray was interested in it."

"Why didn't they go after Bradbury?" Mason asked.

"Because they got such a live lead on Doray. They happened to check up with the officer who had tagged Doray's car."

Perry Mason squinted his eyes thoughtfully.

"Anything else?" he asked.

"Now," said Paul Drake, "I'm coming to the thing that makes your story look a little funny."

"What is it?"

"The Holliday Apartments," the detective said, "tries to encourage its tenants to turn their keys in at the desk when they go out. For that reason, they have a great big tag that's chained to the key. It has a lot of stuff printed on it about dropping the whole thing into the mail box, with a stamp on it, when it is inadvertently carried away."

"Yes, I know the type," Mason said.

"The police found the key to Frank Patton's apartment in the side pocket of his coat," Drake went on. "Patton had evidently opened the door, then dropped the key into the side pocket of his coat. Perhaps he'd locked the door from the inside; perhaps he hadn't. The theory of the police is that he hadn't. They reason that if he'd locked the door from the inside, he'd have left the key in the lock. They think that he had an appointment with some woman. Perhaps with two women. That he left the door open because he wanted the women to walk in."

"Then," Mason said, "who do the police figure locked the door?"

Paul Drake's glassy eyes regarded Mason without expression; his face remained twisted into that frozen expression of droll humor which was so characteristic of the man.

"The police figure," he said, "that the murderer locked the door when he went out."

"The murderer," said Perry Mason, "might have climbed in by the fire escape and gone out the same way."

"Then who locked the door?" asked Drake.

"Frank Patton," Mason said.

"Then, why didn't he leave the key hanging in the door from the inside?"

"Because he mechanically put it in his pocket."

Paul Drake shrugged his shoulders.

"Sure, that's reasonable," Perry Mason said. "A man frequently locks the door from the inside and drops the key in his pocket."

"You don't need to argue with me," the detective told him. "You can save the argument for a jury. I'm just telling you, that's all."

"How long after the sound of the body falling on the floor before the officer arrived?" Mason asked.

"Perhaps ten minutes," the detective told him. "The woman got up, put on some clothes, went down in the elevator, found the officer, told him her story, convinced him it was something he should look into, and brought him back to the apartment. Then there was the little while that they were talking with you, and then the officer got a key. Make it perhaps fifteen minutes in all; say ten minutes up to the time you first saw the officer in the corridor."

"A person can do a lot in ten minutes," Mason said.

"Not much in the line of cleaning up blood stains. It would mean a pretty hurried job," Paul Drake commented.

"Do the police," asked Perry Mason, "know Bradbury's address?"

"I don't think the police are going to figure Bradbury very heavy one way or another," Drake said. "They don't know where he's staying, but of course they can find out easily enough by making a check of the hotels. Carl Manchester simply knows that he can be reached through you."

"And," Perry Mason said, "I managed to hold him in the background until Doray's name had come in first. I want the newspapers to get the young love angle rather than the sugar daddy viewpoint."

The detective nodded.

The telephone on Perry Mason's desk rang steadily. Mason frowned at it.

"Any one know you're here?" he asked, looking at Paul Drake.

The detective shook his head.

Perry Mason reached for the receiver, paused for a moment with his hand held an inch or two from it; then suddenly scooped his hand down, pulled the receiver up to his ear, and said, "Yes, hello. Perry Mason speaking."

A woman's voice said, "I have a telegram for Mr. Perry Mason. Do you wish me to read it over the telephone?"

"Yes," said Perry Mason.

"The telegram," she said, "is filed from this city. It says: 'CHECK HER ALIBI BEFORE YOU LET HER DO ANYTHING.' The message," went on the purring voice of the operator, "is signed with a single initial 'M', as in mush."

"Thanks," said Perry Mason.

"Do you want me to send a copy over to your office?"

"In the morning," he told the operator, and continued to hold the receiver in his hand. He severed the connection by pressing the hook with his forefinger.

"That," he said slowly, "is one hell of a funny thing. Why should she send me a telegram, and why should it be that kind of a telegram?"

He moved his hand which held the receiver and dialed rapidly the number of the Bostwick Hotel, Exeter 93821.

The detective watched him with a speculation which seemed almost indolent in its careless scrutiny.

Perry Mason heard a voice saying, "Bostwick Hotel."

"Will you please," he said, "ring room 408."

The voice of the operator said instantly, "The occupant of room 408 checked out just a few minutes ago."

"You're certain?" asked Perry Mason.

"Absolutely certain."

"She was," said Perry Mason, "expecting a call from me. Would you mind ringing the room?"

"I'll ring it," said the operator, "but there's no one there. I tell you she checked out."

Perry Mason waited for a few moments; then heard the voice over the wire confirming the previous statement that no one answered.

He once more pushed down the catch which cut off the contact and stood staring at the telephone. He was still staring at it when the bell exploded into life.

"Looks like your busy night on the telephone," Paul Drake commented.

Perry Mason released the pressure of his fingers, and said, "Hello." He spoke with quick, nervous harshness.

The voice of Della Street came to his ears.

"Thank God I caught you, chief. Are you there alone?"

"Except for Paul Drake, yes. What's on your mind?"

"Get this," she said, "because you're going to figure in it. Two detectives just left me. They tried to give me a shakedown. They got pretty rough."

"What for, Della?"

"They claim that I rang up Dr. Doray and tipped him off that the police were looking for him, and told him to get out."

"What gives them that idea?" inquired Perry Mason.

"Listen," she said, "and get this straight, because I think they're on their way to give you a going over. They say that somebody rang up Dr. Doray at the Midwick Hotel sometime between nine fifteen and nine thirty this evening, and told him that Patton had been murdered; that Doray was going to be picked up as a suspect, and that there were some things in the evidence that looked bad for him and Marjorie Clune; that Marjorie was getting under cover and was going to keep under cover. In other words, that she was skipping out, and that it would be the worst thing on earth for her if Bob Doray should be picked up by the police. He was instructed to get out of town and keep from being questioned by the police."

Perry Mason frowned into the telephone.

"What made them connect that with us?" he said.

"Because," Della Street told him, "the voice was that of a woman. The operator at the Midwick Hotel happened to listen in, and the one who was doing the talking said that she was Della Street, the secretary to Perry Mason."

Perry Mason's eyes became hard as bits of frosted glass.

"The hell she did!" he said.

"You said it," Della Street told him. "And there are two dicks on the way to your office. Get ready to receive them."

"Thanks, Della," said Perry Mason, "did they get rough with you?"

"They tried to."

"Everything okay?"

"Yes," she told him, "I made a flat and indignant denial, and that was all they got out of me, but I'm afraid of what they may do to you, chief."

"Why?"

"Because," she said, ". . . you know what I mean."

"All right," Perry Mason told her, "you go to sleep, Della, and let me handle it."

"Do you think it's all right?" she asked.

He laughed in a low, reassuring tone.

"Of course, it's all right," he said. "Night night."

He slipped the receiver back on the hook and turned to face Paul Drake.

"Well," he said, "here's something for you to figure on. Some woman telephoned Dr. Doray at his hotel and told him that she was Della Street, secretary to Perry Mason;

that Frank Patton had been murdered in his room at the hotel; that Marjorie Clune was implicated and that the police were looking for Marjorie; that Doray had better get out of town while the getting was good; that if the detectives located him and questioned him, it might look bad for Marjorie; that Perry Mason was going to represent Marjorie and that he wanted Dr. Doray out of town."

Paul Drake whistled.

"And," Perry Mason said, "with two detectives on their way up here to shake me down, you can figure the sweet angles this case is going to have."

"What time did the telephone call come in?" Drake inquired.

"Somewhere around nine o'clock—between that and nine fifteen. Doray had just reached the hotel when the call came through."

Paul Drake stared steadily at Perry Mason.

"How the devil could your office have known that Patton was murdered at that time? The police were just finding it out."

Perry Mason met his eyes steadily.

"That, Paul," he said, "is one of the questions the detectives are going to ask me."

Paul Drake looked nervously at his watch.

"Don't worry," Perry Mason said. "I'm not going to let the detectives find you here."

"Are you," asked Drake, "going to let them find *you* here?"

The lawyer's rugged face remained expressionless, seeming somehow to be firm and weather-beaten. His patient eyes stared steadily at Paul Drake.

"Paul," he said, "I'm going to be frank with you. That's one of the things I can't afford to be questioned about right now."

He clicked back his swivel chair and pulled his hat down on his head.

Wordlessly, the men walked through the door which led to the outer corridor. Perry Mason pushed out the lights and the door clicked shut behind them.

"Where can we go?" asked Perry Mason. "In your office?"

Paul Drake fidgeted uncomfortably.

"What's the matter," asked Perry Mason, "are you getting gun-shy? You and I have pulled some fast ones together. Now, you act as though I had the smallpox. Just because a couple of detectives want to ask me a question I haven't any intention of answering is no sign I can't go to your office for an informal chat. If they found you in my office, it might not be so hot, but it certainly wouldn't bother you if they found me in your office."

"It isn't that," Paul Drake said. "I've got a confession to make. I was going to tell you when that telephone rang."

"A confession?" asked Perry Mason.

Paul Drake nodded and averted his eyes.

Perry Mason heaved a sigh.

"All right," he said, "let's go get a taxicab and ride around."

10

Perry Mason let the detective precede him into the taxicab.

"Drive straight down the street a couple of blocks, and then circle around the block," Perry Mason said.

The cab driver looked at them curiously for a moment, then snapped the car into gear. Perry Mason turned to Paul Drake.

"Well?" he said.

"It's a peculiar situation," said the detective. "I want you to understand one thing, Perry. I wouldn't double-cross you. I wouldn't double-cross any client, you least of all. I tried to get in touch with you and couldn't. I got in touch with Bradbury, who is my real client, and he said it was okay. There was a couple of hundred bucks in it for me, and I needed the money. Things have been rather quiet, and—"

"Never mind the hard luck story," Mason said. "Go ahead and tell me what happened, and make it snappy because I've got places to go."

"It's this way," Paul Drake said, speaking rapidly. "I came back to my office to wait for you right after I'd found out the facts on the murder case. While I was waiting a young woman walked in. She's a well-dressed, attractive young woman, with a peculiar look about her eyes. I can't tell you just what it is. It's an expression that I don't like particularly. She said that she knew Patton had been murdered, and—"

"Wait a minute," said Perry Mason. "How the devil could she have known Patton had been murdered at that time?"

"I don't know," Drake said. "I'm telling you what she told me."

"Did you ask her?"

"Yes."

"What did she say?"

"She laughed in my face and told me I was to get information, not to ask for it."

"What's her name?" asked Perry Mason.

"The name she gives is that of Vera Cutter. She won't tell me where she lives. She says she'll get in touch with me when she wants to hear from me; that I'm not to try and get in touch with her. She says that she knows Marjorie Clune is mixed up in a murder and that she is friendly with Marjorie, and—"

"Wait a minute," said Perry Mason, "let's get this straight. Is she about twenty-four or twenty-five, with warm brown eyes, mahogany hair, a sun-tan complexion, and—"

"No," said Paul Drake, "it isn't Thelma Bell, if that's what you're getting at. I know Thelma Bell's description.

Remember, I had a man waiting for her at her apartment in order to get Patton's address. No, this woman is around twenty-four, but she's a decided brunette. She's got snapping black eyes, long thin hands that seem very restless, a dead white skin, and—"

"How about her legs?" asked Perry Mason suddenly.

Paul Drake stared at him.

"What do you mean?"

"Has she got pretty legs, and does she like to show them?" Perry Mason asked.

Drake's eyes seemed to regard the lawyer with a contemplative scrutiny. There was a smoldering fire back of the glassy film.

"Wait a minute," Perry Mason said, "I'm serious."

"Why?" asked the detective.

"All of our contact with Patton runs to women who have been selected because of beautiful legs. They've been used for publicity purposes," Mason said. "Now, I'm wondering if this woman might not be connected with Patton instead of with Marjorie Clune."

"I see," Drake said. "Well, she's got pretty legs. She crosses them and lets you see lots of stocking."

"Go on," Mason said.

"This woman," said Paul Drake, "wanted me to accept employment to protect Marjorie Clune's interests. She seemed to know a lot of inside stuff. She won't tell me how she knows it. She says that Dr. Doray has got a devil of a temper; that Dr. Doray was jealous of Patton all the time Patton was in Cloverdale, and that Doray came to this city, not to rescue Marjorie, but to kill Patton."

Perry Mason stared steadily at Paul Drake.

"And you telephoned Bradbury?" he asked.

"Yes, I got Bradbury at his hotel. I explained the situation to him and asked him if I could take the employment. At first he said no, he wanted me to work for him exclusively, and he certainly didn't want me working with some woman and making reports to her. She heard the conversation and said that I could make all my reports to Bradbury; that she only wanted to see justice done; that she would be willing to forego any reports."

"You relayed that on to Bradbury?" asked Mason.

"Yes."

"What did he say?"

"That changed the situation so far as he was concerned. He said if I wanted to it was all right to go ahead."

"You outlined her theory of the case to him?"

"Yes."

Perry Mason made drumming motions with the tips of the fingers of his right hand against the glass windows of the taxicab. Abruptly, he turned to Paul Drake.

"That explains it," he said.

"Explains what?"

"The tip-off on that Doray car."

The detective gave a sudden start of surprise, then caught himself and sat rigidly motionless.

"How did you know it was a tip-off?" he asked.

"This business about the homicide squad getting in touch with the deputy district attorney, and all that sort of stuff, sounds a little bit too fast and a little bit too efficient for the police," Perry Mason said. "You know as well as I do that most of the police efficiency, outside of regular routine stuff, is founded on tips and squeals. Now, who tipped you off that Doray's car was parked somewhere in the vicinity?"

"To tell you the truth," Paul Drake said "—and, incidentally, Perry, this is the only thing I've held out on you—it was this woman who told me that Dr. Doray's car was near the scene of the murder at the time of the murder, that it had been parked in front of a fire plug, and that it had been tagged."

Perry Mason's eyes were glinting with excitement.

"Tell me," he said, "was this car a distinctive car?"

"Yes, I understand it was. It's a light roadster, but it has all kinds of attachments on it—a lot of trick horns and headlights. Dr. Doray thought it was good advertisement to drive a distinctive car. Cloverdale, you know, is a small city, and—"

Perry Mason tapped on the glass to catch the driver's attention.

"I'll get out here," he said.

He turned to Paul Drake.

"You're going back to your office, Paul?"

"Yes."

"And," said Perry Mason, "this woman is there in your office now?"

"Yes, she was with me when you called. I had to wait a few minutes to get away. She was going to wait until I came back."

The cab driver swung the cab into the curb and opened the door. Perry Mason stepped to the sidewalk.

"Listen, Perry," Paul Drake said, "I'm frightfully sorry about this thing. If it's going to make any difference, I'll give her back the two hundred bucks and put her out of the office. I need the money, but—"

Perry Mason grinned at him.

"Paul," he said, "if you really feel remorseful you can pay off the taxicab when it gets back to the office."

He slammed the door and watched the cab turn the corner to the left. Then he sprinted for the all-night restaurant he had spotted, where there was a small enameled sign indicating the presence of a public telephone. He rushed to the telephone and dialed a number.

A woman's voice answered, "Coöperative Investigating Bureau."

"Who's in charge of the office tonight?" asked Perry Mason.

"Mr. Samuels."

"Put him on," said Perry Mason. "This is Mason, the lawyer, speaking—Perry Mason—he'll know me."

A moment later there was the click of connection, and Samuels' oily voice said, "Good evening, Counselor, is there something we can do for you tonight? We have been anxious to get some of your business for—"

"All right," Perry Mason snapped, "you've got some of it. The best way you can show that you can get more is by giving me fast service on this. There's a woman in the Drake Detective Bureau. She's talking with Paul Drake right now. She's about twenty-four or twenty-five, a slender type of beauty, with a figure that's easy to look at. She's brunette, with jet-black eyes and black hair. She's going to leave the office, probably some time soon. I want to know where she goes and what she does; I don't want her out of your sight night or day. Put as many men on the job as you need. Never mind the expense. Don't mail any reports. I'll call you up when I want to know anything. Keep it confidential and get started."

The voice at the other end of the line became crisply efficient.

"Twenty-four or twenty-five, slender, brunette, with black eyes. At the office of the Drake Detective Bureau."

"Check," said Perry Mason. "Make it snappy."

He hung up and dashed out to the curb, looked up and down the street and caught the lights of a cruising taxi. He waved his hand and brought the taxi to the curb.

"Get me to the Gilroy Hotel," he said, "and make it snappy."

The streets were open, the traffic signals, for the most part, discontinued, and the cab made fast time to the Gilroy Hotel.

"Stick around," Mason told him. "I'm going to want you, and I may not be able to pick up another cab in a hurry. If I'm not back in ten minutes, keep your motor warm."

He barged into the lobby, nodded to a sleepy clerk and strode to the elevators.

"Ninth floor," he told the elevator operator.

When the elevator stopped at the ninth floor Perry Mason said, "Which direction is 927?"

The operator pointed down the corridor.

"Just this side of the fire escape light," he said.

Perry Mason strode down the corridor, his feet pounding the carpet. He found 927 at the place the elevator operator had indicated. He swung around to find 925 on the opposite side of the corridor. He banged on the door of 925.

The transom was open. The door was of thin wood. Perry Mason could hear the creaking of bed springs. He knocked again. After a moment there was the sound of bare feet thudding to the floor, then motion from behind the door, and a man's voice said, "Who is it?"

"Open up," said Perry Mason gruffly.

"What do you want?"

"I want to talk with you."

"What about?"

"Open up, I tell you," Mason said.

The bolt clicked, and the door opened. A man, attired in pajamas, with his eyes swollen from sleep, his face wearing a startled expression, switched on the lights and blinked dazedly at the lawyer.

Perry Mason crossed to the window, through which a wind was blowing, billowing the lace curtains. He pulled the window down, gave a swift look about the room, then indicated the bed.

"Get back into bed," he said. "You can talk as well from there."

"Who are you?" asked the man

"I'm Perry Mason, the lawyer," Mason said. "Does that mean anything to you?"

"Yes, I've read about you."

"Were you expecting me?"

"No, why?"

"I was just wondering. Where were you tonight from seven o'clock on?"

"Is it any of your business?"

"Yes."

"Just what makes it your business?" asked the man.

Perry Mason stared at him steadily.

"I suppose you knew," he said, "that Thelma Bell was arrested and charged with murder?"

The man's face twisted with expression.

"Arrested?" he said.

"Yes."

"When?"

"Not very long ago."

"No," the man said, "I didn't know it."

"Your name's George Sanborne?"

"Yes."

"Were you with Thelma Bell this evening?"

"Yes."

"When?"

"From around seven fifteen or seven thirty to around nine o'clock."

"Where did you leave her?"

"At her apartment house—the St. James—out at 962 East Faulkner Street."

"Why did you leave her at that time?"

"We'd had a fight."

"What about?"

"About a man named Patton."

"That's the man she's accused of murdering," Mason said.

"What time was the murder committed?" Sanborne said.

"Around eight forty."

"She couldn't have done it," Sanborne said.

"You're positive?"

"Yes."

"Can you prove she was with you?"

"I think so, yes."

"Where did you go? What did you do?"

"We started out around seven twenty, I guess, and thought some of going to a picture show. We decided we'd wait until the second show. We went to a speakeasy, sat around and talked for a while, and then we got in a fight. We'd had a couple of drinks, I guess I lost my temper.

I was sore about Patton. She was letting him drag her down. He thought of nothing except her body. She had won a leg contest, and Patton continually harped on that. To hear him talk, you'd think her legs were her only asset. She couldn't get anywhere working in choruses, posing as an artist model and having her legs photographed for calendar advertisements."

"That was what the fight was about?" asked Perry Mason.

"Yes."

"And then you went home?"

"Yes."

"Do you know anybody at the speakeasy?"

"No."

"Where is the speakeasy?"

Sanborne's eyes shifted.

"I wouldn't want to get a speakeasy into trouble," he said.

Perry Mason's laugh was mirthless.

"Don't worry about that," he said. "That's their lookout. They all pay protection. This is a murder case. Where was the speakeasy?"

"On Forty-seventh Street, right around the corner from Elm Street."

"Do you know the door man?" asked Perry Mason.

"Yes."

"Will he remember you?"

"I think so."

"Do you know the waiter?"

"I don't particularly remember the waiter."

"Had you been drinking before you went there?"

"No."

"When you first sat down what did you order?"

"We had a cocktail."

"What kind?"

"I don't know, just a cocktail."

"What kind of a cocktail? Martini? Manhattan? Hawaiian . . .?"

"A Martini."

"Both had a Martini?"

"Yes."

"Then what?"

"Then we had another one."

"Then what?"

"Then we had something to eat—a sandwich of some sort."

"What sort of a sandwich?"

"A ham sandwich."

"Both of you had a ham sandwich?"

"Yes."

"Then what?"

"I think we switched to highballs."

"Don't you know?"

"Yes, I know."

"Rye or scotch or bourbon?"

"Rye."

"Both had rye?"

"Yes."

"Ginger ale?"

"Yes."

"Both had ginger ale?"

"Yes."

Perry Mason gave a sigh of disgust. He pulled himself up from the chair and made a wry face.

"I should have known better," he said.

"What do you mean?" Sanborne wanted to know.

"Evidently Thelma Bell had you primed before I telephoned this evening," Mason said. "When I said that I was at the Emergency Hospital you answered that test all right. Now you talk like a school kid."

"What do you mean?"

"Oh, this business of both having the same thing. Both had Martinis. Both had ham sandwiches. Both had rye highballs with ginger ale. What a sweet witness you'd make to fix up an alibi in a murder case!"

"But I'm telling you the truth," Sanborne said.

Mason's laugh was mirthless.

"Do you know what Thelma Bell told the officers?" he asked.

Sanborne shook his head.

"They asked her all about the drinks," he said. "She said that you went to a speakeasy; that you had a Manhattan and she had an old-fashioned cocktail; that you'd had dinner before you went there—both of you; that you didn't eat a thing while you were there; that you got a bottle of wine, with two glasses, and had some of that, and that then you had your fight and went home."

Sanborne ran his fingers through his matted hair.

"I didn't know," he said, "they were going to ask us all about those drinks."

Perry Mason walked toward the door.

"Don't use your telephone," he said, "until morning. Do you understand?"

"Yes, I understand, but shouldn't I call—"

"You heard what I said," Mason told him. "Don't use your telephone until morning."

He jerked open the door, slammed it shut behind him and walked down the narrow corridor toward the elevator. His shoulders were slightly slumped forward in an attitude of dejection. His face, however, remained virtually without expression. His eyes were weary.

The cage rattled upward, came to a stop. Perry Mason climbed in.

"Find your party?" asked the elevator boy.

"Yes."

"If there's anything you want," began the boy, "I can—"

"No, you can't," Perry Mason said almost savagely, and then added, after a moment, with grim humor, "I wish to God you could."

The elevator operator brought the cage to the lobby and stood staring curiously at Perry Mason as Mason barged purposefully across the lobby.

"St. James Apartments—962 East Faulkner Street," said Perry Mason with a touch of weariness in his voice as he jerked open the door of the taxicab.

11

Perry Mason pushed through the swinging door of the St. James Apartment house lobby. A colored boy was seated back of the desk, his feet up, his chair tilted back, his mouth open. He was making snoring noises.

The lawyer walked quietly past the desk, past the elevator, to the stairs. He climbed the stairs with slow, heavy tread, taking the three flights at a uniform pace, and without pausing to rest. He tapped with his knuckles on the door of Thelma Bell's apartment. At the third knock he heard the sound of bed springs.

"Open up, Thelma," he said.

He heard her move to the door, then the bolt came back and she was staring at him with wide, startled eyes.

"What is it?" she asked. "What's gone wrong?"

"Nothing," he told her. "I'm just checking up. What happened with the cops?"

"They didn't notice the coat and hat at all," she said. "They came out here to ask me about an appointment I had with Frank Patton. They didn't let on that he was dead and I didn't let on that I knew it. I told them that I had an appointment with him for nine o'clock in the morning tomorrow morning, and that my friend, Marjorie Clune, had an appointment at the same time; that I hadn't seen Marjorie for some little time; that I didn't know where she was staying and didn't know how to get in touch with her."

"Then what?" he asked.

"I kept moving around so they could see the white coat and hat," she said, "but no one seemed to pay any attention to it."

Perry Mason squinted his eyes thoughtfully.

"I'll tell you what happened," he said. "They came out here because they saw that message on the table in Patton's apartment. They wanted to check up on you. They hadn't talked things over very much with the officer on the beat. They'll do that later, and then some one will remember about that white coat and hat and they'll be back."

"You think so?" she asked.

He nodded moodily and stood staring at her steadily.

"You're not worried about your alibi?" he said.

"Oh, no," she told him, "that alibi is all right. I tell you I wasn't there. I wouldn't lie about it."

"How well did you know Margy?" he asked.

"Not particularly well. That is, I've only known her a couple of weeks. I've sympathized with her a lot, and tried to do what I could for her."

"You wouldn't try to save her from a murder rap by putting yourself in danger?"

Thelma Bell shook her head.

"Not murder," she said, "not me."

"There was a message at Patton's apartment to call Margy at Harcourt 63891," he said. "That's this number. I'm wondering how the detectives—"

"Oh, I explained that," she said. "I told them that I was out around six o'clock, but that Marjorie evidently had dropped in for a visit; that I found a note from her under the door."

"Did they want to see the note?"

"Oh, yes."

"What did you tell them?"

"I told them that I'd slipped it into my purse; that I didn't intend to save it; that I'd torn it up and couldn't remember just where I was when I'd torn it up, but I was in a speakeasy some place with my boy friend."

"They accepted that explanation all right?"

"Yes, they didn't seem interested in me at all; they were interested in Margy and they were interested in finding out about Margy's legs. They wanted to know if I'd ever heard her called 'The Girl with the Lucky Legs.'"

"What did you tell them?"

"I told them yes, of course."

"They didn't know that you'd won a contest at Parker City?"

"No, they didn't know very much about me. They wanted to know how well I knew Frank Patton and I said not at all well; that I'd met him through Margy and that I was to go there for an appointment with Margy;

that Patton had some work for us. I told them I wouldn't go if there was any reason why I shouldn't. They stalled along for a while and then finally told me that the reason I shouldn't go there was because Patton was dead. They looked at me to see how I took it."

"How did you take it?" he asked.

"I told them that it wasn't any surprise to me; that I'd heard he had a weak heart and he lived a pretty fast pace. They told me that he'd been murdered, and I stared at them and said, 'My God!' and sat down on the bed. I let my eyes get big and said, 'To think that I had an appointment with him tomorrow morning! My God! What would have happened if I hadn't known about it and had gone on up to his apartment!'"

"Did they say anything then?"

"No, they looked around and went out."

"And you were wearing the coat and the hat?"

"Yes."

Perry Mason hooked his thumbs in the armholes of his vest and started pacing up and down the carpeted floor of the apartment. Thelma Bell was attired in a nightgown and kimono. She looked down at her bare toes and wiggled them.

"My feet are getting cold," she said. "I'm going to cover up."

He shook his head at her.

"You're going to dress," he said.

"Why?" she inquired.

"I think," he said, "that you'd better go places."

"Why?"

"On account of the police."

"I don't want to," she told him.

"I think you'd better."

"But that would make it look bad for me."

"You've got an alibi, haven't you?"

"Yes," she said slowly and with some hesitation.

"Well," he said, "that's going to be okay then."

"But if I've got an alibi why should I go away?"

"I think it would be better, everything considered."

"Do you mean that it's going to be better for Marjorie?"

"Perhaps."

"If it's going to be better for Marjorie," she said with quick determination, "I'll do it. I'll do anything for her."

She switched on a reading light by the head of the bed, grabbed her kimono more tightly around her waist, stared at Perry Mason and then said, "When am I going?"

"Right away," he said, "as soon as you get dressed."

"Where am I going?"

"Places," he told her.

"Does it make any difference?"

"I think so."

"You mean that you're going to pick out a place I'm going to go?"

"Yes."

"Why?"

"Because I want to be able to put my finger on you."

"Have you talked with Margy?" she asked, her eyes, wide and innocent, fastened upon him with warm candor.

"Have you?" asked Perry Mason.

"Why, no," she said in a tone of rising surprise. "Certainly not."

Perry Mason abruptly stopped in his pacing. His feet were planted far apart, his jaw thrust belligerently forward. He shook off the fatigue which had sagged his shoulder muscles and stared at her with a somber light in his steady eyes.

"Don't lie to me," he said savagely. "You talked with Marjorie Clune since she left here."

Thelma Bell let her eyes grow wide and hurt.

"Why, Mr. Mason!" she exclaimed reproachfully.

"Forget that stuff," he said. "You talked with Marjorie Clune since I talked with her."

She shook her head in mute negation.

"You talked with her," Perry Mason said savagely, "and told her that you'd been talking with me; that I said for her to get out of town, or you told her something to that effect. You told her that she was to get out of town. You told her something that made her go."

"I did not!" she blazed. "I didn't tell her anything of the sort. She was the one that told me—"

"Ah," said Perry Mason, "she's the one that told you what?"

Thelma Bell lowered her eyes. After a moment she said in a low voice, "That she was going out of town."

"Did she say where she was going?"

"No."

"Did she say when she was going?"

"She was leaving at midnight," Thelma said.

Perry Mason looked at his watch.

"About three quarters of an hour ago," he said.

"Yes, I guess so."

"What time did you have the conversation?"

"Around eleven o'clock, I guess."

"Did she tell you where she was staying?"

"No, she said that she had to leave."

"What else did she tell you?"

"She just thanked me."

"Thanked you for what?"

"For wearing her clothes and giving her a break."

"Did she say anything about a message for me?" asked Perry Mason.

"No. She said that you had told her to stay here in the city, to be in her room at the hotel, but that circumstances had arisen which made it absolutely impossible for her to do as you wished."

"Did she say what the circumstances were?"

"No."

"Give any hints?"

"No."

"You," said Perry Mason, "are lying."

"No, I'm not," she said, but her eyes did not meet his.

Perry Mason stood staring moodily down at the young woman.

"How did you know my secretary's name was Della Street?" he inquired.

"I didn't know."

"Oh, yes, you did," he said. "You rang up Dr. Doray and impersonated Della Street. You told him you were Della Street, the secretary to Perry Mason, and that he should get out of town."

"I didn't tell him any such thing!"

"You called him."

"I did not!"

"Do you know where he's staying?"

"I've heard Margy mention his name. It seems to me there's a hotel—the Midwick Hotel, I think it is."

"Yes," Mason told her, "you seem to have a pretty good memory."

"You can't accuse me of things like that!" she flared suddenly, staring at him with indignation in her eyes. "I didn't call Dr. Doray."

"Did he call you?"

"No."

"Did you hear from him?"

"No."

"Did Marjorie say anything about him?"

Her eyes lowered.

"No," she said.

"Dr. Doray was in love with Marjorie?" Perry Mason asked.

"I guess so."

"Is she in love with him?"

"I don't know."

"Is she in love with Bradbury?"

"I don't know."

"Does she talk over her affairs with you?"

"What sort of affairs?"

"Affairs of the heart—tell you who she loved?"

"No, we were never very intimate. She talked mostly about Cloverdale and about the predicament she was in on account of Frank Patton. She said that she was afraid to go back to Cloverdale; that she was ashamed; that she couldn't face them there."

Perry Mason nodded toward the dressing-room.

"Get dressed," he said.

"Can't I wait until morning?"

"No," he told her, "there's a chance the police may come tonight."

"But I thought you wanted me to talk with the police. I thought you wanted me to let them think I was the girl in the white coat that the officer had seen coming from the apartment."

"I've changed my mind," Mason said. "Get dressed."

She got to her feet, took two steps toward the dressing-room, then suddenly turned to face him.

"You understand one thing, Perry Mason," she said in a tone that was vibrant, "I know that I can trust you. I know that you stand back of your clients. There's only one reason that I'm doing this, and that's for Marjorie. I want that kid to get a square deal."

Mason nodded grimly.

"Never mind that," he said. "Get dressed."

Perry Mason resumed his pacing of the floor while Thelma Bell was dressing. When she emerged, fully clothed, including a small suitcase which she carried in her hand, Perry Mason looked at his watch.

"Do you suppose," he said, "you could go a bite of breakfast?"

"I'll tell the world I could go some coffee," she said.

Mason took her arm and transferred the light suitcase to his hand.

"Let's go," he said.

They left the apartment. The negro in the lobby was awake as they went out. He stared at them with round-eyed curiosity, but there was a dazed, sleep-sodden look about his face which made his stare seem uncomprehending.

Mason signaled his taxicab.

"Drive down the street," he said, "and stop at the first restaurant that's open, then wait."

The cab driver found a restaurant within two blocks. Perry Mason escorted Thelma Bell into the restaurant and ordered ham and eggs for himself, and, at her nod, doubled the order. A waiter slid a thick glass filled with water across the counter, pushed knives and forks into position.

Perry Mason suddenly gave a guilty start.

"My wallet!" he said.

"What about it?"

"It's gone," he told her. "I must have left it in your apartment."

"I don't think so," she said. "You didn't take it out, did you?"

"Yes," Mason said, "I was looking for an address. It's got my cards in it. I don't want the officers to know I was there.

"Give me your keys. I'll take a run up and get it."

"I can go," she said.

"No," he told her, "you wait here. I don't want you to get around that apartment any more. The officers may be there any minute."

"What will happen if they find *you* there?"

"I'll tell them that I am looking for you."

"But what about the key?"

"I won't go in unless the coast is clear."

She gave him the key to the apartment. Perry Mason caught the eye of the waiter.

"Put on one of those orders of ham and eggs," he said, "and lots of coffee. Save the other one until I get back."

He strode rapidly out of the restaurant to the taxicab, and told the driver, "Get back to the St. James Apartments as quick as you can. Step on it."

The cab driver spun the cab about in a complete turn and pushed the motor into speed. Within a short time he had traversed the empty street and pulled up in front of the apartment house. Perry Mason ran through the lobby. This time the colored boy was staring at him with eyes that were filled with interest. Mason took the elevator to the third floor, opened the door of the apartment, switched on the light, closed the door behind him, turned the bolt into position so that the door could not be opened from the outside, and then started a swift search of the apartment. He did not look in the drawers of the built-in dresser, nor in the likely places, but prowled around in the dark corners of the closet. It took him but a matter of seconds to find a leather hat box thrust back into a corner of a closet shelf, with clothes piled in front of it so that the hat box was concealed.

Mason pulled out the hat box, snapped back the catch and pulled open the lid.

There was a woman's skirt, a pair of stockings and some white shoes in the hat box. They had been washed and were still damp. The moisture had soaked into the hat box, and it gave forth a steamy smell as the lid was pulled up.

The stockings showed no trace of stain, but there were one or two spots on the skirt which had not been removed, and the shoes showed unmistakable spots of brownish stain.

Perry Mason snapped the lid back on the hat box and left the apartment.

"Does you all live here?" the colored boy at the desk asked.

Perry Mason flipped a round silver dollar across the desk.

"No," he said, "I'm just taking a friend's apartment for the day."

"What the number of it?" asked the colored boy.

"509," Perry Mason said, and pushed through the outer door of the lobby before there could be any further questions. He gave the hat box to the taxi driver.

"Take me back to the restaurant," he said. "Then go down to the Union Depot, buy a ticket to College City, check this hat box on the ticket, bring me back the ticket and the check, hand them to me where the young lady doesn't see them. Do you get that straight?"

The cab driver nodded.

Perry Mason passed him a twenty dollar bill.

"Step on it," he said.

Mason reëntered the restaurant. Thelma Bell looked up from her plate of ham and eggs.

"Did you find it?" she asked.

He nodded.

"Fell out of my pocket," he said, "when I was sitting in the chair. It's a good thing I found it; it was lying right in plain sight. The officers would have picked it up and might have made some trouble because I'd have told them that I hadn't been to your apartment."

The waiter thrust his head through an arched hole in the partition which led to the kitchen and bellowed, "Put on those eggs and finish the ham."

Perry Mason sat down at the counter and stirred the coffee which the waiter placed in front of him.

"Was any one there?" she asked.

"No," he told her, "but they may be at any time."

"You seem to be pretty positive about that."

"I am."

"You know," she said, pausing with a piece of ham halfway to her mouth, "no matter what happens, we have to protect Margy."

Perry Mason said bluntly, "That's what I'm being paid for."

There was an interval of silence. The waiter brought Mason his ham and eggs. He wolfed them down and was finished by the time Thelma Bell was finished.

"All right, sister," he said, "we're going places."

"Can you tell me where?"

"Some place not too far away."

"I've got a couple of appointments tomorrow and the next day to do some modeling work."

"Ditch them."

"I haven't any money."

"You will have," he told her.

He finished the last of his coffee, wiped his lips with a napkin, looked across at her.

"Ready?" he asked.

"Ready," she said.

He took her arm and piloted her to the door of the restaurant. The cab drove up just as they emerged to the sidewalk.

"Here you are, boss," said the driver, holding out his hand palm down.

Perry Mason took the ticket and the check.

"What's that?" asked Thelma Bell suspiciously.

"An errand I had the cab driver do," he told her.

"Have you got enough change to cover the amount of the meter?" Mason asked the cab driver.

"I sure have, and then some," said the cab driver, and added audaciously, "enough to make a mighty nice little tip for me."

Mason stared intently at Thelma Bell.

"Can I trust you?" he asked.

"As long as it's for Margy, yes."

Mason pulled the railroad ticket the cab driver had given him from his vest pocket and handed it to her.

"Here's a one-way ticket to College City," he said. "Go there and register at a hotel. Register under your own name. You're going there to do some modeling work; if any one should start checking up on you tell them that and no more. If it gets serious, get in touch with me and don't say anything until I have given you instructions."

"You mean if the law should come?"

"Yes," he said, "if the law should come."

"Will there be trains running at this time of night?"

He looked at his watch.

"There's one leaves in twenty minutes," he said. "You can make it."

He handed the cab driver the suitcase and assisted Thelma Bell into the cab.

"Good night," he said, "and good luck. Ring up my office or send me a telegram. Leave word the name of the hotel where you're staying, and don't take a powder."

"A powder?" she said.

"A run-out powder," he told her. "I want you where I can put my hand on you."

She extended her hand and smiled at him.

"I'd do anything," she said, "for Margy."

Perry Mason took her hand. The fingertips were cold as ice. The cab driver climbed to the front seat.

"And you don't want me to tell any one about where I was? That is, about George Sanborne?"

Perry Mason shook his head with a fatherly smile.

"No," he said, "we'll save that as a surprise—a big surprise."

The cab motor roared into life. Perry Mason slammed the door, stood on the curb and watched the cab until the pale light rounded the corner. Then he went back to the restaurant.

"Telephone," he said.

The waiter indicated a pay telephone in a corner at the far end of the restaurant.

Perry Mason strode to it, dropped a coin and dialed the number of the Coöperative Investigating Bureau, and when he heard the voice of the operator, said, "Mason talking. Put on Mr. Samuels, if he's still there."

A moment later he heard the voice of Samuels booming with cordiality.

"Mason? We've done just what you wanted. We picked up that party, and she hasn't been out of our sight for a minute."

"Where is she now?" asked Mason.

"Ten minutes ago my men reported by telephone. She left Paul Drake's office about half an hour after you telephoned. She went to the Monmarte Hotel, where she has a room as Vera Cutter, of Detroit, Michigan, but she didn't give any street address when she registered. She took a room in the hotel early last evening. That is, around nine-thirty some time, and here's something funny: her baggage is fairly new and has the initials E. L. on it. She's got a rather ornate handbag, with hammered silver in a monogram, and the monogram is E. L. Does that mean anything to you?"

"Not yet it doesn't," Perry Mason said, "but keep her shadowed."

"And you'll ring up for reports?"

"Yes. Be sure that you know who it is before you give out any information. Talk with me for a minute whenever I call, so that you know it isn't some one else using my name, and keep her shadowed every minute. I want to know everything about her. Better put on a couple of extra men, and if any one comes to the hotel to call on her, try and shadow them and find out all about them. Now, how about telephone calls? Can you arrange with the telephone operator at the Monmarte Hotel to let you listen in?"

"One of our men is working on that right now," Samuels said. "It is, of course, going to be rather difficult, but—"

"Hang the difficulties," Perry Mason said. "The world is full of difficulties. I've got plenty of my own. Listen in on her telephone conversations; I want to know what they are."

"Very well, Mr. Mason," said Samuels, "we'll do the best we can."

Perry Mason pulled down the receiver with the middle finger of his left hand, fumbled in his pocket for another coin, dropped it and called the Drake Detective Bureau.

Drake himself answered the telephone.

"Sitting there waiting for calls, Paul?" asked the lawyer.

Drake laughed.

"You pretty near called the turn at that," he said.

"Anything to report?" asked Perry Mason.

"I've got lots to report," Paul Drake told him. "I think you can go home now and go to bed, Perry."

"Why?"

"The murder mystery is all solved."

"What do you mean?"

"The police have traced the knife."

"You mean the knife that did the stabbing?"

"Yes."

"Where have they traced it to?"

"To the man that bought it."

"Have they identified the man that bought it?"

"Virtually, yes. They have a description that tallies on every essential point."

"Who bought it?" asked Perry Mason.

"Your friend, Dr. Robert Doray of Cloverdale," Paul Drake retorted with something of a verbal flourish.

"Go on," said Perry Mason, "tell me the rest of it."

"That's about all of it," Paul Drake said. "The police tried to check the knife. They've been working on that ever since they discovered the body, and the price mark that was on the blade of the knife. You see, there was a cost price, as well as a sales price, on the knife. There's been an advance in prices on that stuff, and from the cost price they knew that the knife was part of a new stock that had been purchased at the increased price, since there was no other and older cost mark on it, and no sign of one having been on it arid having been erased."

"Go on," Mason said.

"They figured first that the knife came from a hardware store. The wrapping paper was a little bit heavier than is ordinarily used in the ten, fifteen and twenty-five cent stores. They got the heads of the hardware jobbers out of bed, got them to get in touch with their salesmen by telephone and try and find a retailer who used that particular cost code. It looked like a wild-goose chase, but they were lucky. Almost at once they got in touch with a hardware salesman who was familiar with a retail hardware store on Belmont Street that used that cost code, and the hardware salesman remembered this dealer had purchased a dozen of those knives not less than ten days ago. The police got in touch with the dealer. The dealer remembered the sale of the knife and gave a pretty fair description of the man. The description was that of Dr. Doray. The police got in touch with the newspaper offices, found one that had a file of the Cloverdale papers, prowled through the Cloverdale papers until they found a picture of Dr. Doray. He'd been an official in the Community Chest drive, and his picture had been in the paper. It was a newspaper photograph, but had enough to it to furnish the basis for an identification. The hardware dealer has made an absolute identification. There's no question in his mind but what Dr. Doray was the man who purchased the knife.

"The police feel they've pulled a nice piece of work, and they're throwing out a drag-net for Doray. Apparently he's skipped out, and, incidentally, that puts you in a funny light."

"Why?" asked Perry Mason.

"On account of that telephone message which apparently came from your office, and which tipped Doray off to what was happening. The police are pretty much worked up about it. I don't mind telling you in confidence that you're going to have some trouble over it, and, incidentally, I don't think Bradbury likes it very well."

"To hell with Bradbury," Perry Mason said. "I didn't call up Doray, and, what's more, my office didn't call up."

"Well," Paul Drake remarked cheerfully, "if you say that you didn't, and Della Street says *she* didn't, there's not much the police can do about it; not unless they should pick up Doray and he should tell them something different."

"That wouldn't change the situation any," Mason said. "Doray certainly doesn't know the voice of my secretary well enough to have recognized it, or to swear that he did. All that he knows is that some woman said she was Della Street. It's easy enough to do that. I could ring up Bradbury and tell him that I was Paul Drake, and tell him he'd better get out of the country."

Paul Drake laughed. He seemed in a very good humor, indeed.

"Well," he said, "I should waste my time telling you law points. But here's something you do want to be careful of."

"What's that?"

"Marjorie Clune."

"What about her?"

"The police have established in some way that Marjorie Clune and Dr. Doray drove together to the vicinity of Patton's apartment. They've located some one who had a little confectionery store in front of the fire plug where Doray parked his car. He remembers when the car drove up, and remembers that a man and a woman got out of it. The description of the man is that of Dr. Doray and the description of the woman tallies with Marjorie Clune. The confectionery dealer is one of those birds who get a great delight out of other persons' misfortunes. He's seen lots of people park their cars in front of that fire plug and get tagged. He likes to look at their facial expressions when they come back and find the tag dangling on the steering wheel, so he happened to notice Doray and Marjorie Clune pretty closely."

"Have the police explained anything about that blackjack yet?" Perry Mason asked.

"No, that probably isn't going to enter into the case particularly."

"Why not?"

"Because the crime wasn't committed with it. It hasn't anything more to do with the crime than the cane that was lying on the table—not as much, because the cane can be identified as having belonged to Patton, whereas no one knows who that blackjack belongs to."

"In other words," Mason said, "the police figure the case is closed, is that it?"

"That's just about it."

"And you think that I'm going to get in over my necktie?"

"I'm just warning you," Drake said. "I know that you've been working on that Marjorie Clune angle of the case. I just don't want you to get in a jam for compounding a felony, or becoming an accessory after the fact."

"While you're on the line," Perry Mason said, "I'll tell you a little law, Paul: You can't compound a felony if a felony hasn't been committed. On the other hand, you can't become an accessory by aiding a person who isn't guilty of anything. If your principal isn't guilty, you aren't guilty, no matter what you do."

"You figure that Marjorie Clune is innocent?" Drake asked.

"Marjorie Clune," said Perry Mason with grave dignity, "is my client. Is it fair to ask what you're waiting for, Paul?"

"What do you mean?"

"You're waiting in your office. You're sitting right there at the telephone. You're waiting for something. Is it fair to ask what it is?"

The detective's tone was hurt.

"Now listen, Perry," he said, "I told you that I wouldn't accept any employment that was adverse to your interests. I've had that understanding with Bradbury, and I thought I had that understanding with you. The employment that this young woman gave me didn't conflict in any way with the employment you folks gave me. In fact, I figured that it checked right in. She claims that Marjorie Clune is innocent, but that Doray is the murderer; that Marjorie Clune may try to protect Doray, and—"

"I know all that stuff," Perry Mason said. "But that still doesn't tell me what you're waiting for."

"Well," Paul Drake told him, "I was coming to that. I've got a tip from police headquarters that the police interviewed Thelma Bell earlier in the evening. They didn't figure at the time that she was connected with the case sufficiently to warrant them in taking any steps. I think that they feel differently about it now. They think that she's got some important information that she concealed or that she could give. I understand they're going out to pick her up, and I was waiting to hear what she said. Have you any objections to that?"

"None whatever, my dear boy," said Perry Mason. "You wait right there until the police pick her up."

Smiling gently, Perry Mason slipped the receiver back on the hook.

12

Morning sun was streaming through the streets of the city when Perry Mason aroused himself from the couch in the Turkish bath. His eyes were steady and clear. He had been freshly shaven, and his face showed no trace of fatigue.

From a telephone booth in the Turkish bath, he called the Drake Detective Bureau. The desk operator answered him.

"Paul Drake there?" he asked.

"No," she said, "Mr. Drake went out about half an hour ago."

"Do you know where he went?"

"Yes, he went home to get some sleep."

"This is Mason talking," the lawyer said. "Can you tell me how long he was here last night?"

"Oh, he stayed right up until half an hour ago," the girl said. "He was waiting for a telephone call. He expected to get some important information."

"And he didn't get it?"

"No, he waited all night, and then decided he'd get some sleep. He left word for me to call him if there were any new developments in that Patton case. He's working on that for you, isn't he?"

"And others," Mason said, with a smile.

"Do you want to call him at his apartment? I'll give you the number."

"No," Mason said, "I know the number. I just wanted to find out if he was still there. I didn't have anything important."

He hung up the telephone, his face wearing a broad smile, and went to the room where he had left his clothes, dressed, secured his valuables at the desk, and looked at his watch. It was eight thirty-five.

He returned to the telephone booth and dialed the number of his own office. Della Street's, "Good morning, this is Perry Mason's office," sounded crisp, fresh, and businesslike.

"Don't mention any names," Perry Mason said, "but this is the Mayor of Podunk. I want to see about floating a bond issue for—"

"Oh," she said, "I'm so glad you called," and there was relief in her tone.

"What's new?" he asked.

"Lots of things."

"Can you talk?"

"Yes, there's no one here right now except Mr. Bradbury, and I put him in the law library."

"What are the things you've got to tell me?" Mason asked. "Be careful how you mention them over the telephone."

"They all have to do with Bradbury," she told him.

"What about him?"

"He wants to see you, and he wants to see you right away."

"I don't want to see him," Mason said.

"I'm not certain about that," she said. "There's been something of a change come over him. I remember what you said about him, and I think you're right. He's a man who has to be reckoned with, and he's determined to see you. He says that if he doesn't see you within the next hour, it may make a great deal of difference to you; that if you should telephone and get in touch with me, I am to tell you that. That I am also to tell you he is not willing to allow a locked door to stand between the woman he loves and her freedom."

There was a moment of silence, while Perry Mason scowled thoughtfully.

"Do you get what he means by that?" she asked.

"I get it," Mason said, "and I might as well have a showdown with that bird now as later. He's not going to browbeat me."

"I think," she told him, "there are detectives watching the office."

"Yes," he said, "there would be. They want to pick me up. I tell you, Della, what you do. I'm about eight blocks from the office, at the Turkish bath that's right up the avenue. You get Bradbury and get in a taxicab. Drive up to the Turkish bath. I'll be standing in the doorway. You can pick me up."

"Do you think it's safe for me to leave with him? You don't think the detectives will suspect anything?"

"No, I don't think so," he told her, "and I want a witness along. You'd better put a pencil in your handbag, and have a notebook that you can use if it becomes necessary. I'm going to reach an understanding with Bradbury, and reach it right now."

"Okay, chief," she told him, "we'll be there in about ten minutes, and please, chief, be careful."

Perry Mason was scowling thoughtfully as he dropped the receiver into place. He left the Turkish bath, climbed a flight of stairs, and emerged into the warm morning sunshine. He stood back in the recess which opened from the sidewalk, and watched the hurrying pedestrians pounding the pavement on their way to the office buildings in the downtown business section.

His eyes scrutinized the passing faces with the keen, quick interest of a man who has learned to judge character at a glance, and who is sufficiently interested in human nature to read the stories written on the faces of the throngs who jostle about the city streets.

Now and again some young, attractive woman, feeling the impact of his gaze, would glance either furtively or frankly into his keenly searching eyes. Occasionally some man, catching Mason's stare, would frown with resentment, or turn to regard Mason with a stare which said plainly enough that the man thought he had surprised a detective at work.

Mason had stood motionless for perhaps five minutes when a blond young woman came hurrying along the street. She intuitively felt his eyes upon her, and raised her own eyes. Suddenly she smiled. Perry Mason raised his hat.

It was the young woman who ran the cigar counter in the lobby of his office building.

She abruptly turned toward him.

"Why so pensive, Mr. Mason?" she asked.

"Just trying to think of the answer to a question, Mamie. What are you hurrying so about?"

"Just the old grind."

"Do me a favor, will you, Mamie?"

"Sure."

"Forget you saw me here if any one should ask you."

"Dodging clients," she asked, "or the police?"

"Both," he told her, and grinned.

"I don't blame you for dodging your new client," she said.

He stared at her.

"Which one?"

"The one who always wears the brown suit, with the brown tie, the brown shirt, and the socks that go with his tie."

"You mean Bradbury?"

"Yes, the one who bought the cigars that you didn't smoke. Thanks for the business, Mr. Mason. I knew you didn't smoke cigars."

He laughed.

"We can't let any out-of-town money get away from us, Mamie. What's the trouble between you and Bradbury?"

"Oh, nothing," she said, "except that I think he's a small-town sport."

"What gives you that impression?"

"Oh, the way he acts. He stops to visit with me every time he comes in the building, and he keeps getting intimate."

"You mean with things he says?"

"Oh, no. He doesn't say so much; it's his tone and his eyes that get intimate. A girl can tell when a man's taking a personal interest."

Perry Mason looked over her trim figure with an approving eye.

"You can't blame him for that," he said.

She smiled frankly at him, and said, "Don't get me wrong, Mr. Mason. I like to have them look me over. It tickles my vanity, and it brings me business. But what I don't like are these counter loungers who think they can date you up, leave a big package for you to keep, and then expect the profit on a five-cent magazine to pay the traffic."

A taxicab pulled in close to the curb.

"Remember what I said, Mamie," said Perry Mason, as he raised his hat and walked across the sidewalk.

"M'Gawd," she said, "he's got on a new outfit this morning. He's busted into gray . . . and look at the smirk on his face. Damn him. He thinks we're just getting in from a party."

Perry Mason paid no attention to the comment. His eyes held Bradbury as he walked to the door of the taxicab, jerked it open and climbed in.

"Drive straight up this street, buddy, until you come to a good-looking side street without much traffic. Turn down it and park when you find a place."

He smiled at Della Street; then met Bradbury's gaze.

"You're an insistent cuss, Bradbury," he said.

Bradbury's eyes met his steadily.

"I'm a fighter, Mason," he remarked gently.

Mason studied the cold gray eyes, the determined angle of the jaw, and nodded his head. He pulled a package of cigarettes from his pocket, offered Della Street one, saw Bradbury shake his head in refusal and reach for a cigar; then, as Mason took one of the cigarettes, Bradbury scraped a match along the sole of his shoe. Mason also lit a match. Della Street thanked Bradbury with her eyes and accepted Mason's match. Bradbury frowningly diverted his match to his cigar. Perry Mason lit his cigarette after Della had her light, and said to Bradbury, "Well, what's the rumpus? I understand you were going to do things if you didn't see me."

"I have got to do certain things," said Bradbury slowly. "I feel that I am entitled to a conference with an attorney when I have hired him on a basis of fair remuneration."

"Let's not argue about that," Mason said. "You've got your conference now. What do you want?"

"I want you," Bradbury said, "to defend Dr. Robert Doray on the charge of murdering Frank Patton."

"I thought you wanted me to defend Marjorie Clune."

"I do. I also want you to defend Dr. Doray."

"You think they're both going to be indicted?"

"They both have been formally charged with murder," Bradbury said. "I got the news this morning. A formal charge has been lodged against them, and a warrant issued."

"Precisely what," asked Perry Mason, "do you want me to do?"

"I want you to defend Dr. Robert Doray," said Bradbury in close-clipped sentences, "and see that he is acquitted."

"It may not be easy to do either," Perry Mason said slowly, staring speculatively at the smoke which spiraled up from his cigarette. "If they are jointly charged with murder, it may be that for ethical reasons I cannot represent both. In other words, it is possible that Doray might try to throw the blame on Marjorie Clune, and Marjorie Clune might try to throw it on Doray."

"Don't be technical, Counselor," Bradbury said. "The situation is critical. Something has to be done, and done immediately. I want Dr. Doray acquitted. You know as well as I do that there will be no question of a conflict of interest. If there is any chance of any conflict developing, it will be when each tries to take the blame in order to shield the other. That is one thing that I have to guard against. I want you to represent both of them to see that that doesn't happen."

"Well," Mason said slowly, "we'll argue about some of those ethical points when the proper time comes. As I understand it, neither of them has been arrested yet."

"That's right."

"Do you know all of the case that the police have?"

"They've got a pretty strong case," Bradbury said. "A very strong case against Dr. Doray. I doubt if they have a strong case against Marjorie Clune."

"And you want me to get Doray acquitted. Is that right?"

"You have simply *got* to get Doray acquitted."

"Suppose it should become necessary to have separate attorneys representing the defendants?" Perry Mason said, his eyes puckered and staring at Bradbury with such keen concentration that their depths seemed to hold a steely glitter. "Which one do you want me to take?"

"It's not going to be necessary," Bradbury said, "and I don't want to discuss the point. I am going to insist that you represent both, Counselor, and that as a part of your representation, you clear up the question of the door."

Perry Mason's eyes narrowed until the lids were level.

"What question about what door?" he asked.

"The question about the locked door into Patton's apartment," Bradbury said. "There are some things I don't need to go over, Mr. Mason. I am not particularly a fool. I appreciate what you have done. I recognize that what you have done was done for the best interests of all concerned, as you understood those interests at the time. However,

I think the police are going to be able to prove that Marjorie Clune was at the apartment about the time of the murder. If the door of the apartment was unlocked, Marjorie Clune could have walked in, could have discovered the body, and could have walked away in a panic. And guilty of no crime other than failing to notify the officers of what she had found. If the door of the apartment was locked, it would mean that Marjorie Clune must have a key. It would mean that she must have been in sufficient control of her mental faculties to pause and lock the door behind her when she left the apartment. That won't look good for Marjorie. It won't look good for her case, and it won't look good for her character."

"But," said Perry Mason slowly, "suppose Marjorie Clune had been in the bathroom; suppose she had been having hysterics. Suppose some one had heard her cries, and had rushed in and killed Frank Patton?"

"Then," said Bradbury, without hesitation and in a tone of voice which showed that he had carefully thought over that phase of the situation, "Marjorie Clune would still have been the last one to have left the apartment, *unless* she had emerged while the murderer was there. To have found a body, and given no alarm, is perhaps a violation of some technical law. To have found a murderer engaged redhanded in the commission of his crime, and to have aided in his escape, would be to make herself an accessory. I don't want her to be an accessory. All in all, Counselor, the question of that locked door becomes more and more important."

Della Street fidgeted uneasily.

The cab turned down a side street, sped along for two or three blocks; then pulled close to the curb.

"How's this?" asked the cab driver.

"That," Perry Mason said, "is fine." His voice was an even monotone, as though he had been talking in his sleep. His eyes were staring with hypnotic steadiness at Bradbury.

Slowly he said, still in that same expressionless monotone, "Let's understand each other, Bradbury. You want me to represent Marjorie Clune and Dr. Doray."

"Yes."

"I'm to be paid for that representation."

"Yes."

"And, furthermore, you insist upon an acquittal."

"Furthermore," said Bradbury, "I insist upon an acquittal. Under the circumstances, Counselor, I think I am entitled to it. If there is not an acquittal, it will be necessary for me to make a complete disclosure of certain facts, which I need not mention at the present time, but which indicate very strongly, to my mind, that the door was locked sometime after both Marjorie Clune and the murderer had left the apartment where the murder was committed."

"And that," said Perry Mason, "is an ultimatum."

"If you want to put it that way," Bradbury said, "it's an ultimatum. I don't want to be harsh, Counselor. I don't want to have you feel that I'm putting you on a spot, but, by God! I intend to get a square deal for Marjorie Clune. We've been over all that before."

"And for Bob Doray?" asked Perry Mason.

"I expect an acquittal for Dr. Robert Doray."

"Don't you realize," Mason said slowly, "that virtually every fact in the case points unerringly to the guilt of Dr. Doray?"

"Of course I realize it," Bradbury said. "What do you think I am, a fool?"

"Not by a long ways," said Mason, with a degree of respect in his tone. "I was simply remarking that you'd handed me a big order."

Bradbury pulled a wallet from his pocket.

"Now that we have discussed that phase of the situation," he said, "I am perfectly willing to admit that it is a big order, and I am perfectly willing to admit that I expect to pay for it. I have given you a retainer of one thousand dollars. I now hand to your secretary an additional four thousand dollars. I expect to give you further compensation when a verdict of not guilty is returned by the jury."

With the crisp efficiency of a banker, Bradbury counted out bills to the amount of four thousand dollars, and handed them to Della Street.

She looked questioningly at Perry Mason.

Perry Mason nodded.

"Well," Perry Mason said, "we understand each other, anyway. That's one satisfaction. But I want you to understand this, Bradbury. I will endeavor to represent both Dr. Doray and Marjorie Clune. I will endeavor to secure a favorable verdict. I will call your attention, however, to the same thing that you have told me about yourself. That is, that you are a fighter. I, too, am a fighter. You fight for yourself. I fight for my clients. When I start in fighting for

Marjorie Clune and Dr. Doray, I'm going to fight. There are not going to be any halfway measures."

Bradbury's face did not so much as change expression by the slightest flicker of a muscle.

"I don't give a damn what you do," he said "—if you will pardon my French, Miss Street—or how you do it. All I know is that I want to be certain those two persons are acquitted."

Della Street spoke hotly.

"I'm not entirely in the dark about what you have reference to, Mr. Bradbury," she said. "I think you're perfectly horrid. Mr. Mason went out of his way to give you protection for the person you had employed him to protect. He did things that—"

"Steady, Della," warned Perry Mason.

She caught his eye, and was suddenly silent.

"I see," said Bradbury, "that she knows."

"You see nothing," said Mason grimly. "And I want to tell you right now, Bradbury, that'll you'll do a lot better for yourself and for your clients if you keep your finger out of the pie. We understand each other, and that's enough."

"That's enough," said Bradbury.

"Furthermore," Mason said, "I don't want any more of your veiled threats made to my secretary. I don't want you to try and browbeat her into getting any more interviews with me."

"I am not going to ask for any more interviews with you," Bradbury said. "I have given you my ultimatum. It stands. I am going to have nothing whatever to say about methods. I am going to hold you strictly accountable for results."

Della Street opened her mouth to say something, sucked in her breath with a quick intake; then, as she looked at Perry Mason's grim face, became silent.

Mason looked at Bradbury.

"All right," he said, "I'll get out here. You can take Della Street back to the office. You pay for the cab."

Bradbury nodded.

"See that he gets a receipt for the retainer," Mason said.

"Needless to say," Bradbury warned, "time is of the greatest value. The police are building up a dangerous case against Dr. Doray."

"Did you know they'd identified him as the purchaser of the knife?" asked Perry Mason.

Bradbury's face showed surprised consternation.

"You mean that they've proven he was the one that bought the knife that stabbed Patton?"

"Yes."

"Good God!" said Bradbury, and slumped back against the cushions of the cab and stared at the lawyer, his mouth sagging slightly open, his eyes wide.

"You knew that they'd located his car as having been parked near the vicinity of the crime?" asked Mason.

"Yes, I knew that. That's why I thought they had a damaging case against him. But, this other, my God, that's conclusive, isn't it?"

Perry Mason made a shrugging gesture with his shoulders.

"May I ask," he said, "why you are suddenly so anxious to have Dr. Doray acquitted?"

"That," said Bradbury, "is my business."

"I had rather gathered," Mason said, "that Dr. Doray was your rival for the affections of Miss Clune; that you didn't have any feeling of friendship for him—that is, no particular love."

"My feelings toward Dr. Doray haven't the slightest bearing on the case whatever," Bradbury remarked in a tone of voice which was doubtless intended as a rebuke. "You are an attorney. You make a business of representing people who are accused of crime, and securing acquittals. I have told you that I shall expect an acquittal of Dr. Doray as well as of Margy. If they're not acquitted on the evidence that the police produce, I propose to take steps, through other counsel, to see that the real facts are called to the attention of the court in order to secure a new trial."

"The facts, I take it," Perry Mason said, "relating to the locked door."

"Correct."

"Well, you're plain enough," Mason told him.

He grinned reassuringly at Della Street.

"Don't worry, Della," he said, "I've been in worse jams than this before."

"But," she said hotly, "how can he—?"

Mason frowned and shook his head.

"Della," he said, "the weather is delightful."

"Yes?" she asked.

"And," said Perry Mason, "whenever you discuss any subject with Mr. Bradbury, I want it to be the subject of the weather. The weather is always a very engrossing subject of conversation. It is virtually inexhaustible. Please see that Bradbury confines himself to it."

"Don't worry," Bradbury said, with a sudden frank smile twisting his lips. "I fight a fighter, Mason. I don't pick on women. I couldn't help observing that your secretary was fully familiar with the point I was making as I made it. That would seem to indicate that—"

Perry Mason interrupted with firmly insistent tones.

"The weather, Mr. Bradbury," he said, "is delightful for this time of year. It is unusually warm."

Bradbury nodded.

"And, as I was about to remark," he said, "I shall attempt to take no advantage of you because of anything Miss Street might say or do."

Perry Mason pulled open the door of the taxicab, climbed to the sidewalk, and cocked an appraising eye at the cloudless sky. Then he raised his hat.

"There is a chance," he said, "that it may cloud over this afternoon."

Bradbury started to say something, but the banging of the taxicab door cut off his sentence, and Perry Mason was striding down the side street back toward the avenue.

13

Perry Mason took a taxicab to the airport. Within ten minutes, the young woman at the information desk in the office had placed him in touch with an aviator who was willing to charter a fast cabin plane by the hour. The lawyer sized up the aviator with eyes that showed approval. He pulled a wallet from his pocket, took out crisp, new bills, and handed them to the aviator.

"You're ready to go?"

"It'll take a very few minutes to get it warmed up," the aviator told him. "She's all ready—that is, all filled with gas and inspected."

"Let's go," Perry Mason said.

The aviator smiled.

"You haven't told me yet where you want to go to," he said.

"I'll tell you that while you're getting the plane warmed up," Mason told him.

They walked down the wide cement walk. A small, snub-nosed cabin plane glistened in the sun.

"That's the job," said the aviator.

Perry Mason looked it over while two mechanics swung it into position, put blocks under the wheels, and started the motor warming up.

"There's a mail plane leaves here around midnight," Mason said. "I want to follow that mail plane."

The pilot stared at him.

"You'll never catch it. Why it's as far as—"

"I don't want to catch it, I want to follow it. Where's the first stop?"

"Summerville."

"How long will it take us to get there?"

"About an hour."

Perry Mason said, "That's our first stop. We may not go any farther. Again we may."

The pilot opened the door of the small cabin.

"Get in and sit down," he said. "You've been up before?"

Mason nodded.

"Don't get worried over air bumps," the pilot told him. "They don't amount to anything. The novice gets worried over them."

He made a circle about the plane, as Mason adjusted himself in the seat, then climbed in at the controls, pulled shut the door of the cabin, locked it into position, waved a hand to the mechanics. They pulled away the blocks of wood. The pilot opened the throttle, and the plane roared into motion.

During the ensuing hour, Perry Mason sat almost without motion, his eyes staring at the scenery with the same abstract speculative interest with which he sometimes regarded the smoke which curled upward from his cigarette.

Once or twice the aviator stole a puzzled glance at his preoccupied passenger, but it was not until the plane was over Summerville that he spoke.

"That's Summerville below," he said.

Perry Mason regarded the airport without interest, and only nodded his head slightly.

The pilot nosed the plane forward. It lost altitude rapidly. When the wheels were jolting on the ground, Perry Mason shouted to the pilot:

"Don't stop too close to the hangar."

The pilot cut the throttle down, and the plane droned into a stop. Two men came walking down the hard surface of the packed ground which served as a runway.

Perry Mason got out of the plane, strode to meet the men, looked them over with a swift glance, and said abruptly, "Was either of you men on duty when the mail plane got in—the one that arrives around one o'clock in the morning?"

"I was," said the taller of the two.

Mason motioned him to one side, and lowered his voice.

"I'm looking for a young woman," Perry Mason said, "who was a passenger on that plane. She's in the early twenties. Has very blue eyes, a slender, well-formed figure, and—"

"There wasn't any girl on the plane at all," the man said positively. "There were just two men. One of them got off, and one of them went straight through."

Perry Mason stared at the man with a frown creasing his forehead. His eyes contained a hard glitter which caused the mechanic to shift his own eyes momentarily.

"Describe those men, can you?" he asked.

"One of them was a fat fellow with a bald head. He was about fifty, I guess, and he was pretty well crocked. He had fishy eyes, and I don't remember much about him. He went on through. The fellow that got off was a young chap, wearing a blue serge suit. He had dark hair and black eyes. He asked if there was another plane that was due to arrive before morning. I told him there wasn't. He seemed a little undecided, and then he asked me how he could get to the Riverview Hotel."

Perry Mason's eyes shifted past the mechanic, focused themselves upon distance. He stood for a few seconds absorbed in thought. Then he pulled a five dollar bill from his pocket.

"I wonder," he said, "if you can get me a taxicab."

"There's one right this way," the man said.

Mason turned to the aviator.

"Check your plane over," he said; "get ready to go on from here."

"In which direction?" asked the aviator.

"I don't know," Mason told him. "Wait until I get back and I'll tell you."

He followed the mechanic to the taxicab.

"Riverview Hotel," Mason told the driver.

During the ride the lawyer sat back against the cushions, his eyes patient, steady and unseeing, paying no attention whatever to the buildings which flowed past on either side of the cab windows. When the cab drew up in front of the Riverview Hotel, Perry Mason paid the driver, entered the lobby and approached the clerk.

"I'm in rather a peculiar position," he told the clerk. "I was to meet a man here for a business conference. The man came in from the city on the plane that gets in at one twenty in the morning. I never was very much of a hand at remembering names, and I forgot to bring the correspondence concerning the deal. The sales manager will can me if he finds out about it. I wonder if you could help me out."

The clerk turned to the register.

"I think so," he said. "We rented a room about one thirty to a Mr. Charles B. Duncan."

"What's the room?" asked Perry Mason.

"The room," the clerk told him smilingly, "is the bridal suite—601."

Perry Mason stared steadily and unsmilingly at the clerk for a matter of a second or two, his eyes calm and patient, boring straight into those of the man behind the counter.

"The hell it is," said Perry Mason, and turned toward the elevator.

He got off at the sixth floor, asked the direction of 601, walked down the corridor, started to pound imperatively upon the panels of the door, then suddenly arrested his hand in mid-motion. He unclenched the fist, and tapped gently upon the door with the tips of his fingers, making the knock sound like the timid knock which would have been given by a woman.

There was the sound of quick steps thudding the floor back of the door. A bolt clicked, the door flung open, and Perry Mason gazed into Dr. Doray's eager eyes.

The face ran through a gamut of emotions—disappointment, fear, anger.

Perry Mason pushed his way into the room, kicked the door shut.

Doray took two or three backward steps, his eyes fastened upon Perry Mason's face.

"Bridal suite, eh?" said Perry Mason.

Dr. Doray sat down abruptly on the edge of the bed, as though his knees had refused to carry his weight.

"Well?" said Perry Mason.

The man on the bed said nothing.

Perry Mason's tone was edged with impatience.

"Come on," he said, "start talking."

"About what?" asked Dr. Doray.

"I want the whole story," Perry Mason said.

Dr. Doray took a deep breath, stared up at the lawyer.

"I haven't any story to tell," he said.

"What you doing here?" Mason asked.

"Just running away. I thought things were getting pretty hot for me. You gave me that message, and so I came here."

"What message?"

"The message that your secretary gave me, telling me to get out and keep under cover."

"And so," said Perry Mason sarcastically, "you took the midnight plane out of the city, came here and registered in the bridal suite."

Doray said stubbornly, "That's right. I registered in the bridal suite."

"Why didn't Marjorie Clune join you?" Perry Mason asked.

Dr. Doray jumped up from the edge of the bed.

"You can't talk that way," he said. "That's an insult to Marjorie. She's not that kind of a girl. She wouldn't think of any such thing."

"Oh," said Perry Mason, "you weren't going to be married then. I thought perhaps you were going to be married and spend your honeymoon here."

Dr. Doray blushed.

"I'll tell you I don't know anything about Marjorie Clune. I came down here because I thought things were getting too hot for me. She wasn't going to join me at all."

"I tapped on the door," said Perry Mason slowly, "with the tips of my fingers, making the same kind of a noise a woman might make if she was very certain of who was on the other side of the door. You rushed to the door with an expression of eagerness on your face, saw me, and then acted as though some one had slapped you in the face with a wet towel."

"It was a shock to me," Doray said. "I didn't know any one knew I was here."

Perry Mason hooked his thumbs in the armholes of his vest, thrust his head slightly forward and started pacing the floor.

"I'm telling you," began Dr. Doray, "that you're all wet. You have the wrong idea about—"

"Shut up," said Perry Mason, calmly and without emotion. "I'm thinking. I don't want to be interrupted."

He paced the floor in silence for more than three minutes, then suddenly whirled to face Dr. Doray. He kept his thumbs in the armholes of his vest; his head was thrust forward, the jaw protruding.

"I was a fool to have come here."

"You were?" asked Dr. Doray, startled.

Perry Mason nodded.

"I'm in this thing deep enough already. I came here in the first place because I thought I'd find Marjorie Clune. I wanted to give her a break. God knows she's going to need it. Why didn't she join you on the midnight plane?"

"I tell you I don't know anything at all about her. I haven't seen her and haven't talked with her."

Perry Mason shook his head, almost sadly.

"Let's reason this thing out," he said. "None of her friends heard anything about her. You became alarmed. So did Bradbury. Both of you love her. Bradbury has money; he's an older man. You're nearer Marjorie's age. You've been practicing dentistry for a year or two and haven't very much saved up. You had a lot of equipment to pay for, and you've been building up a practice. You borrowed what money you could and came to the city to find Marjorie. You also wanted to bring Patton to justice.

"You drove your car in from Cloverdale. It's a distinctive car. You got in touch with Marjorie Clune. I don't know how. Through her you learned where Patton was living. You didn't know that when you talked with me. Therefore you must have reached Marjorie Clune after that. You didn't have any way of getting in touch with Patton except through Marjorie. You didn't have any money to hire detectives with. Marjorie Clune had an appointment with Frank Patton. Your car was tagged in front of a fire plug. It's better than an even money bet you drove Marjorie Clune to keep the appointment with Patton.

"Patton was found murdered. The weapon used was a knife. The police have traced that knife. They've found out the hardware store where it was purchased. The man in the hardware store identified your photograph as that of the one who bought the knife."

Doray's face was suddenly white.

"I'm not making any statements," he said.

"You don't have to," Mason told him in a calm, deliberate tone of voice. "I'm the one who's making the statements. I found Marjorie Clune. I got her to go to a hotel and register. She was to wait for me to call her. She wasn't to leave her room. She looked like the type of woman who would keep her promise.

"Something happened so that she didn't keep that promise. She walked out on me. In tracing her movements, I find that she intended to take the midnight plane. I trail the midnight plane and find you were on it. Therefore it's a fair inference that it was through you she violated the promise she had given to me. Now, what argument did you use?"

"I didn't use any," Doray said. "I tell you I don't know anything at all about Marjorie Clune."

"Then she wasn't to join you here?"

"No."

"You didn't talk with her on the telephone?"

"No."

Mason stared down at Dr. Doray with glittering, savage eyes.

"What a fool you are," he said, "a small-town dentist who's practiced dentistry for three or four years, and you think that fits you to give me a run-around in a murder case, which is *my* specialty. Young as you are, and dumb as you are, I wouldn't think of arguing with you about how you were going to fill one of my teeth. And yet you have the audacity to sit there and jeopardize the safety of the woman you love by trying to lie to me."

"I'm not lying to you, I tell you," Doray said.

There were beads of perspiration glistening on his forehead and on his nose.

Perry Mason took a deep breath.

"I sized Marjorie Clune up as a sweet kid, a straight shooting kid, a kid who had had the cards stacked against her. I decided to give her all the breaks I could. I didn't sit in my office and wait for the cops to arrest her, and then go into court to help her. I went out on the firing line and risked my own safety in order to give her a break. I wanted to put her in a position where she could cope with the police. I wanted to be where I could go over her story and find out what was wrong with it—what she had to forget, what she should emphasize. I wanted to coach her a little bit on what the police were going to do when they picked her up. I had her where I could do that. You came along and talked her out of it because you wanted her to come down here to Summerville on a week-end petting party."

Dr. Doray started to get up from the bed.

Perry Mason reached out with a rough hand and pushed him back.

"Sit down," he said, "and shut up. I'm not done talking to you yet. She was to have joined you on the midnight plane. She didn't. You can figure what that means. That means that the police picked her up somewhere and have held her without booking her. They've probably 'buried' her in some outlying town. That means that we won't have any trace of her until after they've given her all the third degree they can think of. They'll try every trick that's known to the police.

"When she talks, she's going to tell plenty, including the fact that you're here in Summerville, registered at the hotel under the name of Charles B. Duncan. That means you can expect the police here at any time. Now laugh that off."

Dr. Doray pulled a handkerchief from his pocket, mopped the perspiration from his forehead.

"My God!" he said.

Perry Mason said nothing.

Dr. Doray put his elbows on his knees. His hands hung limply between the knees, his head dragged forward as he stared at the carpet.

"I can tell you one thing," he said, "on my word of honor, and that was that I didn't talk her into coming down here. It was . . ."

"It was what?" asked Perry Mason quickly.

Dr. Doray caught himself.

"It was a complete mistake on your part," he said. "Marjorie Clune wasn't to join me here. She doesn't know where I am. She hasn't any idea where she can find me. I haven't communicated with her since I left Cloverdale."

"Just to show you," said Perry Mason, "what a poor liar you are . . ."

There was the sound of quick steps in the corridor, a tapping on the door.

Dr. Doray stared at Perry Mason with eyes that were wide with consternation.

Perry Mason jerked open the door before Doray could so much as move.

Marjorie Clune stood on the threshold, her blue eyes deep with emotion.

An expression of incredulous dismay came over her face as she stared at Perry Mason.

"You!" she said.

Perry Mason nodded, stood slightly to one side. She saw Dr. Doray.

"Bob," she cried, "tell me what's happened!"

Dr. Doray covered the distance between them in four swift strides, took her in his arms, held her to him.

Perry Mason walked across the room to the window, stood with his hands thrust in his coat pockets, staring moodily down at the street below.

"Why didn't you get the plane, dearest?" Doray whispered. "We thought you'd been arrested."

"There was a taxicab accident. I missed the plane. I came by the first train."

Perry Mason, still standing with his back to them, his face toward the window, called over his shoulder, "Why didn't you follow my instructions, Marjorie, and stay in your room?"

"I couldn't," she said.

"Why?"

"I can't explain very well."

"I think," he told her, with his back still turned to her, "that it's very important that you tell me."

There was a period of silence. Dr. Doray started to whisper in her ear.

Perry Mason caught the sound of the hissing sibilants, and spun around on his heel.

"Cut it out," he said to Dr. Doray. Then, as his eyes held the blue eyes of Marjorie Clune, he said, "Come clean, Marjorie, it's important."

She shook her head, her face white to the lips.

Perry Mason watched her shrewdly.

"All right," he said, "suppose I tell *you*. You telephoned to Dr. Doray. He talked you into coming down here with him. You were either going to be married and face the music together, or else you were going to try and hide here. Which was it?"

"No," she said in a firm, steady voice, "that isn't right, Mr. Mason. Neither of them is. I was the one who rang Dr. Doray. I suggested this trip. I rang his hotel. He had checked out. I left a message for him to call me at the Bostwick Hotel. He had checked out of his hotel, but he called in later and got the message. He called me. I asked him if he would come down here with me for a week. We were to get the bridal suite and be together. At the end of that time, I was going to surrender to the police."

"Here?" asked Perry Mason.

"No, of course not. We weren't going to let any one know where we had been. We were going to return to the city."

"And both were going to surrender to the police?" Perry Mason asked.

She nodded.

"What was the reason," asked Perry Mason, "that you broke your promise to me and came down here on this trip?"

She stared at him with frank, steady eyes.

"Because," she said, "I wanted a week with Bob."

Perry Mason regarded her unflinching eyes with speculative appraisal.

"You're not the type of girl who would do that," he said. "You have seen Bob Doray off and on for months, and yet you haven't shown any desire to week-end with him—at least I don't think you have. Now, all of a sudden, you want to give him a week, and then you don't care what happens. You—"

She came to Perry Mason, put her hands on his shoulders; her lips were white and quivering.

"Please," she said, "don't tell him. You're going to figure it out in a minute. Please stop. You'll know if you'll only take time to think."

Perry Mason frowned at her, and then his eyes narrowed.

"By God," he said, "I believe I do know."

"Please don't tell him," Marjorie Clune pleaded.

Perry Mason turned away from her, walked to the window, and stood with his hands jammed into his pockets. He heard Dr. Doray rush to Marjorie Clune, clasp her in his arms.

"What is it, sweetheart? Please tell me."

"Don't, Bob, you're going to make me cry. Remember the bargain. I was to give you one week. You weren't to ask any questions. You promised that—"

Abruptly, Perry Mason's voice cut through the low tones of their conversation. His voice was like that of a radio announcer reporting some news event.

"There's an automobile," he said, "that's just parked across the street. A big man, wearing a black, broad-brimmed hat, is just getting out of the car. He's a typical country sheriff. There's another man getting out of the other side. He's a man in a uniform with a police cap with gold braid on it. He looks like a chief of police. The men are talking together. They're looking across here at the hotel."

The room behind Mason became suddenly silent. Mason continued, in the same impersonal tone of voice:

"They're starting to walk across the street toward the hotel. I don't think there's any question but what they have been tipped off to come here and look for at least one of you. Perhaps they trailed Marjorie. Perhaps they found out about Dr. Doray coming down on the midnight plane."

Perry Mason whirled to face the pair.

Dr. Doray was standing very erect, his face white. Marjorie Clune was at his side; her lips were unquivering, her eyes were fastened upon Perry Mason.

"All right," she said, "if we have to, we can take it right on the chin. You're going to represent Dr. Doray as well as myself, Mr. Mason. That's understood, is it not?"

"That," said Perry Mason, "is understood. And I'm going to do it in my own way."

"What's that?" she asked.

Perry Mason's eyes shifted to Dr. Doray.

"You've got to play the part of a man," he said. "I'm going to throw you to the wolves. You're going to take it and like it. You're going to promise me one thing. It's going to be the most difficult thing you ever did in your life, but you're going to do it."

"Will it help Marjorie?" Doray asked quietly.

"Yes," said Perry Mason.

"What is it?"

"You're going to keep absolutely quiet."

"What else?" asked Dr. Doray.

Perry Mason laughed grimly.

"That's going to be plenty," he said. "They're going to work every trick on you that's known to police psychology. They're going to tell you that Marjorie Clune has confessed to the murder; that she's done it because she loves you, and that she wants to save you. They'll make you believe it. They may even show you a signed statement that they claim she's given to them. They'll ask you if you're going to be a man, or if you're going to hide behind her skirts and let her take the death penalty for a crime that you committed. They'll try everything they can think of to make you talk. Perhaps it will be a bluff. Perhaps it won't. I want you to promise me that you won't try to do any thinking about whether it's a bluff or whether it isn't. I want you to promise me that you'll leave the question of Marjorie's defense absolutely and entirely up to me; that no matter what they tell you, you'll keep quiet. That you'll tell them I am your attorney and that you want to communicate with me. Will you do that?"

"Yes."

Perry Mason turned to Marjorie Clune.

"Where's your suitcase?"

"I left it at the depot. I wanted to make sure Bob was here."

"Good girl," he said. "Come with me."

Doray circled her with his arms, drew her hungrily to him. His lips sought hers.

Perry Mason jerked the door open.

"You haven't got any time for that stuff," he said. "Come on, Marjorie."

She continued to cling to Dr. Doray for a moment; then she turned and ran to Perry Mason.

"Close and lock the door, Doray," Mason said. "Don't be in a hurry about opening it."

He grabbed Marjorie Clune's arm and ran down the corridor. Near a corner of the corridor, he knocked on a door. There was the sound of motion behind the door.

"Quick," said Perry Mason, and whisked Marjorie around the corner of the corridor. He knocked on another door. There was no answer. He pulled a bunch of skeleton keys from his pocket, inserted one, unlocked the door and held it open.

"Go on in," he told Marjorie Clune.

Marjorie Clune walked across the threshold, and had just entered the room when the door of the elevator clanged open and two men, one wearing the uniform of a police officer with a gold-braided cap, the other wearing a black, broad-brimmed Stetson, stepped into the corridor, and pounded toward Perry Mason.

Perry Mason moved with calm, even-spaced tranquillity. He entered the room, standing so that his broad shoulders blocked the officers from seeing Marjorie Clune. Slowly, he groped for the door with the back of his heel, and kicked the door shut.

"There's a sign in the closet, Marjorie," he said, "a sign printed on pasteboard, 'PLEASE DO NOT DISTURB.' Get that and bring it to me."

She opened the closet door, found the sign and handed it to him wordlessly.

Perry Mason was standing by the door, his head cocked slightly on one side, after the manner of one who is listening.

The sounds of rumbling conversation carried to them through the open transom. Then the sounds became more indistinct, and faded out entirely.

Perry Mason turned the knob, opened the door, slipped the string of the pasteboard placard over the knob, closed the door and twisted the bolt which locked it from the inside. He gave the hotel room a sweeping glance of inspection.

"It's unrented. Probably we'll be undisturbed here for some little time," he said.

"What are you going to do?" asked Marjorie Clune.

"Try to get you out of here and back to the city, where you should have been in the first place. Keep quiet. Don't say anything. Sit down in that chair."

She dropped obediently into the chair.

Perry Mason stood leaning against the door, listening.

Minutes passed.

At length there sounded pounding steps in the corridor. Perry Mason pulled a chair close to the door, climbed on the chair, and stood with his ear on a level with the open transom.

Voices were raised in the rising inflection which marks questions. After each question, there was a pause. There was no sound of an answer.

Perry Mason sighed with relief, stepped down from the chair, and smiled over at Marjorie Clune.

"There's just a chance," he said, "that he's man enough to stand pat."

"Of course he is," she said.

14

Perry Mason stared at Marjorie Clune as she sat in the uncomfortable overstuffed chair and met his gaze with unflinching eyes.

"You decided to marry Bradbury," he said slowly, "because you thought that Bob Doray was guilty of the murder."

She said nothing.

"And Bradbury," said Perry Mason, "was going to put up the money for Bob Doray's defense. Is that right?"

"Of course," she said. "I was afraid that you'd say something that would let him know. He'd have taken a dozen death sentences, rather than let me make such a sacrifice."

"Why did you do it?"

"Because it was the only way to raise money for his defense."

"And you think he needs a defense that bad?"

"Of course he does," she said. "You're a lawyer, you know that."

"Then," said Perry Mason slowly, "Bradbury has been in communication with you since you were in communication with me and promised me that you would wait at the Bostwick Hotel."

She stared steadily at him and said nothing.

"Did you call Bradbury," he asked, "or did he call you?"

"That," she said, "is something I cannot tell you."

"Why?"

"Simply because I can't."

"In other words, you've promised not to?"

"I am not even going to answer that question."

Perry Mason hooked his thumbs in the armholes of his vest, started pacing the floor.

"The officers," he said, "have got Bob Doray, they're working on him right now. If I'm going to represent him, it's important as hell that I know what the facts are. Are you going to tell them to me?"

"Yes."

"All right," he said, "go ahead."

She spoke in a low, steady voice. Once or twice there was a throaty catch in her voice, but her eyes were dry, and she continued to speak steadily through to the end.

"I was naturally elated when I won the contest in Cloverdale. I thought that I was going to be a big movie star. I guess perhaps it went to my head; I'm young. I wouldn't be human if I hadn't become conceited.

"I went to the city in a blaze of glory. I found out that I had been trapped; naturally I was too proud to write home and explain. I determined that I had the stuff in me to make good, and that I'd stay on here in the city and make good. That if Patton had defrauded me into thinking I was going to be a picture star, I would let him go to the devil and become a picture star on my own hook."

Perry Mason nodded.

"I didn't know," she said, "what I was up against. You probably know, you live in the city. I tried everything, then I met Thelma Bell; I met her through Frank Patton. I kept in touch with Frank Patton, because I was trying to get some sort of a settlement out of him. My cash was running low, and I wanted to get enough money to stay on for a while."

"Go on," Perry Mason said. "I know all that stuff, or can surmise it. Tell me what happened."

"I had an appointment," she said, "with Frank Patton the night he was killed. The appointment was for eight o'clock. I saw Bob Doray driving his car on the street that afternoon; it was just a glimpse that I had of him, but I knew he was in town. I started in calling up the hotels, finding out if they had a Dr. Doray registered there. It was an interminable job. I used a girl friend's telephone that was on a flat rate. I won't tell you who she was; I don't want to bring her into this. I spent the entire afternoon telephoning. Finally I found him; he was at the Midwick Hotel. I left word for him to call me as soon as he came in. He came in and called me, I told him where I was and he drove out and picked me up.

"I was frightfully glad to see him; I wept and made something of a scene, I guess. I was so happy that the tears streamed down my face.

"He found out that I had an appointment with Frank Patton. He didn't want me to keep it. He swore that he was going to kill Patton. You understand, he really didn't mean it, it was just a manner of expression."

"Go ahead," Perry Mason said as she paused, looking at him with anxious eyes.

"He had that knife in his car," she said. "God knows what had persuaded him to do any such thing, he must have been almost crazy. I wanted to keep my appointment with Patton, but I didn't want Bob to drive me there. Bob insisted that he was going to drive me there. Finally we compromised. I agreed to let Bob take me to Patton's place, and I would go up and tell Patton that I was finished with him once and for all, that I was going to marry Bob Doray. Bob was to go back to his hotel. I didn't give Bob Frank Patton's exact address, I simply told him where to drive me. When we got there, I told Bob to go on and I'd meet him at the hotel.

"Bob didn't want to leave me, he begged me to let him go up to Patton's apartment with me. I became absolutely terrified. Bob parked the car, I guess he parked it in front of a fire plug; I guess he was so excited that he didn't notice what he was doing, and I know I didn't. I told Bob I was thirsty and got him to take me to an ice-cream parlor. I went into the ladies' rest-room and waited and waited and waited. I sent the maid out to see if Bob was still there. He was, so then I had her go out and tell Bob that I had gone out through the back way; there really wasn't any back way, but I did that in order to get rid of him."

"And you continued to wait in the rest-room?" Perry Mason asked.

"Yes, I continued to wait in the rest-room."

"For how long?" asked Perry Mason.

"I don't know, it may have been five minutes, perhaps longer."

"So then what?"

"So then when I thought the coast was clear, I went out to the street. I couldn't see any sign of Bob; I went just as fast as I could to Frank Patton's apartment."

"Now just a minute," Perry Mason said. "Before that you'd telephoned and left a message that you were going to be late for your appointment?"

"Yes. You see, I'd found Bob and I was so happy, and I wanted to be with him just as long as I could. I knew that I was going to be just a little bit late."

"So Thelma Bell had an appointment with Frank Patton for that night?"

"Of course, her appointment was for the same time as mine."

"All right," Perry Mason said, "now we're getting somewhere. Go on and tell what happened."

"I went through the lobby of the apartment house," she said. "I took the elevator to the third floor, and walked down to Patton's apartment; I knocked on the door, there was no answer. I mechanically tried the doorknob; the doorknob turned and the door opened. I found myself in the apartment. I noticed the lights were on and that Patton's hat, gloves and stick were on the table. I called out, 'Oh, Mr. Patton,' or something like that, and walked through to the bedroom. Then I found him."

"Just a minute," said Perry Mason. "Was the bathroom door open or closed?"

"It was open."

"And he was dead when you entered the bedroom?"

"Of course, I tell you he was lying there with the blood all over the floor. It was awful."

"What happened after that?" Perry Mason inquired.

"Nothing," she said. "I turned around and walked right out. I pulled the door shut behind me; I didn't lock it, I didn't have any key; it was unlocked when I went in and it was unlocked when I left it. I went down the corridor, took the elevator down to the lobby; there was no one in the lobby; I walked out of the apartment house and had just started to walk down the street when I saw you. You looked at me in a peculiar way, with a searching look as though you were trying to find out something that I knew, and it frightened me. It was the first time I realized that I might be involved in some way."

"In what way?" he asked.

"Oh," she said, "questions and things like that. You know, the kind of things that you read about in newspapers, where I'd be cross-examined by lawyers and have my photograph in the paper, and perhaps have my word questioned."

"You wore white shoes," he said. "Where are they?"

"Thelma Bell took them."

"Why did she take them?"

"Because they had blood on them, of course."

"Did you know it at the time?"

"Not at the time. I found it out after I got to the apartment. Thelma saw the blood stains on the shoes."

"How did that happen?"

"I walked in some of the blood and some of it spattered on my shoes."

"There was none on the coat you wore?" he asked.

"No," she said, "none. There wasn't any on my stockings, just on my shoes."

"Are you certain," asked Perry Mason, "that there was none on your stockings?"

"Of course, I'm certain."

"Nor on your dress?"

"Of course not. How could any blood get on my dress if there wasn't any on my coat?"

Perry Mason nodded slowly.

"That sounds reasonable," he said. "Now tell me some more about how you happened to leave the Bostwick Hotel, instead of staying there the way I told you to."

"I've already explained that," she said. "I left because I wanted to be with Bob."

"When you went to see Patton, you intended to tell him that you were finished with him, that you were going to marry Bob Doray?"

"Yes," she said after a moment's hesitation.

"When I saw you at Thelma Bell's apartment, you felt the same way about it?"

"I was terribly afraid at that time," she said. "As soon as Thelma found the blood on my shoes, she wanted to know what had happened. I told her just what had happened as well as I knew. She was afraid that I was going to get mixed into it."

"She told you that?"

"Yes."

"She had an appointment with Frank Patton that night?"

"She had an appointment, but she didn't keep it. She broke her appointments with Patton lots of times; this time her boy friend wouldn't let her keep the appointment; he was out with her. George Sanborne is the name. She told you all about it. You remember, you called Sanborne and found out that it was true."

"We'll let that go for the moment," Perry Mason said. "What I'm getting at is that you were still intending to marry Doray when I talked with you there at Thelma's apartment?"

"I guess so. I wasn't thinking much about marriage then, I was frightened, particularly after you came there."

"But as far as matrimony was concerned, you still intended to marry Bob Doray?"

"If I had thought about it, yes."

"Now, sometime before midnight," Perry Mason said, "you had determined you were going to marry Bradbury. Why?"

"Because," she said, "I knew that was the only way I could get money to save Bob Doray."

"You think Bob Doray did it?"

"I'm not thinking anything about it. All I know is that he must have the best legal service he can get."

"When you saw the body," said Perry Mason, "you saw the knife that was lying there by it?"

"Yes."

"You recognized that knife?"

"What do you mean?"

"You knew that Bob Doray had purchased a knife?"

"Yes, I had seen it in his automobile."

"You knew what he intended to do with it?"

"Yes. He had told me."

"That is one of the reasons you were afraid to let him know where Frank Patton lived?"

"Yes."

"Then when you saw the knife on the floor, you must have jumped to the conclusion at once that Bob Doray had killed him."

"What sort of a conclusion would you have reached under the circumstances?" she asked.

"Now let's see," Perry Mason said, "you went to the candy store. You went into the rest-room; you stayed there and persuaded Dr. Doray that you had gone out the back door?"

"Yes."

"He left perhaps five minutes before you did."

"Yes."

"How long had Patton been killed before you entered the door? Have you any idea?"

"It couldn't have been long," she said, "just a minute or two.... Oh, it was ghastly!"

"Was he still moving?"

"No."

"Was blood flowing from his wound?"

"Lots of it," she said and shuddered.

"Therefore," Perry Mason said, "you immediately concluded that Doray had done the killing. You thought that when you didn't show up, but sent word that you had already gone to keep your appointment with Patton, Doray became enraged."

"Yes."

Perry Mason regarded her thoughtfully.

"Do you know what I'm doing with you?" he asked.

"What do you mean?"

"I'm risking my entire professional career," he said, "simply on the strength of the impression that you make, plus certain things that I have observed in connection with the case. You're wanted for murder. I'm helping you escape. If I'm caught, that's going to make me technically an accessory after the fact. In other words, I'm going to be guilty of murder as an accessory."

She said nothing.

"I didn't have that same confidence in Dr. Doray that I have in you," he told her; "that's the reason I left

Dr. Doray in the room to take the rap. I knew that if the police found an empty room, they'd make some effort to search the hotel. If they found Doray and he didn't talk, they might not have known whether you were in the hotel or not. That's the chance I took."

"But," she said, "won't they be watching the hotel when we leave?"

"Exactly," he told her. "That's why I've got to figure out some way of getting us out of it; we're both of us mixed in it now."

He strode to the window, stood once more staring moodily down at the street.

"And you won't tell me," he said, "what changed your mind between the time I saw you and midnight, why it was that you so suddenly decided you were going to marry Bradbury?"

"I've told you," she said, "I knew that was the only way that I could get the money to defend Bob. And I knew that if Bob didn't have first-class legal defense, he would be convicted of the murder. I got to thinking things over; I knew that Bradbury had retained you to represent me. I thought that Jim would also retain you to clear Bob, if he knew that I would marry him."

Perry Mason's eyes glinted.

"Now," he said, "you've said exactly what I was waiting to hear you say."

"What do you mean?"

"He would put up the money for Doray's defense, if he *knew* that you would marry him."

She bit her lip and said nothing.

Perry Mason stared at her with moody speculation for a few moments.

"I'm going to play ball with you," he said, "and when I play ball, I play ball all the way."

She watched him with wide anxious eyes.

"Take your clothes off," he told her, "and get into bed."

Her face didn't change expression by so much as the flicker of an eyelash.

"How much must I take off?" she asked.

"I want your skirt hung on a chair," he said. "I want your shoes under the bed. You'd better have your stockings over the foot of the bed. I want you to have your waist off, so all that will show above the covers are shoulder straps."

"Then what?" she asked.

"Then," he said, "I'm going to have a man come in the room; he's going to look at you. You're going to act the part of the kind of girl he'll think you are."

She searched for the fasteners at the side of her skirt.

"You're playing ball with me," she said, "I'll show you that I've got just as much confidence in you as you have in me."

"Good girl," he told her. "Have you got any chewing-gum?"

"No."

"Can you move your jaws as though you were chewing gum?"

"I guess so. How's this?"

He watched her critically.

"Move the jaw a little bit to one side at the bottom of the chew," he said. "Give it something of a circular motion."

"It's going to look frightfully common," she said.

"That's just the way I want it to look."

"How's this?"

"That," he told her, "is better. Go ahead and get your clothes off."

He walked once more to the window and stared down at the street until he heard the creak of the bed springs.

"All right?" he asked.

"Yes," she said.

He turned and regarded her critically. Her skirt was over the back of a chair, her stockings were hanging on the foot of the bed, her shoes were under the bed.

"Let's see the gum-chewing business," he told her.

She moved her jaws regularly.

"Now if this man looks at you," Perry Mason said, "don't lower your eyes. Don't act as though you were ashamed. Look at him with a 'come-hither' look. Can you do that?"

"Who is it going to be?" she asked.

"I don't know just yet," he told her, "it'll probably be the porter in the hotel. He won't do anything except look at you, but I want you to look the part."

"I'll do my best," she said.

Perry Mason came over and sat down on the edge of the bed. She met his speculative appraisal with steady blue eyes.

"There was quite a bit of blood on your white shoes?" he asked.

"Yes."

"Did Thelma Bell have any white shoes?"

"I don't know."

"And Thelma took your white shoes to clean them?"

"Yes."

"What was Thelma doing when you got to the apartment?"

"She had just finished taking a bath. She looked at my shoes and told me to get out of them right away, and get out of my clothes, to take a bath and make sure I didn't have any blood on my feet or ankles."

"Did she look at your stockings?"

"No, she told me to make it snappy."

"You took a street car to her apartment?"

"Yes."

"And about the time you were ready to take a bath I called at the apartment?"

"That's right."

"So you don't know what Thelma did with the shoes?"

"No."

Perry Mason slid around on the bed, so that he sat with his left elbow resting on his left knee, his right foot on the floor, his left leg on the bed.

"Margy," he said, "are you telling me the truth?"

"Yes."

"Suppose I should tell you," he went on, "that I made a search of Thelma Bell's apartment; that I found a hat box in the closet; that the hat box was packed with clothes that had been washed and hadn't had a chance to dry; that some of the clothes showed evidence of having been washed to remove blood stains; that there was a pair of white shoes, a pair of stockings and a skirt."

The blue eyes stared at him with fixed intensity. Suddenly Marjorie Clune sat bolt upright in bed.

"You mean that the skirt and the stockings had blood stains on them?"

"Yes."

"And they'd been washed?"

"Very hastily washed," Mason said. "And the blood stains were the spattering type of blood stains, such as would have been made from a stab wound."

"Good heavens!" she said.

"Furthermore," Perry Mason told her, "some one was in the bathroom having hysterics about lucky legs. Now one of you girls is lying. Either you were in the bathroom, or it was Thelma."

"It might have been someone else," she said.

"But you don't know any one else it could have been?"

"No."

"I don't think it was any one else," Mason said slowly.

Marjorie Clune blinked her eyes slowly, thoughtfully.

"Now," said Perry Mason, "we're coming to another phase of the situation. Do you know a girl named Eva Lamont?"

"Why, yes, of course."

"Has Eva Lamont got contest legs?" he asked.

"What do you mean?"

"Legs that would win a prize?"

"They didn't," Marjorie Clune said.

"But she had them entered?"

"Yes."

"In other words, she was one of the contestants?"

"Yes."

"Where?"

"In Cloverdale."

"Is she," asked Perry Mason, "a young woman with dark hair and snappy black eyes, a woman with a figure something like yours?"

Marjorie Clune nodded.

"Why?" she asked.

"Because," Perry Mason said, "I have every reason to believe that she's in town, registered under the name of Vera Cutter, and that she has taken a most unusual interest in the development of this murder case."

Marjorie Clune's eyes were wide with surprise.

"Now then," Perry Mason said, "tell me where she gets her money."

"She gets it lots of ways," Marjorie Clune said bitterly. "She worked as a waitress for a while. She was working that when Frank Patton came to town with his contest. After that, she did lots of things. She got chances to show her legs and there were lots of people who admired them. She said that whether she won the contest or not, she was going to the city and go into pictures."

"And after you won the contest," Perry Mason said, "then what?"

"Then," she said, "she swore that she was going to come to the city and make a success of her own, which would make mine look sick. She said that I won the contest because I had curried favor with Frank Patton, and that I had an inside track."

"Did you?" asked Perry Mason.

"No."

"You're not telling me very much about Eva Lamont," he said, "and it's important that I know more about her."

"I don't like her."

"That doesn't make any difference, this is a murder case. What do you know about her?"

"I don't know very much about her, but I've heard lots."

"Such as?" asked Perry Mason.

"Oh, lots of things."

"Do you know," Mason asked, "if she looked up Frank Patton after she came here to the city?"

"She would have," Marjorie Clune said slowly, "she's the type that would."

"Has she any reason to be bitter against you, Marjorie?"

Marjorie Clune closed her eyes, slid back into the bed and pulled the covers up around her shoulders.

"She was madly infatuated with Bob Doray," she said.

"And Doray is mad about you?"

"Yes."

Perry Mason took out his package of cigarettes from his pocket, extracted one, had it raised halfway to his lips before he caught himself and extended the package to Marjorie Clune.

"Do you want me to smoke?" she asked.

"Just suit yourself."

"No, I mean when this man comes in. Would it look better if I was smoking?"

"No, it would look better if you were chewing gum, you'd hardly be doing both."

"Then I'll smoke now," she told him.

She took a cigarette. Perry Mason brought an ashtray from the dresser, set it on the bed between them, held a match to Marjorie Clune's cigarette.

"Give me that other pillow, Marjorie," he said.

She handed him the pillow, he propped it against the foot of the bed and settled his back against it.

"I'm going to think," he told her, "and I don't want to be disturbed."

He smoked the cigarette for a few puffs, then held it in front of him and watched the smoke as it curled upward, with eyes that seemed to be filmed with a dreamy abstraction. The cigarette had almost burnt down to his fingers before he nodded slowly, and let his eyes snap into sharp focus on Marjorie Clune.

He ground out the cigarette in the ashtray, jumped to his feet and pulled down his vest.

"All right, Marjorie," he said, in a voice that was kindly, "I think I know the answer."

"The answer to what?"

"The answer to everything," he told her. "And I don't mind telling you, Marjorie, that in some ways I've been a damn fool."

She stared at him and shivered slightly.

"You look perfectly cold, when you look at me that way," she said, "as though you were capable of anything."

"Perhaps," he told her, "I *am* capable of anything."

He pulled another cigarette from his pocket, walked to the dresser, tore the cigarette in two, picked out a couple of grains of tobacco, pulled out the lower lid of his left eye and dropped the grains into place. Then he pulled out the lower lid of his right eye and dropped a couple of grains of tobacco into that, as well. He rubbed his eyes with his knuckles.

Marjorie Clune sat upright in bed to stare at him with curious fascination.

Tears streamed from Perry Mason's eyes and trickled down his cheeks. He groped his way to the wash stand, splashed cold water in his eyes, dried them on a towel and regarded himself in the mirror.

His eyes were red and bloodshot.

He nodded his satisfaction, moistened his fingers in water from the tap, drew them around the inside neck-band of his shirt until his collar was moist and crumpled, then he pulled his tie slightly to one side and once more surveyed the effect in the mirror.

"Okay, Marjorie," he said, "wait here until I come back, and remember to chew gum."

He walked to the door, opened it, stepped into the corridor without a single backward glance, and pulled the door shut behind him.

15

Perry Mason walked the length of the corridor, looking for the freight elevator. At length he found it and pressed the button, waiting for the cage to come lumbering up to the sixth floor. When it arrived, he pulled open the door, got in the cage and pressed the button marked "BAGGAGE ROOM."

The big elevator moved slowly down the shaft and came at length to a jolting stop. Perry Mason opened the two doors, and stepped out into the baggage room. A uniformed porter, seated at a desk, looked at him with questioning, uncordial eyes.

Perry Mason staggered against the door of the elevator, lurched for two steps, paused, took a deep breath, and grinned fatuously at the man in uniform.

"Came f'r m' trunk," said Perry Mason.

"What trunk?" asked the porter, with hostility in his voice.

Perry Mason grinned and fished around through his pockets, finally bringing out a roll of bills. He pulled out a one dollar bill and lurched across to the porter. He handed over the bill; then, just as the porter was about to take it, jerked it back.

"Thash not 'nuff," Perry Mason said.

He took a five dollar bill from the roll, regarded that speculatively, shook his head in solemn negation, explored the roll of bills, and pulled out a twenty.

The porter's palm was eagerly extended. The porter's fingers clutched at the bill. The look of unsmiling hostility left his face. He pocketed the bill, got to his feet with an amiable grin.

"Have you got the check for the trunk?" he asked.

Perry Mason shook his head.

"Can't find it," he said.

"What kind of a trunk?" asked the porter. "What did it look like?"

"Big trunk," said Perry Mason, "great *big* trunk. Shalesman's trunk. You know, got all my shtuff in it. Gotta have it. Two daysh late now."

The porter moved toward a pile of trunks. Perry Mason became garrulous.

"Two daysh late now," he said, "wife's showing up. 'Magine that. Jush got tip from friend, wife'sh coming down from city to look me up. Maybe she'sh got detectives trying to get goods on me. Got 'nawful nice little girl friend. Can't get her mixed up in it."

The porter indicated a large trunk.

"This it?" he asked.

Perry Mason shook his head.

The porter moved around a stack of trunks.

"This one," he said, "was left here. . . ."

Perry Mason's face broke into smiles.

"Thash one," he said, and patted the trunk affectionately. "Lesh go."

"What's your room number?" asked the porter.

"Six forty-two," said Perry Mason.

"I'll bring it right up," the porter said.

"Gotta come *right now*," Perry Mason insisted. "Maybe detectivesh watchin' hotel."

The porter was sympathetic.

"All right," he said, "let's go right away. That's no way for a woman to check on a man who's on the road a lot of the time. He's got to have a little pleasure sometime."

Perry Mason patted the porter's shoulder.

"You shaid mouthful," he confided. "Little pleashure now'n then ain't gonna hurt nobody."

The porter got a hand truck, put the trunk on it, and wheeled it into the freight elevator. Perry Mason stood beside him as the elevator went up to the sixth floor, walked by the side of the truck down to the room. He opened the door of the room and stood to one side.

The porter pushed the hand truck into the room. Marjorie Clune turned her face toward the porter and made chewing motions with her jaw.

The porter stole a surreptitious glance, then averted his eyes.

"Gotta get half cashe whiskey in thish trunk," said Perry Mason, waving his hand in the general direction of the bureau. "Put'er down anywhere. Goin' out in about fifteen minutes," said Perry Mason, "maybe ten minutes. Wife may have detectives watchin' hotel. You get me taxi-cab, wait by trade entrance, will you?"

He flashed his hand once more toward his trouser pocket.

"You've already given me . . ." said the porter, then let his voice trail into silence as Perry Mason gravely pulled out the roll of bills, took another twenty from it and dropped it into the porter's palm.

"Just give me a ring," he said, "whenever you're ready. I'll have a cab waiting."

He walked to the door, paused with his hand on the knob for one flashing glance at the girl on the bed.

Marjorie Clune was ready for him. She met his eyes with a bold glance of ready invitation.

The porter slipped out into the corridor and closed the door.

"All right," said Perry Mason, "get out of bed and get into your clothes."

Marjorie Clune jumped from the bed and struggled into her dress. Perry Mason pulled the ring of skeleton keys from his pocket, started working on the lock of the trunk.

Marjorie Clune had her dress on, her hair adjusted, and her face powdered before Perry Mason had the trunk open. It was filled with feminine garments, each garment on a hanger, and placarded with a cost tag and catalogue number. Perry Mason pulled the garments from the hangers and tossed them to Marjorie Clune.

"Hang these in the closet," he said, "and then close the closet door."

She took the garments wordlessly, made half a dozen trips to the closet. Perry Mason surveyed the interior of the trunk.

"It isn't going to be pleasant," he told her, "you've got to brace yourself. You'll probably be bruised. The air won't be any too good, but it won't be long."

"You mean I have to get in that?"

"I mean," he said, "you've got to get into that, and like it. You can sit in the bottom if you double your knees up under your chin. I'm going to tell the porter I've got half a case of whiskey in there, to handle the trunk carefully, and to keep it right side up. There's a taxicab waiting by the freight entrance. The trunk will be strapped on the side of the taxicab.

"I'll have the cab take me to another hotel. I'll get a room and have the trunk sent right up. I'll bribe everybody to handle it carefully. But you're going to get shaken some, and bruised some, and it isn't going to be pleasant."

"Then what's going to happen?" she asked.

"As soon as I can get you into another hotel, I'll open the trunk," he told her. "You can get out and we'll take a cab to the airport. I've got a fast cabin plane waiting there. We'll take it."

"Take it where?" she asked.

"Back to the city," he told her.

"What will we do in the city?"

"When we get there," he told her, "we're going to bring things to a head."

She put her hand on his arm.

"Those clothes," she said. "Those garments of Thelma's that had blood stains on them. Do you know where they are?"

"Yes."

"Where are they?"

"They're where we can get them when we want them, and if we want them we can still tie them up with Thelma Bell."

"It would mean," she said, "a lot to Bob if those garments were discovered. You know Bob was my boy friend. They might figure that he had a motive to kill Patton, but Sanborne was Thelma's boy friend, and he had more motive than Bob Doray could ever have had. You see, Patton was . . ." Her voice trailed into silence.

"Was what?" asked Perry Mason.

"Nothing," she said. "It doesn't make any difference. I was just wondering about those garments."

Perry Mason gestured toward the trunk.

"Get in," he told her.

16

As the plane slanted downward toward the landing field, Perry Mason turned to Marjorie Clune, cupped his hands and shouted, "There's a taxi standing over at the north end of the airport. You go directly to the taxi stand. Get in a car and tell the driver to wait for me. I've got some telephoning to do. I want you to keep out of sight as much as possible. Don't be rubbering around. Keep your eyes straight ahead. Understand?"

She nodded.

"I won't be over ten minutes," he said. "Perhaps not that long."

The plane swung in a slight curve, straightened, dropped, and the wheels skimmed lightly along the paved runway. The pilot throttled the motor into speed as the tail-skid dropped to the ground, and taxied up to the hangars.

"Is that all?" he asked when the motor had been stopped.

Perry Mason nodded, took his wallet from his pocket, passed the pilot a bill, nodded to Marjorie Clune.

"You get in the taxi," he said. "I'll join you in a few minutes."

He walked to the telephone booth and called his office. Della Street's voice came over the wire to his ears.

"Are you alone, Della?" asked Perry Mason. "Can you talk, or is there some one in the office who can hear you?"

"Just a moment," she said, "I'll see what's wrong with the connection. You say it's in the law library? Very well, it must be a receiver up."

She added in a low voice, "Hold the line, please."

Perry Mason waited.

After a moment, he heard her voice again.

"I'm in the law library now, chief. There were two detectives in the outer office, and Bradbury is waiting."

"There's no one in the law library?"

"No one."

"All right," he told her, "let's get this thing cleaned up. Have you heard anything from College City?"

"There's a telegram simply saying, 'Am at College City Hotel.' It's signed by the initials T.B."

"Anything else?"

"That's all, except that the detectives are hanging around here. They've been in a couple of times."

"What does Bradbury want?" asked Perry Mason.

"I don't know," she said. "He's worked up about something. He's lost that air of cordial affability, and he's hard—hard as nails."

"I'm pretty hard myself," Mason said. "That is, I can be if the going gets rough."

"Something seems to tell me the going will be rough," she said. "How about things? Are you okay?"

"I'm fine."

"Paul Drake," she said, "is acting very mysteriously. He's called a couple of times. He seems to think that you're in an awful jam somewhere along the line, and he doesn't want to get mixed into it."

"Anything else?" he asked.

"That seems to be about all."

"All right, Della," he said, "perhaps you'd better make a note of this: Telephone Thelma Bell at the College City Hotel. You can't put the call in from the office; you'll have to either get an extension or go out to a telephone booth. Tell her who you are. Tell her that I'm very anxious to know if Marjorie Clune had a telephone call at her apartment after I left her apartment on the night of the murder. Tell her that it's very important that I know."

"Then what?" she asked.

"If she had such a telephone call," he said, "take the Code of Civil Procedure and put it on the desk by your telephone switchboard. If she didn't have such a conversation, put your ink stand by the switchboard. If there's nothing there, I'll know that for some reason you haven't been able to talk with Thelma Bell and get an answer to the question."

Della Street's voice was troubled.

"Chief," she said, "you haven't spirited Thelma Bell away, have you? You haven't been mixed up in that?"

"We'll talk that over later," he told her.

"But, chief, the police are—"

"We'll talk all that over later, Della."

"Okay, chief."

"You can put Bradbury," he said, "in the law library. Put him in there to wait. You can tell him in confidence that I may see him within an hour."

"Okay."

"Now, about the detectives," Mason said, "have they been there steadily?"

"They've been in two or three times. They are trying to find out if you intend to come to the office sometime today. They kept asking if I've heard from you."

"Are they the same detectives that were in the other night?" he asked. "I think their names were Riker and Johnson."

"The same ones."

"You don't think they'll stay?"

"I don't think so. They come in, stick around for a few minutes, ask questions, and then go out. This is the third time they've been in today."

"Do you know if any detectives are watching the building?"

"No, but I think some one followed me when I went out to lunch."

"You don't think you're being followed as you move around the building?"

"No, I don't think so."

"Take twenty dollars out of the cash drawer," he said, "take the elevator to the basement. Tell Frank, the janitor, that I'm working on a hot case and that there are some private detectives trying to shadow me. Be sure and tell him they're private detectives. Tell him I want to get to my office without any one knowing it. Tell him to keep a watch on the door of the furnace room. When I drive up in a taxicab, he can open the door of the furnace room and have one of the elevators drop down to the basement to pick me up. Tell him to fix it with the elevator starter and operator, so the elevator will shoot me right up to the sixth floor."

"All right," she said. "Is there anything else?"

"I think that's all," he said. "I'll be—"

The voice of J. R. Bradbury came booming over the wire with firm insistence,

"Counselor, I insist upon seeing you right away!"

"Who's talking?" asked Perry Mason.

"Bradbury."

"Where are you talking from?"

"From your private office."

"How the hell did you get on the line?"

"I put myself on the line," Bradbury said, "if you want to know, and don't swear at me."

Perry Mason could hear a quick, gasping intake of breath.

"Are you on the line, Della?" he asked in a low voice.

"Yes, chief," she said.

"Talking from the law library?"

"Yes."

"How did you know who was calling, Bradbury?" Mason asked.

"I'm not a fool," Bradbury said. "I've tried to convince you of that on two separate occasions."

"What do you want?" Mason inquired.

"I want Dr. Doray to plead guilty and take a life sentence."

"Listen," Perry Mason told him, "I can't talk with you over the telephone. I'm going to come to the office. You wait for me in the law library, and, Bradbury, you keep your hands out of things. Do you understand? I don't like the idea of you manipulating my switchboard, and I'm perfectly capable of running my own office. I don't need you to prowl around in my private office, and I don't need you to interfere with my telephone calls."

"Listen," Bradbury said, "I've got to talk with you before you see any one else—any one—do you understand?"

"I'll talk with you," Mason told him, "when I get to the office."

"No, you've got to talk with me now. I've got to tell you what's happened. The police are hot on your trail. They've found your taxicab."

"What taxicab?"

"The taxicab," Bradbury said, "that you took from your office, down to Ninth and Olive, where you met Paul Drake. Then you took the taxicab directly out to the Holliday

Apartments, where you went to call on Patton. Then you kept the same taxicab, took it to a drug store, where you telephoned to me, and then took the taxicab right out to the St. James Apartments, where you found Marjorie Clune and tipped her to make her escape. It was a bad blunder, and the police are going to hold you responsible. It makes Marjorie's flight look the more incriminating."

Perry Mason gripped the receiver until perspiration from the palm of his hand slimed the hard rubber.

"You've said that much," he said, "go ahead and say some more."

"I want Marjorie Clune kept out of this," Bradbury said. "No matter what else happens, Marjorie Clune has got to be kept out of it. I've sounded out the district attorney's office through some influential friends. The district attorney feels that Dr. Doray is the guilty person. If Dr. Doray will plead guilty, they'll dismiss the case against Marjorie, if Doray's statement will exonerate her."

"What will they do with Doray?" asked Perry Mason.

"They'll give him a life sentence. He'll escape the death penalty that way. It's really for his best interests to do that."

"I'm the one to determine what his best interests are," Mason said.

"No, you're not," Bradbury told him, "you're working under my orders."

"I'm defending Dr. Doray."

"You're defending him because I employed you."

"I don't give a damn who employed me," Mason said, "the man that I'm representing is the man that is entitled to my best efforts."

Bradbury's voice was coldly insistent.

"You are a man of strong will, Mason," he said. "I am a man of considerable will power, myself. The police are very much interested to learn whom you telephoned to from that drug store, and what you said over the telephone. While you're on your road to the office you might think over the situation in the light of the facts."

"Okay," Perry Mason said, "I'll see you when I get there. Good-by."

"Good-by," said Bradbury.

Perry Mason waited until he heard a click in his ear, then he said in a low voice, "You still on the line, Della?"

"Yes, chief," she said.

"Did you hear what he said?"

"I've got it all down in shorthand," she told him.

"Good girl," Mason said. "Put him in the law library. I'll be there inside of an hour. You keep Bradbury where he can't do any mischief. Tell him I may be in at any moment. Keep him in the law library and watch that telephone. Evidently he knows how to work that switchboard connection. He must have figured what you were doing, plugged himself in on the line and gone into my private office."

"Is it true," she asked, "about the police and the taxicab?"

Perry Mason grinned into the telephone.

"You know just as much about it as I do, Della," he said. "Why don't you talk some more with Bradbury?"

"But that means you're in an awful spot, chief."

"I always get in a spot before I get done," he said, "and I always get out of it. I'll be seeing you, Della. 'By."

He hung up the receiver and dialed the office of the Coöperative Investigating Bureau.

"Mason talking," he said. "Any more reports on Vera Cutter?"

"Just a moment," said the telephone operator.

A man's voice came on the line.

"Who is this talking?" he asked.

"Perry Mason."

"Are you acquainted with Mr. Samuels?" asked the voice.

"Yes."

"What's his first name?"

"Jack."

"When did you first meet him?"

"About a year ago," Perry Mason said. "He came to my office soliciting business."

"What did you tell him?"

"I told him the Drake Detective Bureau did all of my work, but I'd give him a break if there was anything they couldn't handle."

"Okay," the voice said, "I guess you're Mason all right. Here's the latest: Vera Cutter stays in her room at the Monmarte Hotel. It's room 503. From time to time she calls the Drake Detective Bureau. We haven't been able to plug in on the conversations. She doesn't call any one else, but at irregular intervals some man calls and asks for her."

"Is she in her room now?" asked Perry Mason.

"Yes."

"That's all," he said. "I'm going to drop in for a chat with her. Don't have your detectives waste time trailing me when I leave. I'll have a young woman with me."

He hung up the telephone and went to the taxicab where Marjorie Clune was seated, her face held rigidly straight ahead.

"Margy," he said, "would you know Eva Lamont's voice if you heard it?"

"I think so," she said.

Mason nodded to the cab driver.

"Monmarte Hotel," he said.

Mason dropped into the cushions beside the girl.

"What's Eva Lamont doing here?" asked Marjorie Clune.

"If it is Eva Lamont," Perry Mason said, "and I think it is, she's trying her damnedest to get Bob Doray mixed into the murder case."

"Why should she do that?" Marjorie Clune asked.

"There might be two reasons," Mason said, his eyes squinting thoughtfully.

"And what are those?"

He was staring out of the cab window, watching the scenery with speculative, thoughtful eyes.

"No, Margy," he said, "I'm not going to bother you with a lot of things to think about. Just promise me one thing, that is if the police should pick you up, you won't say anything to them."

"I'd made up my mind to that long ago," she told him.

Perry Mason said nothing, continued to stare at the traffic. The cab driver worked his way toward the right-hand curb.

"Go right up to the hotel entrance?" he asked.

"Yes," Mason said, "that's as far as we're going."

He paid off the cab, took Marjorie Clune's arm, escorted her to the elevator of the hotel.

"Fifth floor," he told the operator.

As they left the elevator on the fifth floor, Perry Mason bent forward so that his lips were close to Marjorie Clune's ear.

"I'm going in the room," he said. "I'm going to get that woman in an argument of some sort. I'll try and get her to raise her voice. You keep your ear close to the door and see if you can recognize her voice. If you can recognize it, okay. If you can't, knock on the door, and I'll open it."

"If it's Eva Lamont she'll recognize me," said Marjorie Clune.

"That's all right," he told her, "that's one of the things we've got to figure on. But I've *got* to know whether that's Eva Lamont."

He piloted Marjorie Clune around the bend in the corridor.

"Here's the place," he said. "You'd better stand against the wall there. I'll try and get her to talk while the door's open. I'm afraid you aren't going to be able to hear through the door."

Perry Mason knocked at the door.

The door was opened from the inside just a bare crack.

"Who is it?" asked the woman's low voice.

"A man from the Drake Detective Bureau," Mason said.

There was not another word. The door swung wide open. A woman attired in street costume smiled invitingly at him.

Perry Mason entered the room.

"Well," he said, "it looks as though you were getting ready to leave us."

The woman stared at Perry Mason, then followed his gaze to the wardrobe trunk which stood by the side of the bed partially filled with clothes, to the open suitcase on the bed, and the closed suitcase on the chair.

She looked back at the open door, then wordlessly crossed to the door, closed it and locked it.

"What was it," she asked, "that you wanted?"

"I want to find out," Perry Mason said, "why it was that you registered under the name of Vera Cutter, and yet your baggage has the initials E. L. on it."

"That's simple," she said. "My sister's name is Edith Loring."

"And you're from Cloverdale?" asked Perry Mason.

"I'm from Detroit."

Perry Mason walked over to the wardrobe trunk. He picked up a skirt which hung on a wooden hanger and turned the wooden hanger so that it showed the imprint "CLOVERDALE CLEANING AND DYEING WORKS."

The dark eyes regarded him with glittering malevolence.

"My sister," she said, "lives in Cloverdale."

"But you're from Detroit?" he asked.

"Say, who are you?" she asked in a voice that was suddenly hard. "You aren't from the Drake Detective Bureau."

Perry Mason smiled.

"That," he said, "was just an excuse to get in and talk with you. What I really wanted to ask you was . . ."

She recoiled from him and stood staring, with her face white, her eyes glittering and cautious, one hand gripping the post on the foot of the brass bedstead.

"What I wanted particularly to know," said Perry Mason, "is where *you* were when Frank Patton was killed."

For more than ten seconds she stared at him without making any motion or saying any word. Perry Mason met her eyes accusingly.

"Are you an officer?" she asked at length in a low, throaty voice.

"Suppose you answer the question first," Perry Mason told her, "and then I'll answer your questions."

"I'm going to refer you," she said, "to my attorney."

"Oh, then you have an attorney?"

"Certainly I have an attorney," she said. "Don't think that I'd let any cheap heel come in here and start browbeating me about a thing like that. I don't know anything at all about the murder of Frank Patton, except what I've read in the newspapers. But if you think you're going to come in here and pull a fast one on me, you're going to get fooled."

"And you can't tell me where you were when Frank Patton was killed?"

"I won't tell you where I was."

"Suppose," Perry Mason said, "I should take you down to police headquarters, then what would you do?"

By way of answer she crossed to the telephone, took down the receiver and called the number of Perry Mason's office. There was a moment's silence, then the receiver made a squawking noise and the woman said in a cold, haughty voice, "Is Mr. Mason in? I would like to speak with Mr. Perry Mason. You may tell him this is Vera Cutter."

The receiver made more noise.

Perry Mason, studying the expression on the woman's face, was unable to detect any slightest change in it. After a moment she said cooingly, "Oh, good afternoon, Mr. Mason. This is Miss Vera Cutter again. You told me to get in touch with you if any one questioned me concerning my reason for being here in the city. There's a man in the hotel who claims to be an officer, and . . . what's that?"

The receiver made more noise.

Vera Cutter's face broke into a smile.

"Thank you *so* much, Mr. Mason. You say that if he is an officer he is to come to your office, and if he is not, I am to notify police headquarters and have him arrested for impersonating an officer? Thank you so much, Mr. Mason, I was sorry to have bothered you again, but those were your instructions—to call you if any one questioned me. Oh, thank you *so* much."

She hung up the telephone and turned to Perry Mason with triumphant countenance.

"I guess you know my lawyer," she said, "Perry Mason, just about the biggest lawyer in the city. He's representing my interests while I'm here, and he says that if you're not an officer, he's going to see that you're arrested for the crime of impersonating an officer. If you *are* an officer, you may go to his office and talk with him personally."

"Were you talking with Perry Mason personally?" asked the lawyer.

"Of course I was talking with Perry Mason personally. With the size of the retainer that I paid him, I wouldn't waste my time talking with any law clerks."

"That's funny," Mason said. "I want to see Perry Mason, myself. I called him less than ten minutes ago. They told me he wouldn't be in any more today."

Her smile was patronizing.

"It always makes a difference," she said, "who's calling when you're *trying* to get Perry Mason on the line. He's a very busy man and he doesn't bother with cheap detectives or peddlers."

"And you're not going to tell me why you were getting ready to leave town?" asked Perry Mason, indicating the baggage.

She laughed mockingly.

"Listen, brother," she said, "I'm not going to tell you anything except to scram. Get out of here! Beat it! If you're an officer, you can see Perry Mason; if you're not, you can get the hell out of here."

There was a knock at the door. Perry Mason turned toward it.

Vera Cutter blazed at him, "Don't you dare to open that door!"

She rushed past him, twisted the knob and flung open the door.

Marjorie Clune stood on the threshold.

"How do you do, Eva Lamont?" said Marjorie Clune.

Eva Lamont stared at her for two or three seconds.

"So," said Perry Mason, "your name is Eva Lamont?"

Eva Lamont pointed a rigid index finger at Perry Mason.

"Are you with him?" she screamed.

Marjorie Clune looked inquiringly at Perry Mason.

Before Mason had a chance to give her a signal, Eva Lamont suddenly whirled and raced toward the telephone.

"Just a minute, *dearie*," she called over her shoulder, "I know a man who wants to ask you all about your nice moving picture contract."

She grabbed the receiver from its hook.

"Police headquarters!" she screamed. "Police headquarters! Get me police headquarters at once!"

Perry Mason grabbed Marjorie Clune's arm and swung her about. Together they raced down the corridor. Behind them, they could hear Eva Lamont's voice screaming, "Police headquarters! Police headquarters! . . . Is this police headquarters?"

Perry Mason took the stairs to the fourth floor, then rang for the elevator.

"Steady," he warned Marjorie Clune.

Perry Mason piloted Marjorie Clune through the lobby of the hotel, holding her back when she would have rushed into rapid flight.

"Take it easy," he cautioned in a low voice.

He signaled a cab at the sidewalk.

"Mapleton Hotel," he told the driver. As Mason seated himself in the cab, he extended a cigarette to Marjorie Clune.

"Smoke?"

She took a cigarette. Perry Mason lit it for her, then lit one for himself.

"Settle back against the cushions," he told Marjorie Clune. "Try to think about something besides the case. Relax as much as you can. Don't interrupt me, because I'm going to be thinking, and don't try to think yourself, because it's simply going to make things that much more difficult for you. Think about something else. Relax and rest. You're going to have a trying time."

"Are we going to police headquarters?" she asked.

Perry Mason's tone was grim.

"Not if I can help it," he told her.

They completed the ride in silence. Perry Mason told the cab to wait; told Marjorie Clune to stay in the cab and to keep her hand up in front of her face as much as possible. A uniformed doorman opened the cab door and Perry Mason walked with quick, purposeful strides through the revolving door of the Mapleton Hotel and directly to the desk of the cashier.

"You have a J. R. Bradbury," he said, "staying here in room 693."

The cashier raised her eyebrows inquiringly.

"Yes?" she asked.

"I'm his attorney," Perry Mason said. "There's a possibility I may have to take him out of town on a matter of important business. I want to have his bill all paid up so he can get away if he has to."

"You're checking out for him?" asked the cashier.

"No," he told her, "I'm simply paying his bill to date."

She opened a filing drawer, pulled out a sheet of paper, crossed to an adding machine, manipulated the keys, took the total and returned to Perry Mason.

"The total bill," she said, "is eighty-three dollars and ninety-five cents."

"On 693?" asked Perry Mason.

"He has 693 today," she said, "but he has been connected with 695 and has been paying the bills on both rooms."

Perry Mason pushed a one hundred dollar bill through the window. The cashier inspected it, crinkled it crisply between efficient fingers, then crossed to the cash register. She rang up the amount and handed Perry Mason the change, together with a receipted bill.

Mason studied the bill.

"These telephone calls," he said, indicating the bill with his finger, "are they local or long distance?"

"The long distance calls are marked," she said. "Those others are local."

"I think," Perry Mason told her, "that I would like to have an itemized account of those local calls. You see, I'm paying this bill for Mr. Bradbury. The other amounts are quite all right; he can't question them, but I'd like very much to have an itemized statement of the local telephone calls."

She puckered her forehead for a moment, then said,

"I can get them for you. It will be a little trouble and will take a few minutes."

"If you would be so kind," Perry Mason said, smiling. "You can mark them right on the back of this receipted bill."

The cashier took the receipted bill, crossed to the telephone desk and spoke with the operator. A moment later she brought back to the desk a leather-covered notebook, opened it and started writing with nimble fingers. When she had finished, she returned the receipted bill to Perry Mason.

"The calls," she said, "are all marked on there."

Perry Mason thanked her, folded the receipted bill without even bothering to look at it, thrust it into his pocket and turned from the cashier's window.

"Thank you," he said, "very much indeed."

17

Perry Mason pushed open the door of his office and stood to one side for Marjorie Clune to enter.

Della Street, who had been seated at the secretarial desk by the switchboard, jumped to her feet and stared from Perry Mason to the blue eyes of Marjorie Clune.

"Della," said Perry Mason, "this is Marjorie Clune, the girl with the lucky legs. Margy, this is Della Street, my secretary."

Della Street made no effort to acknowledge the introduction. She stared at Marjorie Clune, then shifted her eyes back to Perry Mason's face.

"You brought *her* here?" she said. "You?"

Perry Mason nodded.

"But there have been detectives in," Della Street said. "They'll be coming back. They've got the building watched. You got in, but you can't get out, and Marjorie Clune is wanted for murder. It will simply cinch the case against you as an accessory."

Marjorie Clune clung to Perry Mason's arm.

"Oh, I'm so sorry," she said. Then, facing Della Street, added, "I wouldn't have done it for the world if I'd known."

Della Street crossed rapidly to Marjorie Clune, put an arm around her shoulders.

"There, there, dear," she said, "don't you care. It isn't your fault. He's always doing things like that; always taking chances."

"And," said Perry Mason, smiling, "always getting away with them. Why don't you tell her that, Della?"

"Because," Della Street said, "some day you're not going to be able to get away with them."

Perry Mason glanced meaningly at Della Street.

"Take her in my private office, Della," he said, "and wait there."

Della Street opened the door of the private office.

"You poor kid," she said maternally, "it's been frightful, hasn't it? But don't worry. It's going to come out all right now."

Marjorie Clune paused in the doorway.

"Please," she said to Perry Mason, "please don't let me get you into trouble."

Della Street exerted a gentle pressure with her arm and piloted Marjorie Clune to the inner office and sat her in the big leather chair which flanked Perry Mason's desk.

"Wait there and try and get some rest," she said. "You can lay your head right back against the cushions and curl your feet up in the seat."

Marjorie Clune smiled at her gratefully.

Della Street rejoined Perry Mason in the outer office.

Mason walked to the door of the outer office, opened it and pushed the catch into place which put on the night latch.

"I don't want to be disturbed for a few minutes," he said. "Where's Bradbury? In the law library?"

Della Street nodded her head, then glanced toward the door of Perry Mason's private office.

"Where did you find her?" she asked.

"You can take a lot of guesses," Perry Mason said, "and then you'll miss it."

"Where was she, chief?"

"In Summerville."

"How did she get down there?"

"By train. But I got there before she did."

"You did?"

"Yes. I was following some one else."

"Who?"

"Dr. Doray. He went down on the midnight plane."

"And they were there?" she asked.

Perry Mason nodded.

"Together, chief?"

Perry Mason pulled out his package of cigarettes, regarded them ruefully.

"Two left," he said.

"I've got a package here," Della Street told him.

Perry Mason lit a cigarette, and sucked in a huge drag of smoke.

"Were they together?" asked Della Street.

"In the bridal suite," Perry Mason told her.

"She's married then?"

"No, she wasn't married."

"Were they going to get married?"

"No, she was going to marry Bradbury."

"Then," said Della Street, "you mean . . . that . . . that . . ."

"Exactly," he told her. "She was going to marry Bradbury because Bradbury had jockeyed her into such a position that she had no other alternative. But, before she did that, she was going to give a week of her life to Bob Doray."

Della Street motioned toward the book which stood by the telephone.

Mason nodded.

"Yes," he said, "I got the signal as soon as I came in. That was particularly important. It was something I had to know, but I was afraid there might be some detectives in here and I didn't want you to tell me in front of them."

"Well," she said, "there's the signal that you told me to arrange. Marjorie Clune got a telephone call just about five minutes before she left Thelma Bell's apartment."

"Did Thelma Bell know who was on the other end of the wire?"

"No, she said that Marjorie stood and talked a few minutes and then said, 'I'll call you back within an hour,' or words to that effect; that Marjorie didn't seem at all glad to have the telephone call. She was frowning when she hung up the receiver."

Perry Mason studied the curling smoke from the end of his cigarette with thoughtful eyes.

"How about Bradbury?" she asked. "Are you going to follow his instructions?"

"To hell with him," Perry Mason said. "I'm running this show."

The door of the law library swung noiselessly open. J. R. Bradbury strode into the office, his face white and drawn, his eyes cold and determined.

"You may think you're running this show," he said, "but I've got the whip hand. So, the little double-crossing, cheap tart had to two-time me, did she? She went to the bridal suite with Doray, did she? Damn them. I'll show them both!"

Mason regarded Bradbury with sober speculation.

"Were you listening at the keyhole," he asked, "or did you bring a chair up to the transom?"

"Just in case you're interested," Bradbury said in cold fury, "I was listening at the transom, which I'd previously opened so that I could hear."

Della Street turned from Bradbury to Perry Mason, her eyes indignant. She sucked in a rapid breath as though to speak; then, catching Mason's glance, remained silent.

Perry Mason lounged upon the corner of her desk easily, swinging his foot lazily back and forth.

"Looks as though we're going to have a show-down, Bradbury," he said.

Bradbury nodded. "Don't misunderstand me, Mason," he said. "You're a fighter; I've got a great deal of respect for you, but I'm a fighter, myself, and I don't think you have the proper respect for me." His voice was harsh, flat and strained.

Perry Mason's eyes were steady, calm and patient.

"No, Bradbury," he said, "you're not a fighter; you're the type who takes advantage of another person's mistakes. You've got the banking type of mind. You sit on the sideline, watch, wait and pounce, when you think the time is ripe. I don't fight that way. I go barging out, making my own breaks and taking chances. You don't take any chances; you sit in a position of safety. You never risk your own skin."

There was a swift change of expression in Bradbury's eyes.

"Don't you ever think I don't risk my own skin," he said. "I take plenty of risks, but I'm smooth enough to always cover them."

Perry Mason's eyes were patient and contemplative.

"You're partially right at that, Bradbury," he said. "Perhaps I should amend my original statement."

"All this isn't getting us anywhere, Mason," Bradbury told him. "I thought you and I understood each other perfectly. I'm accustomed to my own way. I get it by hook or by crook, but I get it. A lot of people hate me; a lot of them think I use unfair tactics, but every one has to admit that when I say I'm going to do a thing I do it."

Della Street glanced from one man to the other.

Perry Mason smoked in silence.

"I told you," Bradbury said, "that I wanted Bob Doray to plead guilty."

"That isn't what you told me originally," Mason said.

"I've changed my mind, and, incidentally, my plans. It's what I'm telling you now," Bradbury said.

Mason pursed his lips thoughtfully, glanced at Della Street, then back to Bradbury.

"I would never have accepted the employment if I had known that was to have been one of the conditions, Bradbury," he said. "You remember that you forced me to represent Dr. Doray. I told you that if I represented him, I would represent him to the best of my ability; that I would put up a fight for him, and that his interests and the interests of Marjorie Clune would be the only things I would consider."

"I don't care what you told me," Bradbury said impatiently. "Time is getting short here. We've got to have some action, and . . ."

There was the sound of a man's weight lunging against the door of the outer office. The frosted glass showed the shadows of two men silhouetted against it. The knob rattled once more and then imperative knuckled pounded on the door.

Perry Mason nodded to Della Street.

"Open the door, Della," he told her.

Bradbury spoke swiftly.

"Let's not misunderstand each other, Mason. I'm absolutely determined about this thing. You're working for me; you're going to follow my orders."

"I'm working," Perry Mason said, "for the best interests of my clients. I accepted the employment on the understanding that I was going to secure a complete vindication, and . . ."

He broke off as Della Street swung the door open.

Riker and Johnson pushed their way past her into the room.

"Well," said Riker, "we've got you at last."

"You boys looking for me?" asked Perry Mason.

Johnson laughed.

"Oh, no," he said with heavy sarcasm, "we weren't looking for you at all; we just wanted to see you about a little legal advice."

Riker motioned toward Bradbury.

"Who's this man?" he asked.

"A client," Perry Mason said.

"What's his business?"

"Why don't you ask him?" the lawyer replied. "It's confidential as far as I'm concerned."

Bradbury faced the two men and said nothing.

"They want you at headquarters for some questioning," Johnson remarked.

"It happens," Perry Mason observed, "that I've been out of the office for some little time and I've got quite a bit of business to attend to. I'm afraid I can't go to headquarters right now."

"We told you," Riker said, "that you were wanted at headquarters for questioning."

"Got a warrant?" Perry Mason asked.

"No," said Riker grimly, "but we can get one and it won't take very long."

"That's nice," Mason observed. "Go ahead and get one."

"Look here, Mason," Johnson said, "there's no use acting like a damn fool. You know we can take you down to headquarters. If you insist on a warrant, we'll get a warrant. If we get a warrant, there's going to be a prosecution. You're mixed up in this thing so that it looks as though you've laid yourself wide open on a felony rap. The chief is going to give you a break; he's going to let you explain before he presents the evidence to the Grand Jury. It's a break for you. If you can talk your way out of it, it suits us. We don't care one way or another. We were just sent here to bring you down."

"You boys said you wanted some legal advice," Perry Mason told them. "I guess, perhaps, you were right. Apparently you do. You can take me down to police headquarters when you've got a warrant for my arrest. You can't take me there before that."

"We can take you there right now as far as that's concerned," Johnson told him.

Perry Mason looked them over with a speculative and belligerent eye.

"Well," he said, "perhaps you can, and, again, perhaps you can't."

"Oh hell," Riker said, "go to the telephone and call police headquarters."

Perry Mason looked at the two detectives and laughed sarcastically.

"Come on, boys," he said, "let's cut the comedy. You're not talking with a dumb hick who doesn't know his rights; you're talking to a lawyer. If you folks had enough evidence to get out a warrant for my arrest, you'd have the warrant with you right now. You haven't got a warrant and you're not going to get one; not right away, anyhow. Perhaps the Grand Jury will mill the thing around and return an indictment, or you may find some one foolish enough to sign a complaint, but what you're trying to do is to get me on the defensive so you can inquire into a lot of my private affairs. I'm telling you you can't do it. There's the telephone. Go ahead and call police headquarters."

He turned to Della Street.

"Call their bluff, Della," he said. "Go ahead and get them police headquarters."

Della Street picked up the telephone and snapped in the plug with a vicious click.

"Police headquarters," she said.

Perry Mason grinned at the detectives.

"When I get ready to come to police headquarters," he said, "I'll come. When you fellows want to arrest me, go ahead and arrest me, but be damn sure that you do it in a legal manner."

"Now listen," Johnson said, "we've got a lot of stuff on you, Mason, a lot of stuff that's got to be explained. You're mixed into this case all the way through it. You started in messing around, getting Marjorie Clune out of the way."

"Do you know I got her out of the way?" asked Perry Mason.

"You had a taxicab running around to her apartment, and she left right after you were there."

"Indeed?" said Perry Mason, and then added, "How fortunate."

"Here's police headquarters on the line," said Della Street.

Johnson looked at Riker.

"Oh, hell," Johnson said, "let 'em go."

"Hang up, Della," Perry Mason said.

Della Street clicked the key as she cut off the connection.

"Just the same," Johnson said to Perry Mason, "I'll bet you five bucks we're here with a warrant before another forty-eight hours."

"I'll bet you five bucks you're not," Mason said. "Put up your money."

"Come on, Johnson," Riker said.

The men turned toward the door.

Bradbury stared steadily at Perry Mason.

"Just a moment, Mason," he said, "are you going to follow my instructions in the matter?"

Mason took two steps toward Bradbury, stood staring at him with ominous steadiness. Riker, his hand on the doorknob, paused. Johnson turned to stare.

"Get this," Perry Mason said to Bradbury slowly, "and get it straight, because I don't want to have to repeat myself. As far as this case is concerned, you're just Santa Claus, that's all. You're the man who put up the money. Aside from that you haven't got a thing to do with it; not one single . . . God . . . damned . . . thing."

Bradbury turned to the detectives.

"Gentlemen," he said, "if you will open the door of that private office, you'll find concealed in there Marjorie Clune, who is at present a fugitive from justice."

Perry Mason swung toward the detectives.

"You open that door without a search warrant," he said, "and I'll break your jaw."

The detectives exchanged glances, looked at Bradbury.

"I tell you I know what I'm talking about," Bradbury said. "She's in there, and if you don't make it snappy she'll get out through the door in the corridor."

Both men made a lunge for the door of the private office. Perry Mason swung about with the lithe grace of a pugilist. Bradbury jumped on him from behind, wrapping his legs about Mason's waist, pinning his arms. Thrown off balance, Mason staggered slightly. Riker charged into him and sent Mason and Bradbury sprawling to the carpet. Della Street screamed. Johnson banged open the door to the private office.

Marjorie Clune was fumbling with the catch on the exit door which led to the hall.

"Stop where you are," yelled Johnson, "or I'll shoot!"

Marjorie Clune turned to stare at him. She stood motionless, her face white, her eyes wide, blue and startled, staring at the two detectives.

"By God!" Johnson said in an undertone, "it sure is! It's Marjorie Clune!"

Perry Mason scrambled to his feet. Bradbury was carefully dusting the knees of his tweed trousers. Riker tugged handcuffs from his pocket.

"Is your name Marjorie Clune?" asked Riker.

Marjorie Clune's eyes stared at him with an unfaltering scrutiny.

"If you have any questions to ask," she said, "you may ask them of my attorney, Perry Mason."

Perry Mason nodded to Della Street.

"Get police headquarters, Della," he said.

18

Perry Mason caught Johnson by the shoulder as Johnson slipped handcuffs on Marjorie Clune's wrists.

"You don't need to do that, you big heel," he said.

Johnson whirled, his eyes glittering with hatred.

"Just because you're a lawyer," he said, "you think you can do anything you damn please. You said we couldn't arrest you before and, by God, you were right. We knew we couldn't. We didn't have enough on you. But the situation has changed since then. We can arrest you now all right."

"Will you listen to me for a moment?" Perry Mason said.

"Oh, you want to talk now, do you?" Riker commented. "The situation is a little bit different now. You're anxious to talk, huh?"

Della Street entered Perry Mason's private office, waited until she caught his eye.

"Police headquarters," she said.

"Tell Detective Sergeant O'Malley that if he can get to my office inside of ten minutes, I'll give him some inside dope on the Patton murder case," Mason said.

Della Street nodded.

"He won't be here ten minutes from now," Johnson said. "You tell O'Malley to wait at headquarters."

Della Street paid no attention to him, but returned to the outer office.

J. R. Bradbury, his face wearing a smile of cold triumph, pulled a cigar from his pocket, clipped off the end, and lit it.

"This man," Perry Mason said, indicating Bradbury, "is the one who retained me to represent Marjorie Clune. He is the one who told me to beat it out ahead of the police and get her out of trouble."

"I did nothing of the sort," Bradbury said.

"He is the one who told me to represent Dr. Robert Doray."

"I did nothing of the sort," Bradbury repeated.

"What the hell do we care what either one of you did?" Riker said. "We've got you, and we've got this broad. She's wanted for murder. You knew she was wanted for murder. It's been in the newspapers. You had her in your office, and you were concealing her. That makes you an accessory after the fact. It's a felony, and we don't need any warrant to arrest you. We've got the proof on you. It's a felony that was actually committed in our presence, as far as that's concerned, although in a felony case it doesn't make any difference."

"If you'll listen to me," Perry Mason said, "I'll explain the entire situation to you."

"You can tell it to the judge," Johnson said. "I've chased around after you just as long as I'm going to, Perry Mason. You've been giving us the merry ha-ha and the run-around for a long time. Now you're going with us. Put the bracelets on him, Riker."

Perry Mason stared steadily at the two detectives.

"I want to talk," he said.

"I don't give a damn what you want to do," Johnson told him.

"When we get to police headquarters," Perry Mason said, "they will ask me what I have to say. I will tell them that I was on the verge of making a complete confession; that you two dumb dicks wouldn't let me talk; that now the prosecution can go to hell and try to prove me guilty."

Johnson turned to Riker.

"Lock the door," he said. "If the man wants to confess, that's different.

"You want to confess?" he asked.

"Yes," said Mason.

"To what?"

"To things that I shall outline in my confession."

Riker opened the door to Perry Mason's outer office.

"You," he said to Della Street, "come in here and take down what this guy says in shorthand."

"It's his own stenographer," Johnson objected.

"That's all right. She'll take it down if he tells her to," Riker said. "And, if he doesn't tell her to take it down, he won't do any talking."

Mason laughed.

"Don't think you boys are going to bluff me," he said, "but as it happens, I want it taken down. Della, you will please take down every word that is said in this room. I want a complete transcript of what is said, and who says it."

"Go on," Johnson remarked, his lip curling slightly. "Start your speech."

"When I first came into contact with this case," Mason said, "I was employed by J. R. Bradbury, the gentleman standing there. He had been to the district attorney's office. They couldn't help him. He wanted me to find Frank Patton and to prosecute him. At my suggestion, he employed Paul Drake, and Drake's Detective Bureau to find Patton."

"This doesn't sound like a confession," Riker said.

Perry Mason fixed him with a cold eye.

"Do you want to listen, or do you want me to keep quiet?" he said.

"Let him go ahead, Riker," Johnson commented.

"I want it understood I am not bound by anything this man says," Bradbury stated.

"Shut up," Johnson told him.

"I won't shut up until I have expressed myself," Bradbury replied. "I know what my rights are."

Riker reached out and caught Bradbury by the knit of the necktie.

"Listen, you," he said, "we're sticking around here to hear a guy confess, not to hear your solo. Sit down and shut up."

He pushed Bradbury back, and into a chair, then turned to Mason.

"Go ahead," he said, "you wanted to talk. Start talking."

"Bradbury came to my office," Perry Mason said. "Before that I had received a telegram signed Eva Lamont. Bradbury said he had sent that telegram. The telegram asked me to hold myself in readiness to act in a certain case involving Marjorie Clune. Bradbury outlined that case. Marjorie Clune had been victimized by Frank Patton. He wanted me to find and prosecute Frank Patton. Through Drake, I located Patton. In locating Patton, we had occasion to interview a young woman named Thelma Bell who lives at the St. James Apartments on East Faulkner Street. Her telephone number was Harcourt 63891. I have always had an uncanny memory for telephone numbers.

"On the evening that Drake located Frank Patton, I was sitting in my office awaiting a telephone call from Drake. We were going out together and try to shake a confession out of Patton. Bradbury came to my office. I told him to wait. I put him in the outer office. Drake's call came through. I told Drake I would meet him. I grabbed a cab and went down to meet Drake. In the meantime, I sent Bradbury back to the hotel to get some newspapers. He is staying at the Mapleton Hotel. He anticipated it would take him half an hour to make the round trip in a taxicab. That's about right. It would have taken just about that time."

"Are you going," asked Bradbury, in a cold, accusing tone, "to confess about entering Patton's apartment in advance of the officers and locking the door behind you as you went out?"

Johnson turned to Bradbury.

"What do you know about that?" he asked.

"I know that's what he did," Bradbury said.

"How do you know?"

"Because," Bradbury remarked with a triumphant leer at Perry Mason, "this man telephoned me here at his office not much after nine o'clock and told me the details of the murder. He told me how the murder had been committed. Even the police didn't know it at that time. I told him to do what he could to protect Marjorie Clune. I referred, of course, to purely legal methods."

Johnson and Riker exchanged glances.

"Was that the telephone call that Perry Mason put through from the drug store?" asked Riker. "We've traced his taxicab from here to Ninth and Olive, from Ninth and Olive out to Patton's apartment, from Patton's apartment down to a drug store where he telephoned, and from the drug store out to the St. James Apartments."

"I was the one he talked to on the telephone," said J. R. Bradbury. "I want to have it definitely understood that I have made this statement before witnesses, and just as soon as I had any knowledge that the things Mason did were at all illegal. I am not going to be involved in any technical illegality."

Riker looked at Della Street.

"You got that down?" he asked.

"Yes," Della Street said.

"Go ahead," Johnson said to Bradbury.

"Let *him* go ahead," Bradbury remarked, nodding to Mason.

"I went to Patton's apartment," Mason said. "I knocked at the door. No one answered. I opened the door and walked in. The door was unlocked. I found Patton's body. He had been stabbed. I found a blackjack lying in a corner of the living-room. I started out and heard a police officer coming down the corridor. I didn't want to be seen leaving the apartment, and I didn't want to be seen standing there by the open door. I had a skeleton key in my pocket, and I locked the door and pounded on the panel. I told the officer I had just arrived and was knocking to try and effect my entrance."

Perry Mason stopped talking. There was a silence in the office which enabled those present to hear the scratching of Della Street's pen on the shorthand notebook, to hear the sobbing intake of her breath.

"You're a hell of a lawyer," said Riker scornfully. "That confession, and Bradbury's corroboration, will put you in jail for the rest of your life."

"On the table," said Perry Mason, without noticing the comment, "in Patton's apartment, were two telephone messages. One of them was to tell Thelma that Marjorie would be late for her appointment. The other one was to call Margy at Harcourt 63891. I saw those two telephone messages. I remembered the telephone number of Thelma Bell. As I mentioned, I have a photographic memory for such things. I surmised at once that Marjorie Clune could be found at Thelma Bell's apartment. I telephoned Bradbury and asked him for instructions. He told me to protect Marjorie Clune regardless of what I had to do, or what means I had to employ."

"That's a lie," Bradbury said. "I employed you as a lawyer. I didn't expect you to do anything illegal. I'm not a party to it."

"Let it pass," said Johnson; "go ahead, Mason."

"I went out to Thelma Bell's apartment," Mason said. "I found Marjorie Clune there. I found her taking a bath. Thelma Bell had just had a bath. Thelma Bell told me that she had an appointment with Frank Patton but hadn't kept it. That she had been out with a boy friend. I telephoned the boy friend for verification. He verified her statement.

"I told Marjorie Clune to go to a hotel; to register under her name, to call my office and let me know where she was, and not to leave the hotel. She promised me that she would. She subsequently telephoned my office that she was at the Bostwick Hotel, in room 408. The telephone number was Exeter 93821. I returned to Bradbury. I told him what had happened, except that I did not tell him about entering Patton's apartment, or locking the door. Bradbury told me I was to represent Dr. Doray as well as Marjorie Clune. I agreed to such representation.

"I met Bradbury at his hotel because he didn't want to remain at the office. He had returned to the office with the newspapers he had been sent to get from the Mapleton Hotel. His return was just about the time that I telephoned. I believe he had just entered the office when I telephoned him from the drug store near Patton's apartment."

"There was also a brief case," Bradbury said.

"Yes," Mason said, "you telephoned Della Street and asked her if you should bring the brief case. She told you it might be a good plan to bring it as well."

"I telephoned from my room in the hotel," Bradbury explained to the officers.

"Subsequently," Mason said, "I telephoned Marjorie Clune. She had left the hotel. Detectives got in touch with Della Street and accused her of telephoning Dr. Doray to get out of the country. As a matter of fact, Della Street did not telephone to him."

"That's what you say," Bradbury commented.

"Shut up, Bradbury," Riker said.

"I learned," Mason went on, "that Marjorie Clune had intended to take the midnight plane. I chartered a plane and followed the schedule of the midnight mail plane. At its first stop in Summerville, I found that Dr. Doray had disembarked. I went to the Riverview Hotel and found Dr. Doray registered in the bridal suite. At first he disclaimed all knowledge of Marjorie Clune, but while we were talking, Marjorie Clune entered the room. She had missed the plane, and had taken the train. Officers showed up at about that time to arrest them. I spirited Marjorie Clune out of the hotel, and brought her back to this city."

"You did," said Riker.

"I did," Mason said.

"And the damn fool admits it," Johnson commented.

Perry Mason stared at them with cold, scornful eyes.

"If you gentlemen are interested in my confession," he said, "and will keep your mouths shut, I will finish it."

"Cut out the wisecracks and go ahead," Johnson told him.

Perry Mason stared at Johnson steadily; then turned so that he faced Della Street.

Bradbury spoke up.

"If you two men will use your heads," he said, "you'll understand that the question of that locked door is going to be of vital importance in the case. If the door was unlocked, it's almost a certainty that Robert Doray killed Frank Patton. If the door was locked, it means that Frank Patton was killed by—"

"You can keep all that stuff to yourself," Johnson said. "You're going to get a chance to talk before we get done with this thing. You've played 'button, button, who's got the button?' with the law yourself. It seems to me you've been trying to blackmail Perry Mason with the information that you have. Don't think you can pull that kind of stuff and get away with it."

"You can't talk that way to me," Bradbury said, jumping from his chair.

"Set him down, Riker," said Johnson.

Riker grabbed Bradbury by the necktie once more, and slammed him back into the chair.

"Sit down," he said, "and shut up."

There was an imperative banging on the outer door.

"That," said Perry Mason, "will be Detective Sergeant O'Malley."

Johnson fidgeted slightly, said to Riker, "Let him in, Riker."

Riker opened the door. A rather short, paunchy individual, with a round, cherubic face, light eyes that seemed utterly devoid of expression, walked with quick, springy steps through the door and across to Perry Mason's private office. He faced the little group of people.

"Hello, O'Malley," said Perry Mason.

"What you got here?" asked O'Malley.

"This woman is Marjorie Clune, who's wanted for murder," Johnson said hastily. "Perry Mason was hiding her in his office. He's spiriting her around the country."

O'Malley's eyes went swiftly to Marjorie Clune; then to Perry Mason; then to Johnson.

"When Mason does anything," he said to Johnson, "he usually knows what he's doing. Do you have to have the handcuffs on the woman?"

"It's a murder rap," said Johnson, "and Perry Mason is making a confession."

"A what?" asked O'Malley.

"A confession."

"Confessing to what?" asked O'Malley.

"Confessing to the fact that he got into Patton's apartment, found Patton dead, ducked out and locked the door before the police came, and then lied about locking the door."

O'Malley looked at Perry Mason with a puzzled frown on his forehead. Then he looked over to Della Street.

"You taking this down, Della?" he asked.

She nodded.

O'Malley looked once more to Mason.

"What's the idea, Perry?" he asked.

"I am trying to make a confession," said Perry Mason, "but I am being constantly interrupted."

"You mean to say you're making a written confession to a felony and having your own secretary take it down in shorthand?" asked O'Malley, his voice showing puzzled incredulity.

"When I have finished," Mason said, "if I am allowed to finish, the confession will speak for itself."

O'Malley turned to Bradbury.

"Who's that guy?" he asked.

"J. R. Bradbury," Mason said; "he employed me to represent Doray and Marjorie Clune. He's putting up the money."

"Go ahead and finish your confession," O'Malley said to Perry Mason.

"I want to explain my connection with—" Bradbury began.

O'Malley turned to him.

"Shut up," he said.

Perry Mason resumed his comments.

"Obviously," he said, "Frank Patton was killed with a knife. The blackjack didn't enter into it at all. Obviously, however, the murderer had thrown the blackjack into the corner after the murder. After I talked with Marjorie Clune, I learned from her that Dr. Doray had driven her to a place near Patton's apartment. Doray had purchased the knife. He had made threats against Patton. He intended to kill Patton. For that reason, Marjorie Clune wouldn't tell him where Patton was. She went to a candy store, stalling for time; went to the woman's restroom and sent word out to Doray that she'd slipped out through the back way. She hadn't. She was hiding in the restroom. Five minutes after Doray left the place, she went out and went to Patton's apartment. She says that she found him dead. I met her leaving the apartment house.

"I went to Thelma Bell's place, and got her to skip out. I bought her a ticket to College City. She went there and registered at a hotel.

"I made a stall to get back to Thelma Bell's apartment. I searched the place. I found a hat box, and in it were white shoes, stockings, and a dress. All of them had been covered with blood. They had been washed hastily. The white shoes belonged to Marjorie Clune. The other things belonged to Thelma Bell. I checked the hat box to College City and held the check. Then I gave the ticket to Thelma Bell so that she traveled on the ticket that was used to check the hat box."

Perry Mason fumbled in his waistcoat pocket, pulled out a numbered slip of pasteboard and handed it to Detective Sergeant O'Malley.

"That," he said, "is the check for the hat box."

"Just the shoes belonged to Marjorie Clune?" asked O'Malley.

"Just the shoes," Mason said.

"That's what she said," O'Malley said.

"That's what I say," Mason said.

"You're a hell of a lawyer," Bradbury said; "you're betraying the confidences of your client. You're divulging privileged communications. You're—"

"If he won't shut up," said O'Malley to Riker, "you can shut him up."

Riker moved over toward Bradbury's chair.

"Nothing wrong with your hearing, is there, buddy?" he asked, doubling his right hand into a fist.

Bradbury's eyes were cold and scornful.

"Don't think you frighten me a damn bit," he said.

Mason continued talking and by his talk prevented the situation from centering about Bradbury and Riker.

"I made a further check of Thelma Bell's alibi," Perry Mason said, "and found there was nothing to it. I'm convinced that the alibi had been framed, and not too cleverly framed at that. It was an amateurish alibi—one that had been hastily concocted. Thelma Bell was taking a bath when Marjorie Clune returned to the apartment. It is obvious to me that she was taking a bath to wash off the bloodstains."

There was a moment of silence.

"You mean Thelma Bell killed him?" asked O'Malley.

Perry Mason made a gesture for O'Malley to remain silent.

"When Bradbury came to my office," he said, "he didn't know where Patton was, and he didn't know where Marjorie Clune was. When I left Marjorie Clune at Thelma Bell's apartment, she intended to marry Dr. Doray. She was in love with him. When I found her in Summerville, she intended to marry Bradbury. Not that she loved Doray any the less. In fact, she was marrying Bradbury because she did love Doray. She knew that Doray was in a tough spot. He had purchased the knife. He intended to kill Patton. That knife had been used in the consummation of the murder. In her own mind, she felt certain that Dr. Doray had committed the murder. She knew that Bradbury would put up the money to retain counsel for Doray if she would agree to marry Bradbury.

"Before I saw Marjorie Clune at Summerville, however, but after she had left the Bostwick Hotel, I saw Bradbury. He ordered me to represent Dr. Doray as well as Marjorie Clune, and to get Dr. Doray acquitted. Subsequently, I called up my office to make a report. I told my secretary to get in touch with Thelma Bell and find out if Marjorie Clune had talked on the telephone before leaving Thelma Bell's apartment. Bradbury was listening in on the line. He had taken the liberty of going to my private office and manipulating the switchboard so that he was on the line. He broke in and ordered me to have Doray plead guilty, and take a life sentence.

"Now, obviously, Dr. Doray didn't have the knife in his hand when he went into the candy store with Marjorie Clune. Obviously, he didn't know where Patton's apartment was at the time. He left the candy store some five minutes before Marjorie left it. Even supposing that he could have walked to his automobile, secured the knife, gone to Patton's apartment, killed him and escaped, all within a matter of five minutes, the question remains, how did he find Patton's apartment? Marjorie Clune seems to think that he might have followed her to the apartment, but she overlooks the fact that she arrived at the apartment *after* the murder had been committed, not *before*.

"When Bradbury came to my office on the evening of the murder, he didn't know where Patton lived. He didn't know where Marjorie Clune was. Yet, after the murder, he managed to get in touch with Marjorie Clune. That is the only explanation for his instructions to represent Dr. Doray. The only reason that Marjorie Clune would have consented to marry him, and would have disobeyed my instructions to remain in the hotel in order to go to Summerville for a week of happiness with the man she loved. Marjorie Clune didn't know where Bradbury was staying. Yet some one called Marjorie Clune at Thelma Bell's apartment. It was as a result of that telephone conversation that she changed her plans. Therefore, that telephone conversation must have been with Bradbury. She has refused to tell me, but I think it is a fair inference to be drawn from all of the facts."

Perry Mason turned to Bradbury.

"Did you call her on the telephone?" he asked.

"Suppose I did?" inquired Bradbury. "What then?"

"I am simply trying to check back on the circumstances of the crime, and the reason that impelled Marjorie Clune to violate my instructions to remain at the Bostwick Hotel. I am asking you the question frankly and directly, Bradbury, and I want to warn you that if you lie, it will be taken as an indication of guilt."

"Guilt of what?" asked Bradbury.

Perry Mason shrugged his shoulders.

"You'd like to have me lie, wouldn't you?" Bradbury said.

"I don't give a damn what you do," Mason told him.

Bradbury shifted his eyes from Perry Mason to Marjorie Clune. For a long moment he gazed steadily at her. Then he said, with slow emphasis, "I see now what you're driving at, Mason. Marjorie Clune would do anything to save Doray's neck. You're clever enough to hatch up some bit of evidence like this telephone call, make a dramatic presentation of your case which will make this bit of evidence have an exaggerated importance and then, by getting Marjorie to give me the lie, make it appear I have been caught in a trap."

"When you are quite finished," Mason said coldly, "will you please answer the question. Did you or did you not call her on the telephone?"

"I did not," said Bradbury.

"I am warning you," Mason said, "that a falsehood will be taken as an indication of guilt. Did you call her or not?"

"Go ahead," Bradbury said with a sneering laugh, "pile on all the drama you want to emphasize and exaggerate the importance of this lie that Marjorie Clune is going to tell. Use all of the skill of a clever courtroom lawyer to build up a dramatic background for Marjorie Clune's perjury, and when you have entirely finished, the fact will remain that I did not call Marjorie Clune on the telephone."

"Yes," said Perry Mason slowly, "you did. Presently I am going to prove it. In the meantime, the question arises, how did you know that Marjorie Clune could be reached at that telephone?"

Bradbury started to say something; then checked himself.

"I am waiting for an answer," said Mason.

"Wait and be damned," Bradbury told him.

Perry Mason turned to Detective Sergeant O'Malley.

"He knew that she could be reached at that telephone number," he said, "because he had read the memorandum which was on the table in Frank Patton's apartment. He read it when he murdered Patton."

Della Street looked up from her notebook. Marjorie Clune gave a quick gasp. O'Malley turned wary, watchful eyes upon Bradbury. Bradbury sat absolutely motionless for a whole five seconds. Then he smiled patronizingly.

"Never forgetting," he said, "that in the first place I didn't know where Frank Patton was located; that you very carefully guarded that information from me, Mason; that, furthermore, you yourself sent me to the hotel to get some newspapers. I made the round trip to the hotel in exactly thirty-five minutes. That represents average time. I couldn't have done it in less than twenty-five minutes to have saved my life. It would have taken me at least half an hour to have gone to Patton's apartment and returned. Under the circumstances, I think you'll have to get some other method of discrediting the testimony that I have given against you, and find some less drastic means of revenge."

"You knew where Patton was located," Mason said, "because you listened in on the telephone conversation. Your ability to manipulate the switchboard shows that you *could* have done that. The fact that you went to Patton's apartment and read the memorandum giving Marjorie Clune's telephone number shows that you *did* do it. As far as the hotel alibi is concerned, just to show the premeditation and careful planning, you didn't forget the newspapers at all. You brought them with you. The brief case you also brought with you. That business of the telephone was just a little artistic touch. You telephoned from somewhere near Patton's apartment. You told Della Street you were telephoning from your hotel room. Naturally, she had no way of checking that, but when you came to this office building, you left the newspapers and the brief case in a paper package that you left with Mamie at the cigar stand.

"You carried a blackjack with you. You knew that you must rely on a weapon of silence. You knew that if you could get me to go out to Patton's apartment, thinking that you were engaged upon another errand and didn't know where Patton lived, you could murder him and get away with it. You pretended to leave the office in a leisurely manner, stopping to flirt for a moment with Della Street. When you left the office, however, you left in a hurry. You drove to a place near Patton's apartment. And then you got what you thought was a wonderful break. You saw Dr. Doray's car parked there. You discharged the taxi, got out to look at the car and found the knife in the car. You took the knife, went up to Patton's apartment, killed Patton, and started out of the apartment.

"Thelma Bell was in the bathroom having hysterics when you arrived at the apartment. The door was unlocked. You opened the door and went in. Patton was trying to get into the bathroom. He was attired in only his underwear. When he saw you, he started to put on his bathrobe. You walked to him without a word, shoved the knife into his heart. He fell to the floor. You turned and started for the door. Then you remembered your blackjack. You had no further need for it. You thought you might be searched, and you didn't want to have such a weapon in your possession. You pulled it out and flung it to the floor. You ran down the stairs of the apartment house and picked up a cab. You stopped within a block or two to telephone Della Street and tell her that you were telephoning from your room in the hotel, and asked if you should bring the brief case as well as the papers. Then you completed your journey by taxicab to the office building here, picked up the package from Mamie at the cigar stand, tore off the wrapper, took out the newspapers and the brief case, and came sauntering into the office just as I telephoned to find out if you were there, and to tell you about the murder.

"Thelma Bell heard the thud of Patton's body when it fell. She unlocked the bathroom door and went out. She bent over Patton. Some blood got on her skirt, stockings and shoes. She wasn't wearing white shoes. Therefore the stains didn't show particularly, and she was able to cover them with shoe polish. But her skirt and stockings were a mess. She cleaned herself up in the bathroom as best she could, and then went directly back to her apartment and took a bath. She went by taxicab. She had finished her bath when Marjorie Clune came in. Knowing that Marjorie had an appointment with Patton, she looked Marjorie over to see if there were any bloodstains on her clothes. She found the bloodstains on Marjorie's shoes, and made her take a bath. She didn't want Marjorie to become involved in the murder. On the other hand, she didn't want to get mixed in it herself. She had called Sanborne, her boy friend, as soon as she had reached her apartment, and had hastily fixed up an alibi with him. The reason that the alibi was so full of holes was that it had been fixed up over the telephone."

Perry Mason ceased speaking.

Bradbury sneered.

"Would it be asking too much," he said, "for you to produce some evidence other than your own maggoty conclusions?"

Perry Mason's smile was cold and frosty.

"I saw Mamie the next morning," he said; "she told me about you having left the package. She mentioned that you always wore a brown suit. I remembered then that you had been wearing a brown suit that evening at the office. Yet, when I saw you in the hotel, you wore a tweed suit. You had rushed from my office to the hotel and changed your clothes. I wonder why. I wonder if it wasn't because there was blood on your brown suit. Of course, the stains wouldn't have shown very plainly by artificial light. But they were there, and you wanted to get rid of the suit. I have an idea that you may have had some trouble disposing of this suit. I think we'll find it concealed somewhere in your room in the hotel.

"Moreover, in order to carry out your plan, you had to have Doray leave the country. You wanted to throw him in a panic. You therefore had Eva Lamont call Dr. Doray at his hotel. She told him that she was Della Street, my secretary, and that I wanted him to leave the country.

"Dr. Doray left the hotel, but kept calling back for messages. He got Marjorie's message, called her, and she agreed to meet him in Summerville."

"Who's Eva Lamont?" asked O'Malley.

"The woman," Mason said, "that occupied Bradbury's suite in the Mapleton Hotel until yesterday. Then, with Bradbury's money, and under his instructions, she went to the Monmarte Hotel, registered as Vera Cutter, and gave Paul Drake information that implicated Doray in the case earlier than would otherwise have happened.

"When I called Bradbury at my office and told him of Patton's death, he almost had a fit, registering surprise. That's the fault of an amateur. He overdoes it. Surprise becomes consternation, and consternation becomes terror.

"Returning, however, to this Eva Lamont angle, Bradbury used her to involve Doray. Naturally, the blacker the case against Doray, the more willing Marjorie Clune would be to do anything in order to bring about Doray's acquittal.

"When Bradbury, listening in over the telephone this afternoon, heard me instruct Della Street to trace any telephone call which had been received by Marjorie Clune prior to her departure from Thelma Bell's apartment, he knew that I was getting on a hot trail. So he changed his plans immediately and ordered me to have Doray plead guilty and accept a life sentence. He wanted to do that because he realized I was commencing to get a slant on what was actually happening. And he tried then to convict Doray and to get me mixed into it in order to save his own skin.

"That, gentlemen, is my confession," Perry Mason said.

He strode across the room and sat down.

Bradbury faced the accusing eyes of Detective Sergeant O'Malley.

"A pack of lies," he said, "a pack of damn lies. Let him produce one bit of proof."

"I think," said Perry Mason, "that if you will have his room in the Mapleton Hotel searched, O'Malley, you'll find that suit of clothes. I think that if you will check his fingerprints with the fingerprints on the bloody knife, you'll find that they check. And, furthermore, just to show you what a liar he is, I dropped by his hotel this afternoon and paid his hotel bill. In paying it, I secured an itemized account of the telephone numbers that he had called. I have the list here. You will see from this list that he called Harcourt 63891 on the night of the murder. That he also called Grove 36921, which was the number of Dr. Doray, in the Midwick Hotel. You will also see that he was paying the bill on a suite of rooms until this morning; that the woman who occupied the other room was Eva Lamont. If you will rush your men to the Monmarte Hotel, you will find Eva Lamont registered under the name of Vera Cutter, and Paul Drake will identify her as the woman who gave him all of the information which enabled him to tip off the police to the evidence against Dr. Doray."

Perry Mason pulled the receipted hotel bill from his pocket, and handed it to Detective Sergeant O'Malley.

Mason turned to face Bradbury.

"I warned you, Bradbury," he said, "not to lie about that telephone call to Marjorie Clune. I told you that it would be a confession of guilt."

Bradbury stared at Perry Mason. His face had gone white as a sheet.

"Damn you," he said, in a low tone vibrant with hatred.

O'Malley nodded to Riker and Johnson.

"We're going to headquarters."

He turned to Della Street.

"Would you mind getting headquarters on the telephone?" he said. "I'm going to send some men out to pick up Eva Lamont and search Bradbury's room at the Mapleton Hotel."

Perry Mason bowed to O'Malley.

"Thank you, Sergeant," he said.

He turned to Bradbury and made a sweeping gesture.

"As you have so aptly remarked, Bradbury," he said, "we understand each other perfectly. We're both fighters. We use different weapons, that's all."

19

Newspaper reporters clustered about the doorway of Perry Mason's private office, grouped in a semicircle. Newspaper photographers held cameras and flashlights. Perry Mason sat behind his desk in the big swivel chair; standing back of him, with warm eyes and smiling lips, was Della Street. Dr. Doray sat in the big leather chair. Marjorie Clune was perched on the arm of the chair.

"Can you get your heads a little closer?" asked one of the newspaper reporters of Marjorie Clune and Dr. Doray. "Bend down a little bit, Miss Clune, and, Doray, if you'll look up at her and smile a little . . ."

"I'm smiling," said Dr. Doray.

"That's a grin," the newspaper reporter told him. "What we want is something a little more wistful; you're too happy."

Marjorie Clune tilted her head.

Perry Mason watched the pair with an indulgent smile.

Flashlights suddenly illuminated the pair.

One of the reporters turned to Perry Mason.

"Would you mind telling us, Mr. Mason," he said, "when you first knew that Bradbury was guilty?"

"I first realized it," Perry Mason said slowly, "when I became convinced that Bradbury had been in communication with Marjorie Clune, some time after the murder and before midnight. I knew that Marjorie Clune couldn't have called him, because she didn't know where he was. Therefore, he must have called her. He couldn't have called her after she went to the Bostwick Hotel. Therefore, it must have been while she was at Thelma Bell's apartment. I wondered how he could possibly have known that she was at Thelma Bell's apartment. He must have gained that information before I had reported to him. The only way I could account for it was that he had seen the number on the slip of paper."

"So then you laid a trap for him?" asked the reporter.

"Not exactly," Perry Mason said, "but I began to put two and two together. I remembered that he had entered my office reading the latest *Liberty*, that *Liberty* had just appeared on the stand. He had picked it up at the cigar counter that evening. Subsequently, when the young lady at the cigar counter told me he had left a package with her and had purchased a magazine, I knew that he must have left the package when he came to my office that evening, yet he said nothing of it. I then commenced to check on other details, and realized, not only that he could have been guilty, but that it was almost certain that he was guilty. I wanted to find out what numbers he had been calling on the telephone; I couldn't figure how I could do this, until I remembered that the hotel kept a record of them; then it was simple."

"And how did you know that Eva Lamont figured in the case?" the reporter asked.

"Because," Perry Mason said, "the first telegram that I received in connection with the case was signed by Eva Lamont. It appears that Bradbury intended to use her to work through. Then he became afraid that she couldn't carry out his plans, so he kept her with him to use as an assistant in getting Doray implicated. She didn't know the true facts, of course; he only confided in her such facts as he wanted her to know. She did the things that he told her, she was rather clever at it, she obeyed his instructions implicitly, and she fooled Paul Drake. By using her, Bradbury was able to get the officers on Dr. Doray's trail much sooner than would otherwise have been the case."

"When do you think Bradbury first conceived the idea of murdering Patton?" the reporter asked.

"Some time ago," Perry Mason said. "He didn't lay his plans in detail, of course, until facts had shaped themselves so that he could make intelligent plans. He is a clever man, Bradbury, don't make any mistake about that. And then, of course, he had some lucky breaks, but he almost managed to put Dr. Doray in the death chair.

"No jury on earth would ever have believed that Dr. Doray was telling the truth when he said that the knife had mysteriously disappeared from his automobile, when he had parked it near the apartment house where Patton lived. Moreover, at any time that Dr. Doray became convinced Marjorie Clune might have committed the crime, he would have confessed."

"And you reasoned all this out without the aid of Thelma Bell's complete statement?" asked the reporter.

"I realized what must have happened," said Perry Mason slowly. "Thelma Bell never did tell me the truth. The first time I knew her complete story was when I saw the signed interview she had given the press, in which she stated exactly what had happened. How Patton, under the influence of liquor, had tried to lock her in the bedroom. How she had taken refuge in the bathroom, where she had given way to hysterics. She felt that Patton had been dragging her steadily down-hill, through his exploitation of her physical beauty. She was tired and nervous and she gave way to hysterics.

"Bradbury, of course, heard her having hysterics as he came down the hall. He simply opened the door of the apartment and walked in. The time and the place were ideal for his purpose."

"But," one of the newspaper men said, "you confessed, did you not, Mr. Mason, to locking the door and then making false statements to the police?"

Perry Mason grinned, and there was a twinkle in his eyes.

"I did."

"Isn't that a crime?"

"It is not. A man can lie to the police or any one else just as much as he wants to. If his lies tend to shield a murderer, he may be guilty of compounding a felony. If he lies under oath, he is guilty of perjury. But, in this case, gentlemen, the lies tended to trap a murderer."

"But," the reporter pointed out, "weren't you taking risks?"

Perry Mason pushed back the chair from his desk, got to his feet and stood with shoulders squared, staring at the newspaper men with eyes that held a glint of amusement, and a glint of something that was not amusement. There was something almost of contempt in his tone when he spoke.

"Gentlemen," he said, "I always take risks. It's the way I play the game; I like it."

The telephone on Perry Mason's desk rang insistently. Della Street picked it up, listened for a few minutes and then left the room. Perry Mason turned to the reporters.

"Gentlemen," he said, "I think you have everything that you want now. I'm going to ask you to terminate this interview. I'm very tired."

"Okay, we understand," said one of the newspaper men. Perry Mason regarded Marjorie Clune and Bob Doray for a moment as if they were strangers. Then he jerked his head toward the door.

"What are you two children doing here?" he asked. "Your case is over. Get out. You've ceased to be a case, you're just a file. 'The Case of the Lucky Legs'—closed."

"Good-by, Mr. Mason," Marjorie said gently, "I never can thank you enough, you know that."

ABOUT THE AUTHOR

Courtesy of the Harry Ransom Center, The University of Texas at Austin

Erle Stanley Gardner (1889–1970) is a prolific American author best known for his works centered on the lawyer-detective Perry Mason. At the time of his death in March of 1970, in Ventura, California, Gardner was "the most widely read of all American writers" and "the most widely translated author in the world," according to social historian Russell Nye. He was cited by the Guinness Book of World Records as the #1 Bestselling Writer of All Time. The first Perry Mason novel, *The Case of The Velvet Claws*, published in 1933, had sold twenty-eight million copies in its first fifteen years. In the mid-1950s, the Perry Mason novels were selling at the rate of twenty thousand copies a day. There have been six motion pictures based on his work and the hugely popular "Perry Mason" television series starring Raymond Burr, which aired for nine years and 271 episodes.